WHITE ROSES

ALODIA THALIEL

ALSO BY ALODIA

The Wolf's Dungeon Series

The Mask of the Wolf

The Teacher and His Pet

Peaches and Cream

Other Fairy Tales Retold

Braids of Silver

Forbidden Fruit

Fate, Love, and Experience Points

Tales From the Resort - Erotic Short Stories

Volume 1 - Contemporary

Volume 2 - Sci-Fi and Fantasy

Acknowledgments

Dedicated most fondly to those who live for magic, love, and romance.

And, as always, to my husband. The man who made me believe in romance.

PRELUDE

As Landon approached the dragon, sword heavy in his hand, and prepared himself.

This was where it all would end. For three days, they had fought, with Landon hiking over mountains and following the dragon into a cave. He never gave up, never stopped his pursuit, and finally, he was winning.

The dragon couldn't run forever. Couldn't keep ahead of him enough to flee. And Landon was nothing if not determined, his stamina stretching far beyond that of others. He would outlast the dragon.

It was a beautiful creature with shimmering blue scales and eyes that glowed pale in the moonlight and sparkled like diamonds in the sun. He wished there was something else he could do, some way to reason with the great beast, but no… dragons could not be reasoned with.

Normally, they dwelled higher up in the mountains, and he and his father made sure no one went there. They left the dragons their space. But this dragon had come down the mountains and begun attacking villages. It stole livestock and left the carcasses on the roads, razed fields of grain, and pursued children and merchants as they traversed the kingdom.

It was only a matter of time before the dragon killed someone, and they couldn't afford to lose any more grain.

So Landon, as prince and the best warrior in the kingdom, went to slay the beast.

He wished, not for the first time, that he could transform. Facing the dragon as a werewolf would make him quicker and more agile. He'd be able to jump higher and dodge easier. But his ancestors had learned the hard way that dragons' hide was not permeable with tooth or claw, nor could they strike deep enough.

Dragons required steel.

The princes and dukes of other kingdoms never needed to learn combat outside of what came to them naturally. When they fought, they did so as wolves.

But Landon, as prince of Fenestral, had no choice but to become a master swordsman. The best in the country. It was his duty to slay dragons, should the need arise, so when he swung his blade again, aiming for the beast's heart, he did so with surety and power. His blade was an extension of his arm, as much a part of him as his wolf, and it struck true.

The dragon was too tired, and when it tried to jump back and swipe at Landon with its claws, it did little more than sway to the side—the blade sunk in, finding space between its scales, silencing the great beast.

With a wheeze, it fell over, huge body landing with a rumble. The light in its eyes died, and Landon was left alone in a dragon's den, the dragon dead before him.

Staring down at the dragon, Landon wiped the blood off of his blade and then sheathed his sword. Then, he sat down on the ground and cried.

After searching the cave, Landon emerged from it for the first time in nearly a full day. The moon was rising, and a gentle wind picked up from the valley below, sweeping up the mountain in a warm rush of florals and...

Something.

He frowned, lifting his nose to the air, and took a deep breath.

On the wind, there was a scent he'd never experienced before. Something sweeter and fuller than the flowers but with the warmth of honey and the freshness of the ocean. It called to him, his stomach dipping and his heart beginning to race.

A new hunt was beginning, and Landon wouldn't rest until he found his prize.

CHAPTER ONE

Briar

I gasped and sat up.

My lungs *ached* like they had forgotten how to work, and my eyes had trouble focusing on the room around me. They were so dry, and all the lights around me were too bright.

I couldn't make sense of any of it. My whole body wasn't working right. Hadn't I just gone to bed in all good health? What happened to me?

I lifted my hands to my face, pressing into my features, trying to make sense of what I could feel. My eyes were still there, and they were open, as best I could tell. My mouth worked, though no noise came out when I tried to speak. My nose was nestled in the center too, and when I took in a deep breath, I found that it still worked.

It wasn't perfect, and the scents around me were dull and muted, but I could smell nature around me, a soft breeze and... something else.

Something spicy and earthy. Primal, almost.

Was it a person?

I waved my hands in front of me and blinked rapidly, trying to get my eyes to adjust and stop being so abysmally dry. I didn't see anyone, but I mapped out the familiar edge of my bed and nightstand.

Though, I swore my hands came back dusty.

Then, I heard it, a footstep and a sigh.

"Drink this," a deep voice mumbled.

A large, warm hand grabbed one of my wrists and pushed a leather waterskin into it.

Greedily, I gulped down half the skein, dumped some into my hands, and rubbed at my eyes.

It helped.

Almost immediately, my eyes felt relieved, and my throat was leagues less dry than it had been. I kept my eyes closed, giving them some rest from the bright light.

Experimentally, I cleared my throat and tried to speak, "H-hello?"

It was hoarse and barely audible, but the stranger heard me anyway. "Hello, try to relax. What are you doing here?"

"Where?" I croaked.

"In… I don't even know where you are. Fuck," he muttered. "We're in the mountains."

Well, that sounded correct. My home had always been in the mountains. A castle my great-great grandfather had built, standing proudly in the middle of two peaks, with huge gray walls and cozy gardens nestled inside. I'd lived there my entire life, and in the valley around the castle, there was a sprawling town. Nearly a city.

How did he not know where we were?

Everyone knew Skyridge and the village of Verdant Hills.

It was the grandest castle around and a powerful trade partner for countries on both sides of the mountains. Goods did not move across the range *without* the blessing of the Rhoswen family.

"Skyridge?" I whispered to him, suggesting the very obvious information.

"Where?" He asked, sounding confused.

Had I been kidnapped by a foreigner? Someone who didn't know the first thing about the mountains? But if that was the case, why was I still in my bedroom?

I patted the bed again, ensuring it was my own bed. I turned and stroked the headboard, and sure enough, it was the same one I remembered. Carved trees and flowers blooming along the grain… but then I felt it. *Moss.*

Had that grown overnight? What was happening?

I sat there in stunned silence, hand falling away, and just... waited.

I wasn't sure what for, but I knew that wherever I was, it was *not* my bedroom. And this man was not to be trusted.

I could feel his eyes on me, and I opened my own carefully, wanting to see the stranger.

Slowly, I blinked them open, and thankfully it was a much more familiar experience than the last time. Instead of overwhelming and blinding light, it was merely bright, and the dryness was improved, though still not gone entirely.

Around me was... not my bedroom.

Or, it was, if my bedroom had been turned over to the wilderness. My room was situated at the top of a large turret in Skyridge, one of the safest and highest places in the castle. Traditional for previous princesses to use as their quarters, it was well appointed, with gilded furniture, paneled walls, sumptuous carpets and bedding, and a beautiful hand-carved bed frame.

The room before me was a dilapidated version of that beautiful room. Part of the wall was missing, and it had let in both birds and weather. Moss covered much of the stone and wooden furniture, and flowering vines covered the walls and ceiling. Even my sheets were beginning to turn green at the edges, and I yanked them off of me, wanting to get away from the creeping mold.

"Hey, take it easy," the man said. "You're not in any danger."

My eyes snapped to him, and I took him in.

Dirty blonde hair stuck out at all angles from his head, and parts of it were slicked down with sweat and sticking to his forehead. What remained looked like it was trying to curl around his ears and temple. His serious brow was pulled low over bright blue eyes, and his full lips were frowning. There was also blood, a *lot* of blood, all over his suit of armor and splattered at the side of his face.

Reacting on instinct, I sprung back, gasping. "Oh!"

His brows drew down deeper, and his frown grew with confusion.

Then, he glanced down at himself. "Shit." He looked at me, "It's not mine."

I shivered where I cowered, now both confused *and* scared. I didn't care if it was his or someone else's. A man covered in blood in my bedroom was *not* a good thing.

"Please leave me alone," I rasped. "I don't know why you're here, but please leave."

He looked at me, evaluating, and then made a decision. Moving slowly, he crouched down and began methodically removing his armor, piece by piece. The moss softened the sounds of the metal hitting the floor, and soon he was left in just his underclothing, a mix of leather, quilted padding, and black linen meant to protect his skin from the metal.

Then, he held up both hands and said, "I'm Landon. I came to the mountains on the trail of a dragon. I slayed it and then found you here. I didn't have time to wash up after."

"That's *dragon* blood?" I gasped.

He nodded, "Yes. We battled for three days. I only just slayed it when I scented you on the wind."

"I..." I shook on the bed, hugging myself.

Dragons were *sacred,* and killing one was unheard of. We gave them offerings and kept them fed, and in return, the dragons kept strangers from our lands.

We would *never* consider killing one.

Tears sprung to my eyes, stinging and making my nose water. I was too dehydrated for them to fall properly, but still, one fell from the corner of my eye, and I let it drip down my chin and fall off, leaving a cool, salty trail behind.

"It's alright," he said gently, inching closer to me.

It was *not* alright! Why had he killed a dragon? What kind of world was I in?

Nothing made sense, and my heart was breaking at the thought of one of the great majestic beasts killed. I'd spent my life watching them fly over the valleys, bright eyes shining in the sun and scales rippling with light.

What evil would compel him to slay them?

I remained frozen, dry tears trying to force their way out of my eyes until he came to the side of the bed where he kneeled next to it. I scrambled away from him, scared of what else he may be capable of. If he could kill a *dragon,* then he had no sense of morals, and nothing was stopping him from killing me too.

I'm sure I stank of fear because his nose wrinkled, but his voice was still smooth when he said, "I'm sure you've been through a lot, but whatever it is, it's over now. I'll get you out of here and ensure you're safe."

Safe? Outside of the castle? In a world where men like him slayed dragons?

It sounded preposterous. It was antithetical to everything I knew, but one glance around us, and I was reminded again that I knew nothing. Not anymore.

Even if Landon wasn't safe, the castle was a dilapidated ruin around me, and ruins were not safe places to be. If my room was like this, I had no doubt the kitchens were a mess too, and staying in a ruin with no food was twice as unsafe.

First, I needed to take stock. To see if the castle was as bad as I thought.

"C-can we look around?" I asked quietly.

I had to make sure. What if my father was still here? My siblings and my mother?

Maybe they'd woken up just as I had, confused and scared.

I would have gone about it alone, but Landon had that *look* about him like he wasn't about to take no for an answer. He tracked my every small move, the eyes of a hunter, and when I shifted, he shifted with me, mirroring me.

Slowly, I stood.

Landon sighed and nodded, assenting to my request.

Shrouded in my silence, I exited my room and encountered the first sign that something was *seriously* wrong. The spiraling stairway that took me down the tower was missing its roof. Sunlight streamed in from above, and birds chirping echoed around me.

"Hm," I said, glancing up.

I quickly wound my way down the stairs but stopped halfway down to look at chipped pieces of wood that seemed to come out of the wall. When I looked at the other side of the stairwell, there were matching splinters coming out there, too. Almost like the wood had spanned the stairwell, cutting off my part of the tower from the rest of the castle.

Uneasy, I continued, coming to the bottom of the stairs and pacing down the main hallway. The carpets and tapestries were also molding or mossy down here, and plants sprouted up between the stones. Where my father's office had once been was an empty doorway with collapsed stone on the other side. I stood in the archway, its keystone barely in place, and stared out into the space.

What used to be a room was now just a pile of rubble baking in the sun.

I could just see past the crumbled walls, and at least the mountains beyond looked the same.

Turning away, I continued down the hall, making for the kitchens. I took a right into the space which should have held them and was again met with a collapsed room. Among the rubble, I could see old silver serving ware where the butler's pantry once stood and silverware peeking out between moss.

Vivid memories of the smell of fresh bread and meals snuck at the counter with the staff played through my mind. My heart ached. The kitchen had always been the heart of everything we did, and now it was nothing but rubble.

"What are you looking for?" Landon asked me finally.

"I'm not sure," I hedged.

"Alright…"

I turned and headed down a different hall and then up an internal set of stairs. My room had been the only one in the tower, and this wing held the rest of my family's rooms. I walked faster down the narrow hall, practically sprinting, pushing open doors, and searching for *any* signs of life.

I looked in room after room, each one feeling emptier than the last.

Mother and Father's rooms— Empty.

Leticia's room— Empty.

Harry's room— Empty.

Carson's room— Empty.

My entire family was gone.

All of the staff was gone.

And my childhood home was a crumble of ruins.

Landon tagged along behind me, a silent shadow as I desperately searched for *anything* familiar, but in the end, there was nothing. I walked slowly to the main hall and then stood there, dejected.

Landon, the dragon killer, was my only option.

I didn't know what was happening to me, I didn't know what kind of backward world I was in, but I knew I was adrift at sea, and he was a rock I could reach for. The waves could bash me against it, taking me away as surely as drowning would... but I was willing to take my chances.

I turned to face him, dejected. "Um..."

He watched me with confused but kind eyes. Like he wanted to ask me a question or say something. I braced myself, but all he said was, "Are you ready to leave?"

Shrugging, I said, "Okay."

He nodded and walked away, expecting me to follow.

So I did.

CHAPTER TWO

After settling me on his horse, Landon went and retrieved his armor and then climbed up behind me. He didn't put back on his plates and instead strapped it to his saddles so he wasn't all sharp edges when he pulled me against him.

Instead, he was warm, but the closer I got to him, the more he began to stink.

My sense of smell was still dull, but it was impossible to ignore the smell of dragon blood this close to Landon. It clung to him everywhere and made my nose and eyes sting.

"T-the dragon..." I murmured, curling forward, trying to get away from the stink. I buried my nose into the horse's mane, breathing deeply.

My stomach churned every time I remembered where the smell came from. Every time I remembered the majestic creature whose life he had ended.

"It's gone now," he assured me, completely misunderstanding. "It won't harm us on our way."

It.

As if the guardians of the mountains were just things and not beings in their own right.

One of his hands gently held my waist in place as he kicked his horse into motion, setting us off on a narrow path down the mountain.

Before, a wooden bridge had led into the castle, but that had deteriorated too, leaving the only way out a winding path out the back of the castle. It took us down into the valley, and for the first time, I could see the entirety of Skyridge and its desecration.

It was as if giants had dismantled it overnight and given it back to the earth.

The great gray stone walls had fallen and collapsed into themselves, none of them at their usual height of thirty feet and most down to a height that was hardly taller than me. The turrets still remained, although they were all in various states of deterioration, and everything was covered in vines and moss, with some trees taking root in the debris.

But the trees weren't small either. They were huge hulking forms.

If nothing else, those trees told me that something was *very* wrong.

"Where are we?" I asked Landon quietly.

He frowned at me, "The mountains."

"Yes, but *where?*"

"We're in the Kingdom of Fenestral, window to the North. Last lands before the vampires." Landon said like it was obvious. "Our land is home to werewolves and fae alike, a melting pot for our kinds. We also see the occasional vampire here, though it's rare. Our ruler is Queen Noe Bleddyn—my mother. "

None of those names sounded familiar. The only familiar words in the bunch were *vampire* and *fae* and *werewolf*.

"Mother and I are both wolves," he continued. "As are my father and siblings."

"Ah," I said, trying to be polite. My throat stung even at that syllable. I needed more water and more time to think. Time away from Landon and the stink of congealed dragon's blood.

Fenestral. Why wasn't that name familiar?

"What is your name?" He asked me. "Do you remember?"

"I do," I admitted.

But did I want to share it?

I didn't know yet.

Sharing my name with this strange man seemed ill-advised. What if this was a trick? Some kind of magic to make me think everyone was dead? Giving my name would reveal to him who I was.

More horrifyingly, what if I told him, and he didn't recognize me?

From his telling, Landon was a prince! A prince should know a neighboring princess, should he not?

I chewed on my lip, still thinking, when Landon sighed. "It's probably best you don't talk either way. Your throat still sounds rough." Then he muttered to himself, "Perhaps she caught an illness…"

I pretended not to hear it.

An illness was as good an explanation as any, I supposed.

But I was still considering the magic angle. It seemed far more likely, and fit more of what I knew of my present situation. A convenient savior, my sudden isolation, the destruction of the once mighty Skyridge. All of it pointed to a *very* powerful magic.

Landon didn't press me for any other answers, probably in deference for my voice, and I was grateful for it.

At first, anyway.

My thoughts were coming at a rapid speed, trying to remember what had happened yesterday, looking for clues in my past about where I was in the present. But even just the other day seemed foggy in my mind. Hadn't I just been out with Mother yesterday, picking flowers from the garden for Leticia and Grandmother?

Grandmother and Grandfather were supposed to arrive today, and we were going to take a trip to the sea. I wanted to watch the boats and the waves and perhaps meet a mermaid.

I supposed now I was never going to see the sea.

Would I ever see my family again?

Were they okay?

Dark despair clutched at my heart as I thought of my younger siblings. I was the eldest. How were they going to get along without me? Little Carson is only ten. What will he do without his stories and playing horsies out in the garden?

Desperately, I turned as much as I could, asking, "Do you have more water?"

I wanted to *cry,* but all I got was pain as my poor dehydrated tear ducts refused to work.

His brows knit, but he passed over another full waterskin.

Without hesitation, I downed it, quenching my thirst again. It was like I hadn't had a drink in *years* with how my body reacted. I felt a little more alive and awake as I handed back the empty skein.

"Thanks."

"Mm."

I'm sure Landon found me strange, but he was gentlemanly enough not to comment on it.

The rest of the trek out of the valley was smooth, and Landon took us East, through the pass, and out into the sloping, gentle hills.

It was the land of the wolves, of my people.

And it was windy.

Shivering, I hugged myself and scanned the horizon, searching for something familiar. Not even the trees were the same as I remembered. Yesterday, it had been Fall, with the leaves turning yellow, gold, and orange.

Now, it looked to be spring, with bright green fresh leaves on the branches.

Different, too, were the towns and villages dotting the landscape. They weren't at all where I remembered them being. Even the river had moved, winding a slightly different path than what I remembered.

But what struck me the most were the trees. Not just their leaves but *the trees.*

Distinctly, I knew there was a large golden wood tree right after the pass, where the road forked. One road led south to the sea, and the other north and east to the vampires and fae, respectively.

There was no tree. In fact, there was no fork in the road either. Instead, the road wound straight and pointed directly at a small settlement before us at the top of a hill. From there, I saw the paths branch out in a giant crossroads. One North, one continuing East, and one South, where we approached from the West.

Instead, there was a stump where it once stood. One well-worn and smoothed from years of people stopping there to rest.

All at once, my mind caught up to reality, awakening from its slumber and plummeting head-first into ice-cold realization.

"Landon," I croaked, trying to sound calm. "What year is it?"

"It's Wolf 45," he said as if the words made perfect sense.

"I..." I looked out over the head of his horse, "I'd like to get off the horse, please."

He started, "What for?"

I pointed at the stump.

"Ah," he nodded, understanding. "I'll help."

He pulled at the reins, stopping us, and hopped off. Then he gripped me around the waist and took my entire weight as I slid off the mount.

Belatedly, I realized I wasn't exactly dressed for travel. I was still in my night clothes. But it wasn't like I had other options. My wooden wardrobe had long disintegrated, being taken over by nature like the rest of the castle.

With more calm than I felt, I went to the stump and sat on it, absorbing the truth.

Though I was in my own world and had woken up on my bed, I was far from my time. I looked down at the tree, counting the rings. I reached a hundred before I gave up.

Just how long had I been asleep?

I hoped the tree could give me a better idea than Landon, but even that was a dead end.

Last I knew, we were in the year Dragon 1115. We'd lived in peace with them for so long. Our years had taken their name, another memorial to our partnership.

Landon watched me with sharp eyes. In the light of the day, I could really take stock of the man who had brought me out of the castle.

He was blonde, tall, and had blue eyes that cut right through me, catching every little movement. His curly hair was plastered to his head where his helmet had once rested, and parts of his face and dark underclothes were smeared with blood.

My throat and nose were still much too dry to scent anything properly, but all I could smell from him was the sick scent of dragon's blood.

Truly, he was an unknown. I did not know his designation, just that he was a wolf like me, and I didn't know if he meant me harm. Perhaps he knew exactly what was happening?

Better to hide my confusion.

If I approached this new future with surety, then it would be harder to take advantage of my naivete.

I might be lacking in my material possessions, but I still had my head on my shoulders.

It would have to be enough.

CHAPTER THREE

Landon helped me back onto his horse, and I spent our ride taking in as much information as I could. Thankfully, he seemed to hold deference for my sore throat and didn't ask me any questions.

Instead, he politely held my hip in one hand and the reins in his other, keeping us on track and guiding his horse forward. We passed through the small village I had noted, a few scandalized women looking my way.

After that, Landon had yanked a blanket out of his saddlebags and draped it around my shoulders. I hadn't been cold, but the extra coverage was welcome.

Why hadn't I worn more substantial night clothes?

What I was wearing was hardly a chemise, though it was lacy and delicate. It crossed over my front in two wide, delicate lace straps, covering my breasts and then crossing just at my stomach. There, it attached to a skirt, which flared out from my waist and draped gently down to the floor.

It was beautiful, the silk making me feel delicate. Somehow, it had been untouched by the mold, and was just as beautiful as when I'd donned it last night.

Now it made me feel exposed to the eyes of the passer-byes, and the blanket was a welcome shield.

Even if it smelled like horse.

Pulling it closer, I held it to my chest and tried to keep my body upright. I didn't want to have to lean back into the other man, but the sway of the horse and the shock of suddenly finding myself years in the future had drained me.

As we ambled out of the village, I slowly slumped back into Landon's chest. The warmth of his body and the steady steps of the horse rocked me to sleep.

When I next woke, I was pleased to find, at the very least, that time did not skip again. I was still on the horse with Landon, and the sun had sunk low into the sky.

Yawning, I stretched and realized I was held tight in the circle of the other man's arms.

"Ah, Lan—"

Immediately, he let me go, "My apologies."

"Where—"

"Shh." He chastised me, tone contrasting the seemingly gentle action of holding me to his body. "You need time to recover. Don't try to speak. We're nearing my family's home. Once we're there, I'll have a healer tend to you."

A healer was a good idea, but what if they found something?

What if they examined me and somehow *knew* I was hiding something?

I must have tensed outwardly because Landon spoke again, softer this time, "You'll have your own rooms, and if you like, I'll stand guard outside. Or, if you prefer, I'll be in the room with you. But I promise I'd never knowingly put you in danger. That includes introducing you to dangerous people."

"Thank you," I wheezed.

He had misunderstood me, but the sentiment was nice enough.

I didn't want him in the room with the healer, but it would be nice to have him just outside the room, just in case.

I still didn't know why I was here or what forces conspired to bring me to this future, but until I had an idea, I'd take the security Landon offered.

Even if he was in on it... Better to court the devil I knew than the one I didn't.

That settled, I felt slightly better about my situation. I had a plan. A small one, a short-term one, but it was more of one than I had when I'd awoken, and given how weariness was still heavy in my bones, I was proud I'd managed to muster this much.

Looking ahead of us, the dirt road we'd been on had turned to cobbles, stretching through a proper city and then winding up, coming to a huge walled-in complex at the center of town. Landon made directly for the walls, and I realized it wasn't just walls; there was a moat, too, butting up against the walls, adding another layer of protection. The only way in or out appeared to be a drawbridge.

The horse's hooves echoed on the wood of the bridge, and on the other side, four guards stood at attention.

"Prince Landon," one called. "Welcome home."

"Thank you, Alex," Landon said smoothly. "Is my father here?"

"Aye, he is."

Landon grunted acknowledgment and trotted past the guard.

If the men had any questions about me, or why Landon had a strange woman with him, they held their tongue.

Well trained, Landon's guards were.

Inside the protective ring of the walls, I had my first real look at Landon's home.

Though the walls and moat would have me believe there was a castle on the other side, what lay before me was more manor than castle. A wild garden lay to one side, flowers blooming and crawling across the facade of the building. The facade was pale pink limestone, huge bricks piled up high to meet a dark roof. In some places, the stone was flat and smooth, but in others, it was carved into intricate patterns, or setback to create inlays for marble statues to live.

At the top of the roof was where most of the detail was concentrated, the pink stone giving way to carved flowers and the snarling faces of wolves and vampires, and at the corners, whole statues of wolves and fae jutted out from the walls and growled down at the grounds below, protecting the home's inhabitants. The windows were nearly all stained glass, with more flowers and fae and wolves and vampires carved into them.

It was surreal. I'd never seen any building like it before, but it didn't feel menacing.

In fact, it felt as alive as the vines and flowers crawling along the stone, real blooms sitting next to their carved pink companions.

"What is this place?" I asked him, keeping my voice soft.

It still hurt to ask, but I needed to know.

"This is Fleur," he said. "Throne seat of Fenestral. The Stained Glass Flower."

"It's beautiful," I tried to say, but it came out mostly as a wheeze.

"Hm," he grumbled. Looking around, he spotted a young man to the side, a little grubby, with straw stuck in his hair. "Lad! Deal with my horse."

Dismounting, Landon pulled me down with him and then tucked me into his side, mostly hiding me from view.

"Aye, Sir!" The kid chirped, running over to take the mount's reins.

"Have the contents of my saddle delivered to my rooms. Ensure the guards handle them. Let no one else touch them."

"Aye!"

The kid gently guided the horse away, and Landon, apparently satisfied, steered me towards the front doors.

I looked up at them, unsure how one man could open them, but I didn't have to wonder because they were already opening the second we began to ascend the front steps.

"Welcome home, Prince Landon!" Some people cried, their voices booming in the courtyard.

"Welcome home, Prince Landon," several people echoed.

"Don't mind them," he said into my ears. "We'll have you in a room soon enough."

I'd thought *they* were the loud voices, but I was corrected when we stepped into the manor, and a veritable *crowd* of people were gathered.

As was due for Landon's station, they were curtseyed or bowed as their prince approached, but the second we walked past them, I could feel their curious eyes on my back.

I was *mortified.*

Why were they here?

"My son!" A voice boomed from the front of the room. "You return victorious?"

I looked up, and on a dias at the front of the room, there was a huge throne carved of the same pink stone, and an older man sat upon it, a crown on his head.

"I do, Father," Landon said, voice just as loud. "I slayed the dragon which was plaguing us. Our fields and livestock are now free of its menace."

"Huzzah! Huzzah!" The crowd cheered. "Hail Prince Landon!"

Unpleasant shivers ran up my spine, and a new sadness gripped my heart.

So many people celebrating the dragon's death. It made my stomach turn.

"And who is this woman?" The man, the king, asked.

"I rescued her," he said simply.

I was *desperately* glad he didn't elaborate.

"I see," the king nodded. "We welcome all lost souls at Fleur. Come, find rest. You have fought well, son."

Dipping his head, Landon bowed.

Gently, he squeezed my hip, and I followed suit, curtseying next to him.

"She does not speak?" The king asked, narrowing his eyes at me.

It wasn't necessarily with suspicion or ire, but like he was puzzled by me, the strange woman who'd suddenly arrived home with his son.

"I cannot," I rasped.

The king's brows rose. "I see."

Nodding to himself, he waved his hand, and several butlers and maids came from the walls of the room, sliding in from hidden panels in the wall. They swarmed Landon and me, surrounding us and ushering us out a side door.

As we went, the king called, "Hail, Fenestral!"

The crowd called back, "Hail, Fenestral! Hail! Hail!

Their words echoed around me and Landon, following us down a long, tall hallway flooded with light.

Chapter Four

Landon and I were separated before I had the chance to protest or shout after him. Though to be honest, with my voice as weak as it was, it was doubtful Landon would even hear me protest. I was alone in the castle, surrounded by a gaggle of maids who were cooing and tugging at my clothes and hair, clearly dissatisfied with my state.

With efficient movements, they drew me a bath, disrobed me, and then informed me that a healer would be there shortly to see me and assess my physical health. There was no choice in the matter, I was expected to submit to their ministrations, and I found no point in resistance anyway.

These women had no idea who I was or where I came from. They were just doing their best with the strange lady before them, and that meant cleaning her up and getting her fed.

Pleasantly, I realized that in however long had passed, bathrooms had taken a massive step forward. The bedroom I was in was massive, pale yellow, and bright, and had its own bathroom attached to one side. It was all marble tile, with a huge sunken bath to one side and a dressing table, toilet, and wash table with a basin on top to the other side. The bath was filled with warm, clear water, which sprouted from a tap affixed to the wall.

It was a *marvel,* and I sunk into it gratefully.

Time had not been kind to my hair.

Though I had no right to feel as well as I did, given the circumstances, there was still dust in my hair and a damp smell that clung to my skin. My sense of smell was still dampened, thankfully, so I was spared the full effect of whatever stench I was carrying.

I washed the dust and must out of my hair, using a soap that smelled faintly of lavender to my weakened nose. A cloud of gray bloomed in the water around me, and by the time I was done washing, I was more than slightly embarrassed at how dirty I must have been when Landon found me.

How had he not said anything to me?

My stench must have burned his nose!

"Miss!" One of the maids knocked on the door. "The healer is here. Shall I send them in?"

"Yes," I croaked, hoping she heard me.

She must have taken the sound as an affirmative, and by the time I'd stepped out of the water and wrapped myself in a robe, a kindly old woman had stepped into the bathroom.

"Hello, dear," she said softly. "My name is Mother Mable; how do you do?"

"Hello, Mother Mable," I rasped back to her.

"Oh, don't speak," she instructed, a frown creasing her already wrinkled face. "Please, have a seat."

She gestured at a small stool near the dressing table, and I obediently took my seat there.

I felt fine, all truths be told, but I was curious nonetheless to see if she would discover anything. What if I was ill, and that was why I had slept for so long? What if I was already dead, and somehow I had been brought back to life?

Each possibility was horrible, changing fundamentally how I knew and perceived the world, and this older woman's guidance would at least help me suss out which option was most likely.

I hoped, anyway.

"Let me see here," she mused, taking my head into her hands and turning it this way and that. She peered deep into my pale purple eyes and slid her hands through my blonde hair, feeling for any injuries on my scalp. Then, she pressed her hands into my skin. First, under my eyes, then across my chest. It was no-nonsense and perfunctory, and in quick succession, she listened to my lungs, took my pulse, and then gripped my wrist, assessing my energy and my humors.

"All appears well," she eventually declares. "Fit as a fiddle in a fiddler's hands. Ready to play."

She patted my cheek, smiling at me.

Relief flooded my chest, relaxing my shoulders, "Really?"

"Yes, dearie," she said. "I'd say it's a miracle."

Frowning, I asked, "How so?"

"You slept for five thousand years. One would expect for you to suffer more effects than a sore throat and weak voice."

"I..." I was shocked. *Five thousand years??* It was such a length of time, longer even than most fae's lives. "Five thousand?!"

She shook her head, "Shh. Speak not. Your voice needs to rest."

Confused, I glanced between her and the door.

How had she known I was asleep? Moreover, why did it appear there was a sinister glint in her eyes. As I stared, trying to determine who this woman was and how she knew I'd somehow moved in time, she changed.

The face of the kindle old woman slowly morphed. Soft, wrinkled skin grew young and tight again, and her rounded shoulders and back straightened as she grew taller, a cloak of black, shimmering night draping itself over her shoulders and her lips turning a vivid red. A crown of blood-red laurels bloomed around her head, shimmering in the afternoon light.

"Well, hello, darling," she purred.

Before my eyes, the old woman had turned into Eris, a witch who roamed the mountains and deeply hated Skyridge and all who lived within it.

Gasping, I scrambled back from the chair, putting as much space between me and the witch who stood before me.

"Do you remember now, sweet thing?" She asked, heedless of my fear. "Oh, how I've longed for this day, the day when I would *finally* see the fruits of my labor."

Her *labor?*

Taking leisurely steps towards me, her cape of midnight flared out behind her, caught in an invisible wind. She towered over me, leaning in so close I was forced to lean away from her, trying to put space between me and the evil witch.

Laughing, eyes sparkling with delight, she cooed, "Ah, poor thing. You still haven't figured out what happened, have you?"

I looked at her with suspicion, unwilling to ask her any questions. I knew from experience that if I did, she would just twist her answer, convoluting the truth.

"Well, I'll just tell you," Eris drawled, holding her nails out to examine, all casual as if she wasn't speaking of curses and magic. "Your father, bless his soul, thought it was prudent to try and deny my demands for tribute. I told him, in no uncertain terms, that this was unacceptable. He had no use for the land I required, and I swore I wouldn't interfere with him and his cronies when they made their tributes to the beasts." She sighed, twirling her hand around, gathering her words to her,

"We spent years negotiating until finally I told him that if he continued to refuse me, I would have no choice but to curse his precious firstborn."

That couldn't be the truth. There was no way it was. But without my father here to refute her, I had no choice but to listen to her version of events.

"Of course, this proved to be disastrous for the whole of Skyridge. After all, with you in a deep and unending sleep up in your tower, it was rather bad for morale. Your family tried to hold on to their convictions, and they even made it a few hundred years before they simply couldn't anymore. They tried to forget about you, but you were always there, *sleeping* and reminding them I was out there. Waiting. Did you see how they tried to wall you in? Eventually, one of your successors boarded up the tower and tried to pretend you weren't up there, sleeping soundly."

Sighing, Eris trailed the back of one finger down my face, the sharp end of her nail tickling my skin. "Long story short, I got the land I wanted and all of Skyridge too. But there was one thing I never did get... *You.*"

"Me?" I asked, hoping to sound as outraged as I felt.

What did *I* have to do with her and her quarrel with my father?

"Yes, *you*," she scoffed. "Here, let me give you a little help remembering. When you're all done reminiscing and getting your tears out, do come find me. Someone has to catch you up on at least the last thousand years."

Eris then took my chin into her hands and muttered words I couldn't hope to understand but sounded like stones in a river or a thunderclap on the horizon. My scalp tingled, and a shock shot down my spine, making me jump. It lasted only a moment, and then she released me.

Straightening, Eris tossed her long dark hair over her shoulder and said, "Ta for now."

In a swirling mist of black smoke, she disappeared.

And I fainted.

CHAPTER FIVE

Waking up, I put a hand to my head, groaning.

"Bad dream?" My father asked.

I shook my head, trying to dispel the memories of a broken tower and the witch Eris, "Yes, terrible dreams."

"Mm, I'll call for some tea." He pulled at the rope behind him and then settled back in his desk chair, steepling his fingers. "What was it about?"

I sat up from the comfortable leather couch I often napped on, situated across from Father's desk and near the roaring fire, "Eris was there. The witch."

He nodded, "Of all the fae, she is by far the foulest. Of all the *people.*"

"She said..." I struggled to remember what it was she'd claimed, but it came to me after a moment's concentration. "She said she was trying to get some land from you."

Father laughed, rich and deep. It was so familiar any uneasiness from the dream faded away.

"For years, Eris has been sending me letters asking me for land," he shook his head. "Sometimes she makes threats, but they're all empty. She needs us to keep the dragons happy. She can't do it on her own. She has no love for livestock keeping or animal care."

I frowned, "Is that all that's stopping her?"

Shrugging, he said, "Best any of us can suss out, yes. She asked the same of my father too, and she'll likely ask the same of you. She doesn't just want *any* land. She wants the springs."

"The springs?"

"Mm. And the land around them. To build her own castle and capitalize on the magic from the water."

The springs, the only springs I knew of, anyway, were up the mountain just past Skyridge. It was a natural source of warm water and close enough to the mountain passage that travelers often stopped there to bathe and relax. It was, by far, the best part of the trip through the range. A moment of peace on an otherwise grueling journey.

"What magic could be in the water?" I asked, confused.

I'd never heard the springs referred to in any way other than it being a delightful stop, a tourist destination. But magic? That had never been a part of the equation.

Sighing, he admitted, "I don't pretend to understand that witch. The other fae can deal with her, but I'm not going to give her a part of the pass just because she wants it."

"I see."

"Put it out of your mind," Father assured me. "We're not about to give Eris her own claim to the mountains or allow her to control part of the pass. She'll lose interest eventually."

Distantly, I heard someone laughing.

When I blinked, I wasn't in the study with my father anymore.

Turning quickly in a circle, I realized I was outside of Skyridge, my home, and in front of me, Eris was standing, a smug look on her face.

"Look, girlie," she was saying, her red crown glinting in the moonlight. "I'm tired of trying to negotiate with your family. So let's cut a deal, woman to woman. As the next heir to your family throne you can make me a few promises. And in return, I *won't* curse you."

"This is hardly a negotiation," I pointed out. "You're threatening me."

"Mm. Your idiot father seems to think I won't follow through on it. But I will."

"*Don't* call him an idiot," I insisted, glaring at her. "If we're to barter, it *will* be civil."

Rolling her eyes, Eris said, *"Fine.* Your *highly intelligent* father seems to believe I won't curse you. But I will. Gleefully, even."

"Tell me why you want the springs," I insisted. "I can't promise you anything unless I know."

"It's none of your concern *why* I want it," Eris told me. "You wolves could never hope to understand me and my magic anyway."

"Your fellow fae don't even deal with you," I pointed out. "It seems to me the problem is with your magic, not my understanding of it."

"What would you know," she hissed, eyes narrowing, swooping even closer to me. She was so close I could feel her breath when she spoke. "You'd do well not to try me, little girl. You might be queen one day, but right now, you're just a pathetic little princess doing her father's bidding."

"He doesn't know I'm here tonight," I reminded her. "I came here in good faith."

"And good faith to you is insults?"

"You threw the first insult," I pointed out. "You besmirched the name of my father."

"And I'll continue to do so," she declared, coming to her full height. "For as long as your family insists on denying me, you are *all* fools. Idiots. No smarter than *dogs.*"

I growled at her, "Silence! Tell me why you want the spring, or I'll leave here and now. And hear this, you will *never* get another chance to negotiate with me again. Nor my progeny. I will make it my life's goal to see it through."

"Hah!" She laughed. "Oh, that's rich. The first of your line to show any sense of a backbone, and it will be your doom. Poor thing, you don't even know."

"You don't scare me."

"Oh, but I should," she cooed.

"Last chance," I declared. "Tell me why you want the spring."

"No."

Turning on my heel, I began to walk away from her. It was dark, but not so dark that I couldn't see. I picked my way across the grass, but froze when behind me, a delighted, sickly laugh began to come from the witch.

"Oh, Briar," she sighed. "You're going to live to regret this, and I can't wait to see the look on your face when you realize what you've done."

Whirling, I found Eris smiling at me. Then, she began to rise up from the ground, her cloak billowing out behind her, the edges shadowy and filled with galaxies, and her dark hair flying around her face. She raised her arms, hands curled into claws, as a red circle of magic began to form on the ground below her.

Suddenly, she began to chant, weaving her spell. The words grated, and I turned, running from the witch and her evil.

Whatever was happening here, I knew I needed to get away from it, and *fast*.

I should have transformed, but in my panic, I kept going on foot, sprinting all the way back up into the castle, and then ascended my tower, heart beating wildly and my mind racing.

She couldn't really hurt us, could she?

I threw off my outer dress and vaulted into bed, fearful Eris would follow me or that one of my maids would discover I was missing.

But no one was there.

I was surrounded by nothing but eerie silence and eventually, I went to sleep.

Gasping, I came to in the bathroom, still perched at the dressing table, head throbbing.

I was alone among the cold, pink marble tiles and the even colder truth.

Eris had cursed me. Made me sleep for five thousand years.

It was as I feared. Everyone I knew, everything I loved, was *gone*. Lost to time. My family had left this world while I slept, unaging, right before their very eyes.

Now, I was alone in this world. Everything I knew needed to be cast aside, and I had to start from scratch. The very rivers I once took for granted had gradually shifted over the years, and small paths had grown to major roadways, and the surety with which I once knew the countryside was now gone.

I knew *nothing.*

The life I knew wasn't waiting for me back in Skyridge, and I had no choice but to forge something new.

I couldn't begin to know what that would mean for me, or where to even start, but I was saved from trying to figure it out when the maids who had helped me earlier knocked lightly on the door, and then came bustling in, kind smiles on their faces.

"'Ello, miss," the oldest of them said softly. "We saw the healer leave. We've brought you some tea and honey. It's in the bedroom for you."

I nodded at her, plastering on a smile.

"I'm Anita," she informed me. "And this is Rose, Candela, and Lily. Should you need something, call for any one of us."

They helped me out of my chair and then gently guided me back into the bedroom.

"You need rest," Anita told me.

"A lot of it," Rose agreed.

"And tea," Lily whispered at the end.

As those three helped me into the bed, Candela circled the massive four-poster structure and pointed out a rope to the side of the bed, "Tug this if you need us!"

The girls all nodded in unison, and I was all but thrust between the sheets, covered in a duvet, and settled in. There was no choice for it, and by the time the maids were done with me, they had me tucked in so tight I could barely move. Though, it was shockingly comfortable. The pillows under me were fluffy and delightful, and the sheets smelled faintly of lavender and vanilla.

"Sleep," Anita urged me. "The sun is already set, and an early night never did anyone any harm."

Rose pointed to the teacup on the night table next to me, "Drink that before you sleep. You need all you can get."

I nodded, the extent of what I could realistically do to communicate with her, and watched as all four maids bustled out of the room in a swish of pastel skirts and soft tittering.

The door closed behind them, and I was all alone again.

Reality began to close around me again, but shockingly, so did weariness.

I might have slept for thousands of years, and then some more on Landon's horse, and then fainted when the witch Eris had visited, but it was as if my body was now unaccustomed to being awake. Every minute felt so much harder than the last until even my panic faded, and I again slept.

CHAPTER SIX

Waking up again, this time I immediately noted that the sun was already nearing its peak and that I'd forgotten to drink my tea last night. Rising slowly, I took the cold cup into my hands and sipped it as I thought.

Thankfully, my sleep had been dreamless, but unfortunately, no answers had come to me in that blank state. My mind hadn't come to any conclusions, and nothing about my life seemed any rosier or more obvious in the light of a new day.

If anything, I felt *more* despair and perhaps slightly feverish.

As I sipped, I came to two decisions. First, I needed a plan *fast*. And second, I needed to establish if Landon and his family could be trusted.

His father, the king, seemed to be quite the character, and Landon himself appeared... I wasn't sure. He was warm in his actions, but stoic at the same time. Helping me while watching me closely, as if he was trying to puzzle me out.

I could work with both of those things, I was a princess, after all. Landon didn't know that, of course, but it was true all the same. I had the skills to handle this with diplomacy, and so I would.

My mother might be dead, but there was no reason I couldn't still make her proud. It would take every single lesson, trick, and strategy she had taught me to secure myself a new place in this new time.

Perhaps, I should start where it all began - with Landon.

I finished my tea, set the cup on the saucer, and then yanked the red velvet rope that would call the maids to me.

Within minutes, there was a knock on the door, and Anita, Rose, Lily, and Candela burst into the room in a flurry of activity.

"You're awake!" Anita declared.

"Finally," Rose enthused. "We thought you might sleep *forever."*

I winced. She had no idea that was now my biggest fear, that I might again sleep again for millenia, time passing by me without even knowing it. It was almost uncanny how she immediately targeted that weakness with her offhand comment.

"Sorry," Lily said softly. "We were just worried."

Candela shook her head, "I've never seen anyone sleep as much as you. You were out for nigh on sixteen hours!"

I winced again. That was a *very* long time, but I had to admit that I did feel a little more awake now than I had yesterday. It felt ridiculous to think I needed more sleep, but all signs were pointing to the fact that I was *exhausted.*

With as much efficiency as the night before, the women had me out of bed, whisked behind a screen, a cloth run over my skin, my hair pinned up, and an elegant day dress wrapped around me in no time at all.

"Er," I said experimentally. It hurt, but not as much as yesterday. "Landon?"

"The prince?" Anita asked, brows drawn together. "He's away, I'm afraid."

"Ah."

"The castle is *full* of stories of your arrival with him last night," Rose gushed.

"It sounded very romantic," Lily admitted.

"Like a book!" Candela agreed. "He whisked in, *in the middle of a ball* carrying you in his arms!"

"Um…" I mumbled.

"There's no helping them," Anita assured me. "They're all romantics."

"Plus, anyone with a set of eyes would think Landon was a *catch,*" Rose giggled.

Lily blushed, giggling with her, "He is handsome."

"Um..." I mumbled again.

"Leave her be," Anita insisted.

The girls looked knowingly between each other, but did as Anita asked, leaving me alone and continuing to fuss over me, sliding a dab of perfume behind my ears and then smoothing a cold cream over my face and décolletage.

The fact that Landon departed so quickly threw a wrench into my plans. He was the only person here I knew with any power behind him. He was a *prince*. He was powerful, no doubt wealthy, and both of those things meant he could help me. If nothing else, his influence would deter others from trying to take advantage of me or use me as some kind of pawn.

No one wanted to risk a monarch's wrath. Mother had impressed that into me above all.

People schemed, they planned. That never changed. But the key was to catch them at it. People could be so sneaky, but if you could catch them, they would back away, for no other reason than they wanted to ensure their heads stayed attached to their necks.

Brutal, but it was reality. Treason was dealt with harshly for a reason.

"Where did he... go?" I wheezed after a moment.

"Ummm..." Rose and Lily glanced at each other, and Candela pretended like she didn't hear me.

It was Anita who answered me. "He's away on a mission, again. Though his mother wished him to stay and rest some more. He slept nearly as long as you, but then he was up and away again."

"He never listens to anyone," Candela sighed.

"He has business to attend to, I'm sure," Anita said, cutting a look at Candela. "Not that he shares it with anyone, but he's a prince. Those great men always have business to attend to."

"I heard he was awake for *days* fighting the dragon," Lily said softly. "I don't know how he can be away again so soon."

I winced, because Lily had a point, and at the reminder that Landon had done the unthinkable. It seemed insane to me that he could slay a dragon, but then to be so casual about it that he would leave again, heedless of the time or effort it took to accomplish such a thing... It was unfathomable.

Landon was clearly a man made of steel.

He would make for a powerful ally, even in spite of his deeds. It was too bad he wasn't here.

"I see," I said.

I would just have to find someone else to be my ally. If the Prince was unavailable, then surely there was someone else here in the castle. A brother, or a cousin. I'd even take a visitor who was high ranking. A duke would serve me nearly as well in my quest for an ally.

Settling back, I allowed the maids to pamper me, my mind made up.

It was time to put Landon out of my mind, and focus instead on whatever it would take to survive.

I set about my mission immediately. As soon as the maids finished with me, I asked them where I could go to chat with people, feigning the need for some company.

They looked sad, at first, until I insisted that I knew they had work to do, and I couldn't possibly keep them from it all day. They seemed mollified after that, and I made my way out of my room towards the drawing room.

I kept their directions at the front of my mind, and barely took in the huge lightly pink castle around me. The stone was shimmering lightly in the sunlight, which streamed in through diamond paned, leaded windows, and splashed across the floor, making patterns on the cream carpets.

The drawing room was, thankfully, easy to find, and it was *filled.* The long, tall room contained at least ten seating areas, all consisting of lush chaise lounges, couches, and chairs arranged around a low table. Most of the tables had tiered serving ware on them displaying small cakes, pastries, and little snacks for the nobility.

Clearly, the party last night was not over, and the attendees were not done with their socializing.

Belatedly, I realized I was rather underdressed compared to the other women here. I hadn't exactly been neglected, the girls had done my hair beautifully, and my day dress was fine enough, but the women here were extravagant. Pins tucked into their curls shimmered with gemstones and polished metal beads. In some cases, the pins held in place gently draped chains dripping with yet more gems and shiny gold and platinum. Around their necks too, wealth and bounty shone, with huge necklaces that suspended giant gems at the hollow of their throats, and then draped down over their cleavage. Their dresses even shone in the light, silk shimmering, some of their gowns shot with gold or silver thread, and beaded with real pearls and yet more precious gems.

The men too were wearing crisp, fine white linen shirts, silk velvet coats, and soft leather breaches. Their buttons were shiny metal, some with jewels of pearls embedded into them, and at their wrists and collars, small pins and links winked in the light. It was more subtle than the women around them, but just as elegant, as just as wealthy.

The styles had changed since I'd been princess at Skyridge. The skirts more voluminous, and the necklines lower, but I knew expensive fabric and well-cut gems when I saw them, and it was in this room in spades.

Bizarrely, none of them turned to me when I walked in. Normally, a newcomer to a room would draw attention, and I was used to how people treated me when I was princess. I was accustomed to people rising to greet me, or rushing to my side to try and gain my ear over some matter or another. Here, I warranted nothing more than a sly glance, as people leaned into one another to whisper about the mysterious woman Landon had brought into the castle the previous night.

The attention sent shivers up my spine. It was so covert, so calculating.

I needed to form a plan, and *quickly,* or these nobles would eat me up alive.

Starting with the basics, I went to the wall, and began to pace around the perimeter of the space, returning people's sly glances and assessing them just as much as they were me. If they were any skilled at this game they were playing, they would be able to recognize that I was onto them, and that I wasn't going to be easy prey.

Step one in keeping myself safe was establishing that I was not an easy target for the sharks.

Lap one was all about establishing myself, and lap two was about taking stock of the people I was sharing the castle with. The guest rooms must be stuffed to the gills with all of the people sitting there, and it gave me the perfect opportunity to find myself someone I could rely on.

I carefully looked over each group of conversationalists, assessing those who were in a pair together, and those who were alone. I also took in the variety of people there, pleased to note that there was a vast array of people present. Wolves sat with vampires, and they all sat with fae, chatting amicably and laughing with one another. I noted there were even couples who appeared to be from across different magical races. One fae with a set of elegant horns on her head sat with her arm threaded through a vampire's arm, shiny new wedding rings winking on their fingers.

Such friendly relations were just beginning to develop in my time, and it made my heart glad to see the fruits of that work come to bear.

Among the assembled people, I also spotted one fae with a set of pale white horns that swept elegantly from his forehead back over his dark hair and came to wicked points over his head. He was dressed in all black, in contrast to many of the other men assembled. A black shirt, black velvet jacket, black cravat held in place with a platinum pin, matching platinum rings on his fingers, all of it together looking both stylish and dangerous, making his golden eyes pop. He was seated among a mixed group. There were a few wolves, with gently pointed ears like my own, and some vampires with pointed teeth laughing with them. The fae nearby all had horns or antlers, with sharp points to their ears and eyes that flashed extraordinary colors.

I caught the eyes of the man dressed in black, and he smirked at me.

The first person to openly acknowledge me.

I thought that was interesting.

I smiled back at him and tilted my head to the side. A question and an invitation.

He took me up on the offer, standing and excusing himself from his group with a sharp bow, and came to my side.

"I was wondering if we might see you this morning," he said by way of greeting.

I tilted my head, and responded quietly, "I wasn't sure I would be welcome."

"Because you're a stranger?"

I was shocked he was willing to be so open with me, but I took advantage of it immediately, "Yes."

"Ah, we were all hoping for a bit of drama anyway, and you and Landon's arrival was just what that dull party needed." He smiled at me, flashing a row of perfectly white, straight teeth. "Not that the king throws boring balls, but they all blend in together after a while."

Fae were long-lived, even more than the wolves and the vampires, and I tried to imagine a lifetime that long of balls, each one shockingly similar to the last, and could see his point. "I see. I'm glad to be of assistance."

He frowned at me, "Your voice. It is worse than it seemed last night."

Wincing, I admitted honestly, "I don't know when it will improve."

Nodding thoughtfully, he gently took my hand, and maneuvered it into the crook of his elbow, propelling us forward, continuing my circuit around the room, "You need a healer."

Reminders of Eris from the previous night came rushing forward, and I could feel the blood leave my face.

"Or not," the man murmured.

I smiled at him briefly, and then faced forward again, plastering a bland but pleasant look on my face. Even more attention was on me now that I had this man accompanying me, and it wouldn't do to show them weakness. Not when I was still drifting in unfamiliar waters.

"I'm Elias," he said, leaning down to speak softly into my ears.

"Briar," I whispered back.

"She does have a name," he said, clearly amused. "I am the envy of them all to know it."

I quirked a smile at him, "Are you?"

"Indeed. Everyone wants to know who you are and where you came from. There was a wager that you were Landon's secret lover, but then he departed today without you. Most curious. It only fed the whispers more."

It was unusual for someone to be this open about politics, but it was refreshing too. As many of Mother's lessons as I'd had, I still preferred this open speech, as opposed to sly questions meant to pull things out of me and assess me for weaknesses.

"We're not lovers," I told Elias, glancing up into his golden eyes. They were so bright, they nearly glowed. "He rescued me and then left me here. I'm afraid I have no connections in this land."

"Then allow me to be the first," he grinned, lifting his other hand to cover mine where it rested in the crook of his. "I may not be as powerful as our prince, but I come from a family just as old. I am the Fifth Duke of Trapp. It would be my honor to be seen with you, our mystery woman. Imagine how the tongues will wag at our association."

I laughed, and though it hurt, it felt good too. Elias was amusing and good-natured, and above all, *influential.* A duke would be more than powerful enough to provide me with some safety here. And though I didn't know him well, I was going to get nowhere by being cautious and refusing to associate with anyone.

So Elias it was.

"I cannot wait to hear you laugh without the strain on your throat," Elias told me, smiling with me. "Come, let us get you some tea and some honey. And allow me to introduce you to some people."

He guided us towards the group he had left, allowing me to take his own seat, and having a chair pulled up next to me so he could sit close. In short order, he introduced his group to me, ordered me some minty tea with honey in it for my throat, and managed to do most of the talking for me.

Elias was quite skilled, really, so much so that even my mother would be impressed with how he maneuvered conversing with such a large group. My name he kept to himself, choosing instead to point out each of the others and give to me their titles. We were seated with two wolves from the neighboring kingdom, three fae from the east, three vampires, and the couple, who I was told lived here in Fenestra.

They all watched me carefully and curiously as I sipped on my tea. After a few polite questions, which I all dodged, they got the memo that I was not necessarily open to answering questions about myself and instead turned to gossip.

This was more valuable than gold, and I listened attentively. Elias, I noticed, watched me closely, clocking my closed-off nature, and smiling at me like we shared a secret.

I supposed, in a way, we did.

"It's no wonder the king feels so comfortable," one of the women, a wolf with golden hair named Celeste said. "Landon is the most formidable crown prince we've had in an age. No one can best him in combat, and if they tried, he'd have their heads for it. By claw or by steel."

Her partner, a woman named Lynette, leaned into the middle of the circle, whispering, "I heard he's so dedicated to his training, and to avoiding his king, he spends every night away. Either warming a lucky woman's bed or finding a new challenge."

One of the fae men, named Carlisle, laughed, "I hear that he's broken more than one lady's heart with his antics. Last time he attended a ball he nearly caused a riot. Either lovers whose beds he left, or women convinced they can be the ones to make him stay."

"Good luck to them," Elias laughed. "Landon isn't one to stay anywhere for long."

I leaned in, latching on to any piece of information I could get about my host here at the castle.

"Is it true he never says anything to anyone?" Lynette asked Elias, eyes sparkling with the joy of gossiping among fellows. "You know him better than we, tell us what you know."

I glanced at Elias, surprised. Was he friends with the prince?

Shrugging Elias demurred, "I cannot say. He is not one for conversation, that is true. But anything else, I do not know. Landon does as he will. He is a prince, so this is his right. There's no use in conversing about it."

Lynette looked quite put out, "You're no fun, Elias."

"On the contrary, I am *very* fun," he purred, winking at her. "More fun than talking about Landon."

There was an edge to his voice, something that pushed the woman to change the subject, fanning herself and saying, *"Well,* aren't you the charmer?"

"Always."

Elias smiled wide at her, his eyes then sliding to the side to find my own. He gave me a look, quick as a flash, and then turned back to his companions.

All in all, I didn't know if I understood everything correctly, or indeed if there was anything of real value in their words tonight, but I had a small, tentative hope that Elias might be *exactly* who I needed.

The gathering wrapped up before lunch, every one streaming back to their rooms to change and get settled before the next event, and Elias *insisted* on walking me back to my rooms before he went to do the same.

Tucking my hand into the crook of his arms again, he held my hand there with his own opposite hand and leisurely walked me deeper into the castle.

"I have so many questions for you," he admitted as we strolled. "I wish you could answer them."

I glanced at him, trying to convey my curiosity without needing to sacrifice my throat for the words.

Chuckling, I knew he understood when he began to list his queries. "Where you came from. Where you're intending to go. Who your family is. Where Landon found you. How you came to be with him at the party, looking as if you'd just stumbled out of bed."

I winced. There was no way for him to know how correct he was with his observations, but it hit close to home all the same. Elias, sharp, didn't miss it.

"Gods, Briar. Did you?"

I shrugged at him, "Perhaps."

His laughter exploded, warm and bright in the pink stone hallway, "You're exactly as different as I'd hoped you'd be."

"Hm?"

"Do you remember how I said the parties all blend together?"

I nodded.

"You, Briar, don't blend in."

"Hmmm."

I looked up at him, and his fingers squeezed my own, "It's a good thing, poppet."

Making a face at the taller man, it was all I could do not to smile when he laughed again.

Elias, I was pretty sure, was going to make me a good ally. And maybe even a good friend.

CHAPTER SEVEN

L andon did not return the next day, so though I was still curious about the prince and the circumstances around my awakening from Eris's curse, I pressed forward the best I could without him.

The girls dressed me again when I awoke, and when I was finished, Anita declared, "You'll go to the ball tonight."

"I'm sorry?" I wheezed.

My throat, thankfully, hurt remarkably less today than yesterday. But it still hurt and came out sounding rather weak.

"The ball!" She declared. "We've secured a dress for you, and there's many whispers about your presence here…"

Lily whispered, "Everyone's talking about you."

Candela noted, "And the prince is still absent."

So, Rose finished, "Even the king asked after you."

I flinched. That couldn't be good.

The king, as was his right, could turn me out of his castle onto my behind at any time. I needed allies, a soft place to land, and I needed it sooner than later.

Glancing between the four women, I belatedly realized they were all looking out for me. Sharing knowledge and trying to give me the tools I needed to secure myself. Even as someone unknown to them, they were trying to help.

Touched, I nodded slowly, "I'll go to the ball."

"Huzzah!" Rose cheered.

Even Anita smiled.

I did not venture to the drawing room, nor did I make my way to the grand breakfast the girls informed me was happening. Instead, I found it prudent to head to the library and prepare myself for the ball in the evening.

My absence during the day, I knew, would be noted, and therefore my appearance in the evening would make even more impact.

But before I could make it there, I needed knowledge. One afternoon would not be enough time to learn everything, but it would be enough. Of course, I had all of my mother's lessons, all of my father's teachings, but in five thousand years, anything could change.

Shaking my head, I quickly dispelled thoughts of them and how long I had slept. The tear stains on my pillowcase were enough mourning for now. I needed my wits about me, and I needed *focus.* Crying was *not,* obviously, focusing.

The girl's directions to the library were true, and I found it easily. Slipping in through the massive donors, I assessed the space and found it pleasantly empty, and exceedingly well organized. It took no time at all to locate the history section, as well as the genealogy tables of all of the current noble houses in Fenestral.

Laying them out in front of me, I opened one of the history books and began to read. The words were, thankfully, all ones I recognized, the written tongue had not changed too much in the last millennia.

Scanning the text, I took in the history of my own lands, my own family, hundreds of years after it happened. It happened so long ago, all of Skyridge was barely a footnote in the massive text.

Skyridge, once the seat of a noble house, fell due to disarray in the family. Land and control of the mountain passage merged with that of the Starks.

That was it.

No information about my parents, my siblings. No mentions on if they married or when, or how they lived their lives.

I'd come here for knowledge, that was true. But a small part of me was hoping for some news of my siblings and my parents. Insight into what I had missed while I slept, mere steps away from them.

Misery. This is what Eris wanted from me.

This striking and painful stabbing pain in my heart threatened to overwhelm me. She wanted the tears on my sheets, and I could hear the echoes of her laughter all around me, mocking me.

This was the culmination of her curse. The true outcome.

What Eris desired above all was my deep understanding of all I had lost. Of all my family had suffered.

And even still, all of that suffering, all of that toil, we were but a footnote in history. Easily dismissed. Easily forgotten.

I gave Eris what she wanted then, and let myself cry. Bitter, hot tears streamed down my face and dripped off my chin and into my dress.

The heavy door creaked open, and I slammed the book shut and used my sleeve to dash away my tears, turning to glance at whoever came into the room.

Surprisingly, it was Elias. He was glancing about with open curiosity, looking up the tall shelves, taking in the ladders and lush couches until his eyes caught on me and his steps froze, and he frowned.

"Briar?"

I smiled at him, knowing it was weak, but doing it anyway, "Elias."

My voice was weak, but he caught the word anyway, and dipped his head in a short bow, "Am I interrupting?"

I shook my head, setting the book to the side, feigning a casualness that I did not feel.

"May I join you?"

"Yes," I said, nodding to the seat next to me. "Please."

I took the book, and slid it onto a table in front of me, putting it under some of the other tomes I'd pulled from the shelves, and laid my hands in my lap, trying to appear serene, and not like a woman lost in time, crying over her losses.

Elias wasn't convinced, and as he gracefully dropped onto the chair next to me, his eyes narrowed, and he asked, "Is all well?"

Was there a point in denying it? I didn't think there was. And it was not as if crying would be unusual for someone thrust into a strange castle the way I was, curse notwithstanding.

"I am not a good liar, I think," I laughed, looking down at the hands in my lap.

"No, darling, you're really not," he said gently. "Would you like to talk about it?"

Sighing, I smoothed my hands over the silk of my skirt, trying to figure out how to skirt both the truth and what felt safe to reveal, "I miss my family. I feel rather lost here."

"Hmm," Elias murmured, leaning closer, propping his head in one fist, frowning. "Where are you from?"

Unsure of how to answer that, I said, "Just past the mountains."

Nodding thoughtfully, he said, "It is like a whole other world to the West."

"Mm." I said, "It is. And I miss it. I miss my family and I miss my home." I sniffed, trying to beat back the tears. "I don't know what I'm doing without them."

"Love, do any of us know what we're doing?" He asked me softly, leaning in closer. "It's ok to feel lost."

"Thank you," I warbled. "I know it's unusual to be somewhere so beautiful and be so sad."

"Half the places I've felt despair have been the most beautiful I've ever beheld," Elias told me honestly. "It's like the beauty makes the pain all the sharper."

His voice was so gentle, and his eyes filled with understanding, the tears rushed forward again, overflowing and leaving salty tracks down my cheeks.

"It does," I cried. "It's all so painful."

My hands came to my eyes, and I pressed my palms into my cheeks, trying to stem the flow of sadness. It was ineffective, and the painful sobs came one after the other.

Cooing softly, Elliot stood and pulled me up and into his arms, gathering me close. He tucked my head into his chest, and squeezed me tight, letting me cry my feelings into the soft linen of his shirt.

"Cry all you need, poppet," he said quietly, rocking us gently. "You don't have to be alone right now."

"T-thank you," I said, grabbing onto his shirt, and fisting the fine material, heedless of whether or not I wrinkled it.

Surely Elias was able to employ a laundress, and I was taking his words here at face value. If Elias said it was ok for me to cry, then I was going to *cry*. I leaned into him, letting all of it trail out of me. My sorrow at my lost family, how my heart ached for what I missed, and at the uncertainty of my future.

However long we were there, Elias remained steadfast and strong, holding me close and murmuring softly to me. And when the tears began to ebb, and I mumbled a soft apology, he squeezed me even tighter.

"I won't hear of it. Apologies are for mistakes and slighted lovers. Never for our emotions."

Giggling, I asked, "Slighted lovers?"

"When you live as long as I, you tend to accumulate them," he said, sighing and looking harried.

Pushing against his chest, I took a small step back, wiping at my eyes. Elias kept one arm around my shoulder and used his other to fish out a handkerchief from his pocket, handing it to me. It was soft white, with an elaborate embroidered black and silver E in one corner.

"Thanks," I mumbled, giving my face a thorough wiping down, and then shyly handing it back.

Without a look, or even a flash of disgust at all of the fluids I'd just put onto his hankie, he put it back into his pocket and then took me by both shoulders, squaring us up and stooping down to look me directly in the eyes.

"You need a good time. Something to take your mind off of things."

"Do you think?"

"I *know*. I'm well-versed in all manner of pleasant distractions, and I happen to know that balls are high up on the list. Allow me to escort you to the ball this evening, and I promise to show you how it's done," he said, smiling gently.

"Oh!" I was shocked. I hadn't imagined Elias would be just as gung-ho about spending time with me as I was with him. That he would enjoy me as much as I did him. But his smile was clear and bright and I found myself agreeing. "Alright, that would be lovely."

"I'll come find you and pick you up," he said, thinking aloud. "I'll be wearing black, of course."

"Of course," I said, eyeing his current outfit.

"It's my color," he said with mock defense. "I've tried others, but black is the most flattering."

"It does look good on you," I admitted. "With your hair and horns and things."

Rougeish to the end, he grinned and tilted his head to the left, showing me his good side, "I'm glad you noticed, love."

Laughing, I rolled my eyes and finally felt stable enough to step away from the circle of his arms. "Remind me to limit my compliments in the future."

"I'll do no such thing," Elias said, hand over his heart. "I *live* for your kind words, my lady."

"Do you say that to all your partners?"

"Of course not," he winked. "Just the interesting, beautiful ones."

"Silver tongue."

I shook my head and decided that this was enough for now. If I was going to have a partner for the evening's festivities, I needed to cry less and prepare more. Mostly, I needed to give my girls enough time to wash and pin up my hair.

Grabbing my book from under the cushion, I smiled at Elias, "Until tonight, then."

He bowed, eyes twinkling, "Tonight, my lady."

CHAPTER EIGHT

Though so much emotion took some of the energy out of me, when I returned to my rooms and found Anita, Rose, Candela, and Lily waiting for me, I found my second wind. Their excitement was *contagious*.

"I have an escort for this evening," I told them, giving them the updates. "He said he would be wearing black?"

"Ohh!" Candela cooed.

"That's *perfect!*" Anita said. "Your dress will match his well."

"I'll go get it," Rose said, hustling from the room, Lily hot on her heels.

"This is such good news," Anita told me. "You're too pretty to have to attend alone."

"Thank you," I smiled at her. "I'm just glad to have people I know there. I was worried I'd be facing a room full of strangers."

"Who is the lucky sir?" She asked, pulling me to the seat at the dressing table and assessing the state of my hair, massaging my scalp as she did so.

"His name is Elias. He's a fae." I motioned over my own head, where Elias's horns curled. "He has pale white horns."

"Ah," she smiled knowingly at me through the mirror. "He is handsome."

Blushing slightly, I had to admit, "He is. But I don't think it's a romantic connection."

"Perhaps not now, but anything can happen at a ball," Candela said, swirling around me, a large bowl of warm water in her hands, a few soft cloths already soaking in the liquid. To the water, she added some chamomile tea and lavender, then swirled it around and let it sit on the vanity. "It's the perfect time to make any connection a romantic one."

"If you're interested in men," Anita said quietly. "Elias is a good one."

"Good to know," I smiled at her.

Truthfully, I knew that long-term security in this strange world would mean marriage, but I had barely begun to accept the idea and all that it meant. I'd dreamed for so long of finding a mate, someone who was my perfect match in any way.

Was I willing to give that up?

I didn't know that I had a choice.

Instead of dwelling on it more, which I knew might lead to more tears, I leaned back in the chair, and let Candela wash away the salt and sadness from my skin.

When she was done, Lily and Rose rushed back in with an exquisite bundle of white in their arms, and I knew it was going to be a good evening.

When my hair had been curled, pinned, and piled in waves of blonde on my head, with delicate braids threaded throughout and held in place with sparkling jeweled pins, and the dress had been smoothed over my hips and placed just so over my shoulders, Lily, Rose, Candela, and Anita stepped back, taking me in from head to toe.

"Oh my *gods*," Candela enthused. "You're so pretty, my lady."

"I've never seen a prettier woman," Lily said quietly.

Anita and Rose fussed with the hem of the dress, but both mentioned how the fabric made me *glow*.

Which wasn't, honestly, too far from the truth.

The stark white silk was embroidered delicately in white and silver, from the deep vee neckline, and then down the seams of the skirt to glide along the hem. Flowers danced on silver vines, making the already white fabric seem even more pristine. There had to be magic woven into the dress, because it was so inconceivably pristine, like it was repelling even the oils from my skin to maintain itself.

It made my freckles stand out against my skin, and my eyes glow with a brightness that had been absent since I'd awoken. Where the silk swirled around me in a skirt that moved at the smallest step, it was soft and wrapped around my legs like a gentle caress.

Ordinarily, I would have considered the vee at the front too deep, but the girls insisted it was *all* the fashion. Thankfully, my breasts had always been small, so I wasn't threatening to spill out of the dress, and all the deep cut revealed was more freckled skin.

Altogether, I felt ethereal. Like the mystery everyone seemed to perceive me as, and with Elias in all black next to me, we'd be the perfect pair.

Lastly, Anita came to me, and said, "To match your escort."

In her hands was a small diadem of black and white diamonds that curled around a silver branch like small buds, ready to bloom into something beautiful and dark. It was the most beautiful thing I'd ever seen, delicately made by an artisan who had an eye for details.

She settled the diadem on my head, and then declared, "All done."

Together, the curls stood in front of me, eyes shimmering with a job well done.

"Oh it's wonderful," Rose cooed.

"Where did it come from?" I asked with wonder, lifting one hand to gently prod the diadem.

"An admirer," Candela giggled, winking at me.

"What?" I asked, rearing back. "Elias?"

"Oh we can't tell," Rose said, singing the words as she made one last circle around me, making sure everything was as it should be.

"Take it," Anita assured me. "It was not given with ill intent."

"Alright..." I nodded.

Though it was generally a bad idea to accept gifts from unknown sources, if the girls said it was okay, I trusted them. They had shown me nothing but kindness and care in my time here, and there was no reason for me to start doubting them now. Not over something as small as a gift.

The gift *was* an exquisite diadem, but still.

Lavish gifts were all part of the game Mother had taught me to play at court. I'd give it no more or less credence than she would. Mother would simply accept it, and refuse to give anything in return for it, even if the giver heavily implied they expected something from her.

She was always strong like that, unwilling to bend to any pressure lest it be her will.

As the ladies fussed and fluffed and twirled errant curls around their fingers and laid them into place, Lily stepped close and whispered, "Have fun tonight."

Heart melting, I smiled at the soft-spoken maid, and assured her, "I will."

With perfect timing, a knock came at the door, and Anita rushed to open it.

"My lord," she greeted, curtsying to the person on the other side.

Elias's silky voice responded, "Good evening. I'm here for Lady Briar."

"I'm here," I said, making my way to the door.

Anita obliged me, opening the main door wide, and giving me my first first glimpse at Elias in his finery.

He was wearing black, as promised, but it was nothing like his normal garb. It was *much* finer. An exquisitely tailored black velvet coat accentuated the breadth of his shoulder and the sharp taper of his waist. Across its surface, small flowers and stars were embroidered in black silk thread and stark silver, shimmering as he turned, taking his time to absorb me as much as I was him.

I did my best to ignore his gaze as it moved over me, choosing to instead catalog how his black silk shirt shined, and how his simple but gorgeous cravat was pinned in place with a pin that matched my diadem. To finish it all, he had on perfectly tailored black leather pants, held closed with buttons, and disappearing into tall black leather boots that shone in the low light, silver accents at the calf and just at his heels.

It was effective and so Elias. Arching every part of his wry, mysterious, and engaging personality. One look at him and you knew who he was.

Or at the very least, who he wanted you to think he was.

His eyes were intent, flaring with appreciation as he raked them over me, taking in every last detail of my outfit.

"You look *splendid*," he said quietly. *"Radiant. Ethereal."*

"That's a lot of compliments," I smiled at him. "Thank you, Elias."

I dropped my head, trying to do Mother proud with my etiquette, but he was having none of it. He came to my side, lifted me up, and kissed my cheek.

"We'll have no formalities between us," he declared. "I think we're past that, do you not agree?"

I smiled at him, "I can agree to that."

Really, who would I be if I didn't? I had *sobbed* in Elias's arms. He was right. We were well past formalities.

Reaching up, I tapped on the cravat pin, and said, "You have good taste."

"I do," he said shamelessly.

I waved towards my head, asking, "Do I have you to thank for this?"

Shrugging, he demurred, "I cannot say, love. But whoever gifted you that must also have exquisite taste."

"Well, thank you to him, then," I laughed, smile widening up at him.

"Are you ready to face the ravenous crowd?" He asked me, arching a brow. "You certainly look ready for battle. You'll have them all charmed with but a glance. It'll be splendid."

"I'm hoping you're right," I told him, unease leaking into my words. "I'd like to be seen positively among the court. Or at the very least, not seen as a nuisance or…"

"Or prey," Elias filled in, shooting me a knowing look. "I understand. Your situation here is precarious. But you're making the most of it, you'll find your place soon, I am certain of it."

How was it possible that I'd found this many understanding people after coming out of such an ordeal? What was by far the most challenging and difficult part of my life was made bearable by understanding and kindness, so much so it was almost hard to believe Eris had cursed me.

Until I remembered the book, and then my heart sank again.

These highs and these lows would be my normal, and it was time for me to accept it.

So I put on a wide smile, and said, "I appreciate having you at my side for this, Elias."

He inclined his head, "It's my honor." Then, he held out his arm, offering me his elbow. "Shall we?"

"We shall." I threaded my arm through him and together we made our way through the castle, slowly joining the stream of other guests heading in the same direction we were.

Wolves, vampires, and fae alike were all dressed in their best, with sweeping trains of silk and lush velvet and shiny silk on every person. And the *jewels*. It reminded me of the lavish parties my mother would throw for festivals, and my chest aches with nostalgia.

"Is this a holiday gala?" I asked Elias quietly, leaning in and going up on the toes of my white slippers to whisper into his ear. "Or some birthday?"

He glanced at me, confused, "It's solstice, love."

"Ah, of course," I smiled at him, feigning embarrassment. "In the... well... I forgot."

He smiled, understanding, "I hope one day you'll trust me enough to share your burdens."

It was a nice sentiment, a wonderful one even, but there was no good answer for it, so I settled for squeezing his arm and facing forward again.

Our walk to the ballroom was spent, on my part at least, ignoring all of the stares— and even a few gasps— that we earned. We were going to be the talk of the town, I could sense it, so I did my best to do what I could now. That was: Appear unbothered, smile at Elias, and glide as serenely as I could across the pink stone floors.

On the main floor, we neared the ballroom Landon had first brought me to when we'd arrived at Fleur. I tensed with the memory. I had a lot to make up for when it came to that night and the impression I'd given these nobles.

I lifted my chin and waited with bated breath next to Elias as we joined the line to be announced and let into the ball.

"What shall they announce you as?" Elias asked softly, leaning in to whisper close to my ear.

"Lady Briar Rhoswen," I said proudly.

If Eris could take me away from my family, I was not about to let her take my family away from me.

"A gorgeous name," he murmured. "Suited for a gorgeous lady."

He conveyed our information to the Lord Steward, who noted it down, and then opened the doors for us, announcing proudly, "If it pleased the court, Sir Elias, Fifth Duke of Trapp, escorting Lady Briar Rhoswen."

A polite applause broke out, and Elias propelled us forward.

This was familiar territory, at last.

I smiled my best smile, the one Mother had made me practice a hundred times over, making eye contact with every person I could, making sure I did so with intent.

I wanted them to know I saw them. That I could play this game with them, and that I was *good* at it. I wanted them to see me not as a curiosity, or a plaything, but a potential ally. Hopefully, Elias at my side would bolster that claim.

Behind us, another couple was announced, and more polite applause followed, but eyes remained locked on Elias and I.

"They're ravenous for news of you," he told me softly. "We didn't see you at breakfast, and it made them curious."

"About who I am?"

"About who you were *with* that you missed breakfast."

Curses. I hadn't considered that they'd reach that conclusion. Of course, a grand breakfast like that would *only* be missed if it was spent in the throes of passion with an eligible bachelor.

Likely, they thought I was with Elias.

"It seems I have caused you to be the subject of gossip," I said. "My apologies."

"Oh dear, it's been *years* since I was in the spotlight, it's a delight to be here by your side."

I eyed him carefully, "Are you sure?"

"I'm sure, love," he said, squeezing my hand. "I'm not a fragile man. I have enough reputation that I can afford a little scandal now and then."

Grateful, I squeezed his arm again, and then, from the main doors, trumpets began to sound, and as one the crowd moved to the sides of the ballroom.

"Announcing to the court, His Majesty the King!"

Together, the crowd bowed and curtsied, their heads down in deference for their ruler. The trumpets blared, playing a tune I didn't recognize, and the main doors opened, allowing in the king.

With powerful strides, he crossed the ballroom, headed for the dais at the back of the room, and he did so alone.

"Landon is still missing," Elias murmured.

"Mmm."

I wondered again where he had gone, and why he had left me here without so much of a word. Why had he bothered rescuing me just to leave me here alone?

It made no sense to me, but no matter how many times I thought about it, no answers would come without me being able to speak directly to Prince Landon.

One day, I'd hoped I'd be able to do just that.

The king swept past us all, and when he reached the dias, he turned, cape swirling around behind him, and then announced, "Rise."

As one, the crowd rose, and turned to face their ruler.

He stood before us, and I realized I hadn't properly taken him in the night I'd arrived at the castle. The king looked strikingly similar to Landon, with blonde hair, a strong, clean-shaven jaw, and curly hair. Though Landon had darker blonde hair, the king's was more of a chestnut color that shone in the candlelight. He was dressed in a red and gold formal jacket, heavily embroidered with depictions of a hunt, a pair of black pants and boots, golden rings on his fingers, and with a golden crown on his head made of fleur de lis and inlaid with rubies and diamonds. His cape swept around him, a sea of red velvet trimmed with white fur, held at one shoulder with golden braids, and a large golden aiguillette hanging down at the opposite shoulder as a counterweight, just as jeweled as his crown.

"Greetings all, and Happy Solstice." He boomed. "As we welcome spring and the end of our long winter, I am glad to be doing so in such good company."

The crowd tittered with delight, people smiling up at the king.

"Together we will eat, we will drink, and we will bring in this new era with joy. My son, Prince Landon, has ensured our safety, so revel with peace in your hearts, and gratitude for his strength, and the strength of the crown!" He held out his hand, and a server passed him a drink. He held it aloft, and shouted, "Fenestral!"

Everyone returned his cheer, shouting, "Hail, Fenestral! Hurrah! Hurrah!"

Elias was silent next to me, but made sure to smile, and I followed his lead, smiling and looking delighted to be there. The king was apparently done, as he gestured to a balcony behind us, and immediately a band struck up a waltz, the rich sound of the full orchestra a lively embrace.

Turning to me, Elias smiled wide, and said, "Shall we dance, my lady?"

I slid my hand down his arm, grasping his own, and smiled, "I'd be delighted."

Together, we joined the dance, making our way to the middle of the room, and then starting into a waltz.

It was similar enough to the dances I had learned as a child, and fell into step with Elias easily. As the music played, and Elias expertly led me across the floor, I relaxed into his arms, following where he went, spinning and finding joy in the dance. The way my skirts swirled around my ankles, Elias's warm hands on my skin, and the swell and fall of the music, it was all beautiful.

It was a dream.

Everything about it reminded me of the life I had had. But instead of feeling sad and bitter, I forced myself to enjoy having this feeling again. To be able to be a part of this grandeur again was almost magical.

I kept my eyes on Elias, admiring the gold in his eyes and how it reflected the candlelight just so. I could feel the eyes on our backs, but they were small next to this feeling. Immaterial.

Elias spun me, and then reeled me back in, pulling me close to his body, and then twirled me back into place, whispering as he did, "You look radiant when you dance."

I smiled at him, "Thank you. Do you think that's why people are staring at us?"

He winked, "They're looking at me, love. Of course."

"Ahh, of course," I giggled, spinning again into his arms.

Holding me close, he leaned down to whisper into my ear, "It's because they're all jealous of me."

"Jealous?"

"Mm. I get to have you close. To whisper into your ear. To touch you."

I spun out again, cheeks flushing with the meaning of his words, "I'm sure it's just because of how I arrived here."

"For some of them, perhaps," he admitted. "But I know jealousy when I see it. I'll have to watch my drink tonight."

"What? Why?"

"Some aren't above using a sleeping draught to open up a fine lady's dance card."

Shaking my head, I whispered, "That's horrible."

"No, Briar," he said softly, pulling me close against him. "Horrible would be to never know the warmth of your skin, or how sweet your laugh is."

"Elias," I whispered. "You're too kind."

With his easy charm, he winked at me, stepping away to bow before me, kissing the back of my hand as the music began to wane. "I can be kinder."

My heart skipped a beat when his lips brushed my skin, but before I could properly evaluate that feeling, we were at the side of the dancefloor, and people rushed in from all sides, polite smiles on their lips and their eyes filled with questions.

Elias, sensing the sharks closing in, pulled me to his side, and dipped his head to the assembled crowd.

"Elias, you must introduce us to your enchanting partner," a fae man with an elegant pair of antlers on his head said. "She's been the subject of much intrigue since her arrival." His eyes swept me head to toe, taking me in.

"Esteemed friend," Elias said, gesturing to the small crowd around us. "Please be introduced to Lady Briar."

"Lady Briar," one woman said. "It's a pleasure to meet you. Your gown is lovely."

I smiled at her, trying to memorize her face, "Thank you Lady...?"

"Waterhouse," she supplied for me. "Elizabeth Waterhouse."

"A pleasure," I smiled.

The man with the antlers said, "I'm Lord Brecksville. Damien Brecksville."

I nodded at him, keeping my polite smile in place, "A pleasure, Lord Brecksville."

And so it went, for ten or more people, until my head was swimming with faces and names, and Elias announced, "I think I'll have Lady Briar here for another dance if you'll excuse us all."

I shot him a thankful glance, which got me a quick smile in return, and then I was back in Elias's arms for another dance.

This dance was more formal than the last, with Elias and I making circles and rounds around one another, and then with the people on either side of us. The dance was a rondo of sorts and gave me a view of the entire space and the people in it as we moved.

People still had their eyes on Elias and I, and when I turned and caught sight of the dias, even the king's eyes were turned our way.

Shoot.

The king was an unknown. A *huge* unknown. It hadn't escaped my mind that I was only here by his grace, and he could kick me out of here just as soon. All the better I knew Elias now. If the king decided he was done with me, at least I had him to fall back on.

I hoped, anyway.

I thought back to his quiet words, the compliments he gave even when no one was listening, and my heart squeezed.

I mentally shook myself and forced myself to finish out the rondo, spinning and touching hands with Elias. But there was no shaking the awareness I now had for the king's gaze.

Every time we turned, I saw him sitting there, watching us with narrowed eyes.

When Elias bowed to me, he looked up, face arranged into a rare serious expression, "It seems His Majesty wishes to speak with us."

"He isn't subtle," I noted. "Should we get it over with?"

"Better sooner than later," he said, then smirked. "After, we can locate some champagne."

"You've convinced me," I said, taking a deep breath. "Let's take care of our obligations. Only so we can drink after."

"Such strength," Elias said dramatically, pretending to swoon. "Briar, how do you do it?"

Giggling, I hooked my arm through his elbow, and allowed him to lead us off the dance floor and towards the dias. My heart pounded unsteadily, and I had to take deep breaths to calm myself. I'd met kings before. Hells, my *father,* was a king. This man was just another ruler, and I could deal with him the same as any other.

He watched us approach with eagle eyes, and when we came to stand at the bottom of the dias, he looked at Elias, waiting.

Elias bowed, and I dropped into a deep curtsey as Elias said, "Your Majesty, allow me to introduce to you Briar Rhoswen. Briar, His Majesty Eduard Hugh Charlemagne Bleddyn, King of Fenestral."

"Rise," King Eduard said. "Is her voice much recovered?"

"It is, Your Majesty," I answered, making sure to cast my eyes down at his feet. "Thank you for your concern."

"She's polite," the king noted, sounding surprised. "With how she came to us, I half thought she was a wild thing."

Elias laughed politely, "Indeed, Your Majesty. She is a lady, through and through."

"Good. Then she'll have no trouble remaining here for the duration of the festivities," he said.

Reading between his words, I heard what he wasn't saying. *I was only welcome for the festivities, and no longer.*

"If it pleases you, Your Majesty," I said, keeping the panic from my voice. "I'm thankful for your hospitality."

I needed to get a plan. *Fast.* I knew my welcome here would run out eventually, but I hadn't planned for it to be so soon.

Unable to help myself I asked, "If I may, Your Majesty. Will we be seeing Prince Landon this evening? I've yet to thank him for helping me."

The king was silent for so long, and Elias was so still at my side, I risked a glance up at the king's face only to find him staring down at me with a fierce expression. Just as quickly I looked away from him.

Only then did the king speak, "You're not to concern yourself with my son."

"Yes, Your Majesty," I hastened to say.

"You're dismissed."

Elias and I dipped down again, and then he practically pulled me away.

I was shaking like a leaf and Elias noticed, pulling me to the side of the room, near a towering display of flowers, large enough to hide us from the prying eyes of the masses.

"Are you alright?" He asked me softly, taking one of my hands into his own and sliding his thumb along the back of it.

Back and forth, I thought of nothing except for that touch until my panic subsided enough for me to think.

"I... was not expecting to be dismissed so suddenly," I admitted. "I don't know where I shall go."

"Do you... not have a home?" Elias asked carefully. "Just where did Landon find you?"

Several answers rattled around my brain, some of them lies, some of them the truth. I could settle on none of them. So I smiled at Elias, a weak, apologetic thing, that he read for the answer it was.

"So many mysteries," he mused. "I hope one day you'll trust me with them."

I smiled at him, genuinely this time, "I don't like keeping secrets. I simply don't know how to divulge them."

"Is this why I found you crying in the library?"

I nodded. In a way, it was.

Elias believed me, nodding, and I wished I could tell him the truth so fiercely, my heart burned with it.

But what would I say? *Oh, I've been cursed by a witch who made me sleep for millennia, unchanged. When I awoke, my family and kingdom were dead, and Landon was the one who found me.*

He'd have me sent away to the country to live out my days as an insane woman. Ill of mind and of heart. He'd probably think he was doing me a kindness too, allowing me to live in luxury with my delusions until the end of my days.

Or perhaps he'd abandon me altogether, leaving me to rot on the streets.

A country home was *far* from the worst outcome, and that reminder had me clamping down again on my secrets.

When I had a plan for my immediate future, housing, and protection, I'd need to sit down and think of how to explain my life. Or invent a fake one for myself. Something like I was the illegitimate child of some distant noble. Abandoned because of the shame I brought my family.

It was far more plausible than the truth, far-fetched though it was.

"I'm sorry," I said, putting on a smile for Elias. "We should find champagne. No need to let uncertainty ruin our evening. We're here, and I intend to enjoy it."

He searched my eyes, golden irises boring into my own, and after a moment, he smiled. "Alright, Briar. Let's enjoy this evening to its fullest. We'll leave our worries for the morrow."

"Perfect," I enthused. "First, champagne. Then I insist on another dance."

"If the lady insists, how can I deny her?" He asked, sweeping me away from the flowers and towards a server with a tray of glasses.

Together, we nabbed ourselves some glasses.

And then we danced.

Exactly as I had asked.

CHAPTER NINE

Solstice and its celebrations were meant to conclude in two days.

Which meant I had two days to find myself a new place to go.

The obvious answer was, of course, to use the connections I had, and impose myself on a willing noble person. Someone with power, someone like Elias.

He was a duke, an older fae who was well-connected and, I suspected, quite powerful. Plus, he was hardly bad to spend time with, being good-natured and funny, and he made no bones about enjoying my company in return.

He was the obvious choice.

Guilt turned my stomach at the thought of using him... of lying to him... but there was no other choice. I didn't mean to lie with malice, and that must count for something, right?

Therefore, the morning after the ball, I woke up first with a mission to concoct the story of my life. Something close enough to the truth to ring true when I spoke it, but far enough away to keep anyone from digging into my past.

I didn't need anyone looking for my family, fake or real, and complicating matters.

What I settled on was close to my initial thoughts from the ball, merged with what little I'd told Elias.

I'd be Briar from the West. An illegitimate child who was suddenly orphaned and left without a penny. No family was willing to take me in, and so I was left to fend for myself. I'd bedded down in some ruins for the night on my way through the mountains in search of a new life when Landon found me.

The prince took pity on me and brought me here to Fleur. Of course, I was ever so grateful for his rescue and knew nothing but kindness for both him and the king.

I was a perfectly well-mannered woman of good breeding, and therefore not a risk to bring into your home. I'd bring no danger, no trouble, and no drama. Instead, I would be helpful, and friendly, and do whatever was asked of me in return for my safety.

Hopefully, Elias would be willing to take me in.

My stomach churned with worry, and my skin felt hot and uncomfortable, but I still rose from bed and had my ladies dress me, asking them of the events of the day.

"Well," Anita said, chatting with me as she helped Lily style my hair, "with the festivities last night, there are no morning events today."

"Ah," I said. That was familiar too. And it made sense.

Some nobles had been deep into their cups by the time Elias and I had retired to our own rooms.

"That said, there is an *extravagant* late brunch. You're welcome to it, of course," she said. "As a guest of the prince."

I smiled at her, and she smiled back at me.

I was going to miss her and Lily, Rose, and Candela when I left.

"I would like to go to it, yes," I said to her. "Do you have anything I can wear?"

"Of course we do!" Candela said, walking to the wardrobe and pulling out an emerald green day gown. "We've made sure you're outfitted as good as any lady."

I didn't know how they'd pulled that feat off, but I was grateful for it, and not one to spurn a boon when I was handed one.

"Thank you," I said. "It looks beautiful."

"Oh, it is," Rose said, digging through a small jewelry box, selecting a few pieces. "And I know we have just the earrings for it too. I think there's even a hairpin."

With ample time before the brunch, my hair was curled, emerald chandelier earrings were placed in my lobes, and I was wrapped in yards and yards of emerald green silk velvet with a lush thick pile.

It was a tea gown, pulled directly over a floor-length black silk dress edged with fine black lace. No corset was needed, as the gown was held on with a wide, black silk belt with a large bow at the back. The gown itself was edged with more of the same black lace from the underdress and fell in luscious waves from my waist, and into a short train at the back. It was not fully closed over the black silk underdress, leaving a center parting through which one could just see the low front vee of lace and glimpse at my cleavage.

It was gorgeous, and I was immediately excited for Elias to see me in it.

"Would you send a note for me? To Duke Elias?" I asked Anita, once she had fussed about, and finally pronounced me ready.

"Whatever you need," she nodded. "Shall I ask him to attend you?"

"Please, yes."

Nodding, she hustled off, the other girls following her. "We'll be back with your duke!"

The door closed before I could protest their use of the possessive *your*.

"He's not my duke," I said anyway to the closed door.

Turning again, I looked myself over in the mirror fussing uselessly. The girls knew what they were doing, and there was not a stray thread for me to wipe away.

I fussed anyway though, nervously waiting for their return.

A few minutes later, there was a knock, with Anita announcing, "My lady, Duke Elias is here to see you."

Rushing to the door, I pulled it open and found Elias standing right on the other side, so close I nearly ran into him.

"Woah, there," he said, taking me by the shoulders to steady me. "I'll not have any accidents on my account."

"Sorry," I mumbled, finding my feet again and stepping back. "I should have been more careful."

"Nonsense," he waved his hand in the air. "You were perfectly careful. Was an accident nothing more."

"Well, thank you."

I stood there awkwardly, wondering how to ask him to accompany me this morning, mind torn between thoughts of a luscious lunch and asking him for protection. Both made my stomach churn but in a completely different way from the other.

"I can see by your face, you're conflicted," he said after a moment, looking me over. "You look lovely, but conflicted all the same."

"I... Well. It'd be improper for me to—"

"To hell with propriety," Elias said. "Tell me what's on your mind."

"Alright." I squared my shoulders. "I'd like it if you accompanied me to brunch."

Elias laughed, smiling huge and golden eyes twinkling, "Love, you were nervous to ask me that? As if I'd say anything other than yes."

I blushed, "Well how was I to know?"

"I thought I'd made my stance clear. There's no one here I'd rather spend time with than you, Briar."

"Oh."

"Should you find yourself in doubt of that sentiment, simply ask me and I shall remind you."

I bit my lip, torn between guilt and being pleased.

I was happy he'd said that. Both for myself and because, from all indications, that meant he'd be amenable to my plan. But that, in turn, made me feel guilty, and I was being torn up all over again.

Perhaps it would be better for me to ask him *before* brunch, rather than after.

If for no reason other than my stomach's sake. I'd like to be able to eat a proper meal, and there was no way I'd be able to with this huge question, and the uncertainty of my future hanging over my head.

"Might we find some time to talk before brunch, then?" I asked nervously. "I think there's still an hour until it begins."

"There is," he nodded. "Indeed, I've already scouted us a place to talk. Come."

As was his way, he offered me his elbow, and I took it. Elias led me away from my room, and my girls, who I cast a parting wave towards, and down the large, brightly lit pale pink hall.

"It shocks me every time," I said, looking around me with wonder. "It's so pretty. I can't believe they could find this much pink stone. Let alone that they'd think to make a castle with it."

"Legend has it it was built as a symbol," Elias told me. "A beacon for people of all types and ways of life. A flower blooming on the horizon."

"That's beautiful."

"Indeed it is," he agreed. "Would that all of its occupants shared that message."

"Do they not?"

He shrugged, "Some do, some do not. No king is the same as the last."

Wolves didn't live as long as fae, that was true, but they still lived to be nearly three hundred. If all of the kings had been wolves, like Landon and his father, Elias would have only seen three or four of them in his time.

Which made me wonder what happened to make Elias sound so disgruntled, and reminded me to find another history book to read. I needed to study if I was going to maintain my facade. I'd missed so much of the world, there was knowledge I'm sure others took for granted that I knew nothing of. Sooner or later, that lack would catch up to me.

"I see," I finally said, smiling lightly at Elias.

His eyes narrowed just slightly, and he pulled me closer to his side, dropping his voice to ask, "What is it that bothers you, Briar? Did something happen this morning?"

I laughed nervously, "I'm not very good at hiding my emotions, am I?"

"You're terrible at it."

"Well!" I huffed, looking away from him, out the windows we were slowly passing. Some of them were normal diamond-leaded, and others were stained glass depictions of roses and thorns winding through one another.

"You can tell me," Elias promised, laughing lightly. "It's no trouble to listen to you speak, even if it's about your troubles."

"You say all the right things," I told him, shaking my head. "I hope you're who you seem to be."

Pulling on my arm, Elias dragged us to a stop. In the middle of the hallway, he looked down at me, brows knit together and eyes swimming with questions. "Have I done something to make you doubt me?"

"N-no!" I hastened to say. "No, Elias. Never. I'm just... having a difficult time trusting people at the moment. Our acquaintance is still so new, and I find myself in an awkward position."

His lips pulled down into a frown, "Awkward position?"

Now was it. Now was the time to lie. I'd accidentally created the perfect moment to ask him, and I set about seizing it.

"I told you how I'm far from home here, right?" I said, opening the floor.

"You did."

"I'm... Well, my family..." My voice warbled, and I felt my nose begin to burn. Thinking about my family made me immediately emotional, and I struggled to hold together the tethers of my heart. "I don't have them anymore. I'm alone now. An orphan."

"Gods, Briar," he breathed. "I'm sorry, love."

I smiled briefly at him, sad and small, and then continued on, "My mother died when I was young, and then my father followed her when I was a teen. Without my father around to protect me, and with my mother being dead... There was nowhere for me to go. I came east, across the mountains, in search of something new. A fresh start. Somewhere to *belong.* My father was a lord, I've never worked but I thought perhaps as a maid or... I don't know."

It felt genuine, these thoughts. They mirrored so closely my own concerns and goals, it was easier to speak around the lies, though guilt threatened to clog my throat.

"A maid?" Elias asked, disbelieving.

"I didn't know what else I was suited for," I said, embarrassed. "I've no experience. No practical education. I need to start over, and I knew I had to do it here, where no one knew me."

"You came here with *nothing?*"

I shrugged, "That's how Landon found me. I don't have coin to rent a room anywhere, or to buy a seat on a wagon through the mountains. I set out on my own, and fell asleep in some ruins just near the pass. He took pity on me and brought me here."

"I see..." Elias mused. "I had been wondering where he found you."

"He'd just finished, er... with the dragon..." I couldn't choke out the words. The mere remembrance of the smell of dragon's blood made me angry and saddened and disbelieving. It was still unbelievable, what Landon did. "He found me, and when he did he was covered in blood."

"An unsettling first impression, I'm sure."

I nodded, "I was unsure what to make of him, or his offer to help me. But I had no other prospects. And now I'm here."

"Now you're here," he echoed. "A whole world away."

"It feels like it," I admitted. "I have no idea what I'm doing, or where I'm going. Then last night the king's words."

Elias's brows went up, and his eyes filled with knowing. Stepping closer to me, Elias bent down, peering with concern into my eyes, "Briar, do you really have nowhere to go?"

The obvious and completely sincere concern in his eyes did me in. Though the girls had worked very hard to make my makeup perfect and shimmery and beautiful, I began to cry. It wasn't violent, or sobbing, but an overflow of uncertainty and grief that I could no longer contain. They streaked silently down my face as I shook my head, confirming his words. "I don't."

"Ah, love," he said, one hand coming up to cup my elbow.

"I need to ask you," I said, the words wobbling. "I need to ask you if there's any way— *any chance*— you'd take me with you when the solstice is over. It doesn't have to be forever, or even for very long, but—"

Elias cut me off, "Of course, you can come with me."

His palms cupped my cheeks, and then swept under my eyes, wiping away my tears.

"Are you sure?" I asked uncertainty, holding onto his forearm like the lifeline it was. "I can't do much for you in return…"

"You needn't do anything but be yourself, Briar. It would be a delight to have you travel with me."

Relief so strong it made my knees weak shook me, and I told him with feeling, *"Thank you."*

For now, at least, I had a plan. Finish out the Solstice here at Fleur, then travel with Elias.

"It seems, my companion, that we should chat about my home," he said, musing aloud.

He released my cheeks with one final, tender swipe of his thumb, and then fished out a handkerchief from his pocket and handed it to me.

"I seem to keep crying around you," I said, laughing as I dabbed at my tears.

"It's no trouble," he assured me. "Though I'd prefer to see you smiling."

I did smile at that, and Elias looked pleased with himself. "Well, now that we've settled that, come with me, and we'll spend our time speaking of Trapp and my dukedom."

"I'd love to hear of it," I said, meaning every bit of my enthusiasm.

He took back my handkerchief and then offered me his elbow again, guiding me to a small sitting area at the end of the hall. The walls of the space were curved, as it occupied room in a turret, with windows along all of the exterior walls that overlooked the town and then the fields beyond. It was bright and flooded with late morning light and filled with plush pale blue furniture that complimented the pale pink walls and lush green rug. It felt like spring, and we settled easily down onto a couch, sitting side by side and looking out the windows.

"Alright?" He asked me once I'd arranged my skirts, the dark green velvet brushing against the stark black of his pants leg.

"I'm alright," I said, breathing deeply. "Thank you, Elias. I can't tell you what this means to me."

He looked at me seriously and said his next words with such feeling it was impossible not to believe them, "Briar, I will accept your thanks this once, but hear me— it is my *pleasure* to help you. To have you travel with me, shelter you, whatever it is you need, it is my boon. I will never ask anything of you in return, except that you continue to be yourself and speak with me as we do now. You're not a burden on me. In fact, I fear I may burden you with my company. I'm old and crotchety, and fickle. I've no doubt you'll tire of me."

"No!" I shook my head. "Elias, no. I very much doubt that."

Elias was charming, and there was certainly something brewing behind his congenial surface, but he was eight hundred years old. Of course, there was much about him that I didn't know, but I found myself looking forward to learning about it.

For the first time since I'd woken up, I had something to aim for. A goal.

To get to know Elias and share with him his burdens.

Perhaps, with enough time and trust, I could even tell him the truth of me.

Once I knew he wouldn't cast me out for it, that was. I couldn't blame him for not wanting to tangle with Eris, but I really clung to the hope that he wouldn't condone me for her curse either.

Shaking his head, Elias bumped his shoulder against mine, "I'll hold you to that, poppet."

"Good." I grinned at him and then watched as he settled back into the couch. I followed his lead, settling in beside him.

"Now, let me tell you where we'll be going after the solstice," he said, smiling at me.

And I listened attentively, smiling right back.

The hour passed quickly, and everything Elias said settled something inside of me. He spoke with such surety, laying out his travel schedule for the rest of the season, before assuring me that we wouldn't be on the road forever. Our trip abroad would end back at his manor where I'd be given space of my own. Rooms to decorate, girls of my own to help me dress for occasions, do my hair and the like, and a proper wardrobe of my own.

It was *exactly* what I'd needed, and when I tried to thank Elias or insist it was too much, he shot me down.

"It is my pleasure," he assured me. "I have plenty. The dukedom is not struggling by any means. To have you and your company would be a joy."

"There must be something I can do in return," I tried to insist.

"Worry about that *after* we're back home."

Home.

I was still thinking about that word when we arrived together for breakfast, arm in arm, and a swarm of eyes came to us, locking onto us.

"Ah, of course, they were waiting on us," he said, whispering in my ear.

"Were they?"

"Of course, they love the idea of some drama," he laughed, guiding me towards the table. "And I suspect our meeting with the king raised some eyebrows."

"Oh gods," I whispered, taking a seat next to him.

"Don't worry about them," he said. "Just concentrate on breakfast."

Breathing deeply, I did as he asked and looked at the opulent display sprawling down the middle of the table.

Plates were piled high with pastries, cured meats, cheeses, and all manner of cold items. Aside them were delicate displays of fruit carved to look like animals and flowers, sitting in piles of sweetened sliced fruit that were fresh and vibrant. Next to those were plates of roasted asparagus, brussels sprouts, and potatoes lined up next to boats filled with hollandaise sauce, a dark brown gravy, and bright jams and marmalade. There were displays of bread, and then finally, some roasted chicken, a whole roasted duck, and some sandwiches that were filled with cream cheese and accompanied by either savory veggies or sweet fruits.

And that was just what I could see on the table in front of me, and to the side of me. I could hardly imagine what was down along the others. It was abundant and a *very* good distraction from all of the eyes digging into my back.

I glanced to the side and saw people had already begun to eat, so I followed suit. As delicately as I could, I reached for some pastries, and then some fruit, deciding to start light. The crust on the pastries was flaky and golden, and they were still warm.

Biting into one, I swore I saw stars for a moment.

"That good, hm?" Elias asked, smirking. "I'll have to be sure to employ a good baker at the manor.

Blushing, I realized immediately I'd moaned around.

Putting down the danish that had been filled with sweetened cream cheese and topped with fresh clover honey, I said quickly, "That's not necessary."

"Trust me, love, it is."

I couldn't handle the amused intensity of his gaze, and instead looked across the table, catching the eyes of one of the people Elias had introduced me to my first real day in the castle. Lynette, the werewolf with blonde hair.

She was openly staring at me, curiosity clear in her expression.

"Lynette, right?" I asked her, smiling.

She didn't seem remorseful at all to have been caught staring, "Indeed, yes! I've heard rumors you're Briar?"

"I am," I confirmed. "Briar Rhoswen."

"You sound *much* better," she said, delighted. "We can actually talk today!"

Elias cut in, saying, "Careful, Briar. A *talk* with Lynette could last days."

"Oh hush, you," she said, rolling her eyes. "Honestly, you have a long conversation with a man *once* and he's convinced all you can do is talk."

"I have it on good authority that you can also write letters that double as wallpaper," Elias said dryly.

Lynette narrowed her eyes, declaring, "Elias, were you not so handsome, and were I not hopelessly in love with my Celeste, I would make you pay for those words."

"Promises, promises," Elias sighed.

Then, they both dissolved into laughter, and Celeste came to sit next to Lynette, glancing between them and then at me. "I hope they weren't being too much."

I shook my head, "No. Not too much."

"Ah, just enough then," she said, smiling.

It was so warm. Between their smiles and my newfound sense of security, I found myself laughing with them all.

For the first time since I woke up, I found myself feeling like I'd found a place to belong. A future I could believe in.

Chapter Ten

By the time breakfast wrapped up, and I was full of pastries, cured meats, bread, and jam, the nausea I'd woken up with and the fever I could feel building had gotten worse.

I rose from the table, unsteady on my feet.

"I think I'll retire for the afternoon," I announced. "I'm not feeling my best."

Frowning, Elias asked, "Shall I escort you?"

"No," I shook my head. "Please, stay, enjoy. I'll see you later."

"Tea?" He asked. "This afternoon?"

Nodding, I said, "That would be lovely."

"Get some rest before then," he instructed.

"I shall."

"Feel better, Briar," Lynette said.

"Make sure to have some water," Celeste said. "And some mint tea, if you can."

"I'll keep that in mind," I promised, already forgetting the suggestion.

Something was tightening in my chest, and my cheeks felt hot. I needed a rest.

Perhaps it was all the excitement catching up to me, but I was tired to my bones, and I knew there was nothing for it but to lay down and allow my body to recover. I'd spent so long asleep, but it still wasn't enough, apparently.

I made my way back to my rooms, and when I entered Anita, Rose, Lily, and Candela were busy righting the bed and doing their daily tidying.

"Ah, My Lady!" Rose exclaimed. "You're back so soon?"

"I'm not feeling well," I admitted, smiling faintly. "Can you help me disrobe? I'd like to rest for a bit before tea time."

Anita looked upwards, mentally calculating, "You can rest for two hours. We'll come wake you in time to be dressed."

"Don't push yourself," Lily said gently. "Rest is important."

"Yes," Anita agreed, nodding. "If need be, we'll deliver your excuses to the gentry."

"Thank you," I said. "But I'd like to make it if I could."

"Very well," Anita said and then began to bustle about.

The girls moved with her, turning down the bed, and then rushing to help me disrobe. They pulled the pins from my hair, allowing it to fall down my shoulders, and then ushered me into bed. Lily disappeared and then brought a bowl of cool water and a cloth from the bathing room.

I sighed with relief when she carefully wrung out the cloth and laid it over my skin, saying, "You look flushed, my lady."

"She's ill," Candela declared. "Should we call for a healer?"

On instinct, I sat up and shouted, "No! Don't."

All four women froze, staring at me in shock.

"Er, I mean," I rushed to cover my outburst. "I'll be fine, really. I don't want to be of any trouble. Let me rest and I'll be right as rain in no time."

"Very well," Anita said, clearly not believing me. "We'll be back to check on you soon."

"Thank you," I nodded, settling back into bed, and placing the cloth on my forehead.

In another short but well-choreographed rush, the women gathered their things and left me to my room, and shortly after, I fell asleep.

When I woke, I wasn't any better.

In fact, I felt worse than before. I was warm all over, and my chest was hot and tight with discomfort.

"Ugh," I groaned, rolling over and reaching for the bowl and cloth Lily had left me. I sat up and carefully wrung it out and then settled back. I laid there, an arm thrown over my forehead, cool cloth across my chest, trying to abate the fever, and contemplated whether or not I'd be able to do *anything* other than lay here. I was shaking, the breath wheezing through my lungs, and my arms and legs were numb. I felt weak. Every bit of me was aching, inside and out, and it felt like nothing I did made it better. Whatever sickness this was, it had me firmly in its grasp.

A soft knock came at the door, and I weakly called out, "Come in."

The door opened slowly, and Anita walked in concern knitting her brows together, and then she froze in place, and said quietly, "Oh. Oh, dear."

I winced, "I'm sorry, Anita. I seem to have taken a turn for the worse. I'm not any better."

"W-well!" She huffed, a soft blush coming across her cheeks. "I'd say so. I'll go grab you some food, water, and supplies. I hadn't realized, my lady. I should have... Let me go get those supplies."

"Supplies?" I asked, confused.

Who needed supplies for a cold?

"Heat supplies," she clarified, blush ramping up. "It seems you're *incapacitated,* and we'll be sure to give you what you need. And post a guard at the door who will be... unaffected."

"I... I don't understand," I said, sitting up in the bed, looking at her with wariness.

"Is this... by the Gods, is this the first?" She asked me, eyes wide. "Miss. Briar, have you had heats before?"

Slowly, so slowly it was frankly embarrassing, I realized that I *had* felt like this before. It had been more than five thousand years ago, but this was, in fact, a heat.

"Oh," I said. "No, it's not. I'm so sorry, Anita. Please, forgive me. It's just... I, uh, forgot. I've been so busy it hadn't occurred to me that I was due."

She frowned at me but didn't comment. Because really, who could forget *heats?*

Likely, I was the only person who could. Because in the rush of waking up, waiting for my body to come back into myself, and spending time with Elias, and the girls, and Eris, I really had forgotten heats existed. It hadn't even occurred to me that I would have one coming so soon.

I hadn't had one in years, why should I think I'd have one now? It was like my body had forgotten what it felt like, it'd been so long, even the clear memory of past heats felt like an impossible dream.

What would this one be like?

"I'll bring those supplies, Miss," she said, covering her nose and backing away. "We'll make sure you're squared away."

"Thank you," I told her, embarrassed, but truly, I was grateful.

I could always count on her to help me when I failed to prepare, always.

She dipped into a short curtsey, and then rushed out of the room, quicker than I'd seen her move before. I must have smelled deeply of pheromones, if she could recognize them so quickly coming into the room, the heat would be here soon.

At least I wasn't sick, but I was still going to be out for the count either way with my heat.

I mentally sifted through my schedule for the next week, remembering all of the plans Elias and I had made. I was just finding a place for myself here, people I could depend on, and now I was going to be forced into isolation until the heat passed.

Tea for sure wasn't going to happen. When Anita came back, I'd have to ask her to send Elias word that I'd been incapacitated. I took the cold cloth from my chest, and placed it over my eyes, sighing happily.

I'd forgotten how this felt. Waking up after so long really was like finding myself all over again, discovering my body and starting over from scratch. My heart still bled from the loss of my family, but I hardly had time to mourn them with everything else.

The door opened again a short while later, and I, cloth still over my eyes, told Anita, "You can leave the things over there. On the dresser."

A deep, rich voice I recognized said, "Ah. Well, I came to get you for tea, but it seems I've come at a bad time."

Belatedly, I remembered I was supposed to meet Elias for tea.

"Ah!" I sat up in bed, looking at the man with wide eyes, clutching the sheets to my chest. "Elias!"

He was looking politely away, but said amusedly, "It seems you're unwell." He tilted his head, and said quietly, "Heat?"

I nodded, wincing, "Is it that obvious?"

"To me? No." He mused. "To most fae, in fact. Our noses aren't as sensitive as you wolves are, but I've known a few other omegas, I know the signs."

"Ah..." I settled back in the bed, relaxing and pulling the sheets up around me. "Well, I apologize. I'm afraid I won't be making it to our plans this week."

"I imagine..." Elias trailed off, glancing briefly at me and smiling, before his eyes focused on the wall again. "Will you be ok? Do you have a partner for this cycle? Someone back home?"

"No, to both," I admitted. "I'll just handle things alone. It'll be ok."

"Won't that be uncomfortable?"

"It's more difficult to deal with it alone," I admitted. "It'll last longer, and be more agonizing, but there's no one here I'm involved with, and I don't want to have to seek out a strange alpha."

He glanced at me again, and asked softly, "Would you like for me to join you?"

"You?" I asked, surprised. "Elias, I don't think that's—"

"Before you say no," he said, holding up his hands, "listen. There's some spells out there, ones I can use to keep up with you. It's not the same as laying with an alpha, of course, but it should make it easier for you. Help make the heat shorter."

I flushed, from my head to my toes. I went hot at the idea.

Elias was objectively handsome, well-formed, and tall, with dark hair and tanned skin, elegant ivory horns, and bright golden eyes. It wouldn't be a challenge to spend my heat with him, of course, but he wasn't a wolf. He could keep up with me, using magic, but no magic could make a knot, surely? And my omega *called out* for a knot,

She writhed around in my chest and in the back of my mind, begging for an alpha, begging to be sated and pinned down and shown her place next to his side. It was impossible to ignore her demands, and as tempting as Elias was as a person, she didn't want him.

"I..." I said quietly. *"Elias."*

He smiled gently at me, lips parting before his answer. "I know it's not ideal, love. I know I'm not a wolf, but surely I'm better than nothing, hm? I like you, Briar. You're a beautiful mystery, and it would be *far* from unpleasant to spend your heat with you. I've helped other omegas through their heat, I can help you though yours, too."

I began to wiggle up the bed, piling pillows behind me, mind racing with his offer and with the realities of a heat. It'd been *a millennium* since I'd had a heat. What was going to happen now that it was returning? Would it last much longer than the normal week? Would it be more intense?

With so many uncertainties, it was a bad idea to take him up on his offer, even outside of my omega's protests. But what if... What if I would need help? What if it goes on for too long without someone there with me? So long I begin to lose strength? Heats demanded a lot of energy, even a normal length one sapped me of everything I had. If it went on longer than that, I could come out the other side a shell of myself.

Perhaps it was better to spend it with Elias, rather than risk weakening myself so completely. I wasn't even close to my normal self after waking up yet, and a heat risked to take away what little I had, and then some.

"It might, er, make some sense," I admitted, gripping the sheets tight in my fists, twisting them. "I'm still not feeling very well, and this timing is not the most convenient."

Railing against the walls of my mind, my inner wolf was affronted I would even *consider* Elias for us.

He's not for us! She insisted. *He's not ours!*

Then who is? I asked her. *Who else is there?*

Before she could answer, a deep and familiar voice came from the doorway, "Would you please excuse the lady and I, Elias?"

Standing there looking *very* different from the last time I saw him was Landon. *Prince* Landon. The man who had taken me from my tower and then disappeared the next morning without a word or explanation. And now here he was standing there looking perfectly presentable, with his hair hanging in loose curls to the collar of his dark and deeply blue shirt. The shirt was tucked into a pair of black leather trousers, which disappeared into well-worn but equally well-taken-care of boots. On top of it all was a jacket, made of a fine black velvet, and corded with silver accents, looping and twining over his body, making him every inch the regal prince he was. Everything about it made his blue eyes pop and together with his perfect posture he exuded everything a knightly prince should have.

It was the exact opposite of how I had seen him last, bloody and dirty and weary.

Elias glanced at me, waiting for me to incline my head at him, before bowing to Landon, murmuring, "My Prince."

With a final, slightly confused and concerned look, he left me alone in my bedroom with Landon.

The door closed behind him, and the moment it did, Landon began to walk toward me with long, purpose-driven strides.

"You'll not be spending your heat with him," he commanded, coming to stand at the side of my bed. He looked down at me as I once again scrambled to cover myself with the sheets.

"I don't—" I began to protest, but he cut me off again.

"You'll be spending your heat with me."

I gasped, "Excuse me?"

How could he waltz in here and make such demands? Who did he think he was?

But truthfully, in the days since I'd seen Landon, my senses had awakened fully, and without the stench of dragon's blood on him, I quickly noticed something I hadn't the first time I'd seen him. Landon, the prince, the first man I'd seen after waking from my curse, was an *alpha*.

My omega, of course, delighted in this, begging me to agree with him, to submit to him and let him breed us.

Yes, yes, yes. She was chanting. *He is who we need.*

"You'll spend your heat with me, and afterward we'll be married."

"Excuse me?" I cried again, louder this time.

This was *not* a conversation to be having while I was in my bedclothes, laying down and vulnerable. It pained me, but I left the comfort of my bed, walking past Landon, and wrapping myself in a lilac dressing gown I'd draped over a nearby chair the night before.

Then, I turned to face Landon, crossed my arms, and declared, "We do not know one another. We *cannot* get married."

He raised one eyebrow, and then walked towards me, cupped one of my elbows, and stated, "We don't need to know one another to be wed."

I reeled back, asking, "How can you mean that? What is this? I haven't seen you in *days,* and then you walk in here demanding to marry me? I don't understand."

Sighing, Landon ran a hand through his hair like this was tedious, and he'd rather not be here with me at all. "It's convenient. You're a mysterious woman in want of connection, but clearly well-bred and beautiful enough to entice any man, and I'm a prince who needs a wife, but with no will to wed. We'll marry, find what we need with each other, and spend the rest of our days happily letting the other do as they wish." He frowned, glancing at the door, "Even if you wish to spend them with Elias. You're free to do so the moment you give me an heir."

Blinking, heart pounding, and mind racing, I couldn't even *begin* to sort through Landon's wild proposal. On the surface, it was indeed everything I needed. But there was something about it, a bent which niggled at me and begged to be explored.

"How would you know I am in want of connection?" I asked carefully.

He hadn't even been here, and he was hardly privy to my thoughts. There was no possible way for Landon to know that what he offered me was the exact same boon I needed. He was offering me something too good to be true. *Far* too good to be true.

Which, obviously, I found to be unbelievable. And suspicious.

"I've had people keeping an eye on you," he said plainly. "They kept me apprised of your movements, who you associated with, and the like. It's obvious you're trying to establish yourself. I don't know why, but it's clear to me you need a... sponsor, of sorts. Someone to protect you. You're likely used to a certain lifestyle, a certain way of living, and a certain status. I can provide all of that and more."

Shaking my head, I stepped back from him, "You cannot be serious."

"I am."

"You don't know me."

"I don't need to," he countered. "Why would I?"

"Because you want me to be your *wife!*" When I imagined my husband, I always imagined someone who was caring and kind. Someone who knew me inside and out, and loved me to the deepest depths of his heart. Not this. Not this marriage of convenient strangers. "Don't you want someone you know? Or at the very least, someone whose *family* you know? Wouldn't a political marriage serve your needs better than this?"

Landon narrowed his eyes, "Are you declining my offer?"

"I don't know!" I hastened to say. "But it sounds too good to be true, Landon. It feels like a trap."

"How so?"

"You can't imagine I can trust this, you swooping in here and offering me everything I need, and then acting as if it's not a big deal." I said, demanding. "How could I? I would have to be a fool not to question you and your intentions."

Murmuring to himself, he said, "I knew this wouldn't be easy."

Hysterically, I laughed, "Did you now?"

The prince cut me a piercing blue glare, and then said, "How can I prove to you my intentions?"

"H-how?"

"Tell me. Tell me how to prove myself, and I will. I swear, Briar. I will do what it takes to prove it to you. If for no other reason than I need this as much as you do."

"That isn't true," I said, confused. "It can't be."

"It can and it is." He insisted. "My father needs me to produce an heir. We both need it to provide stability and a clear future for our country. Fenestral lives on the outskirts of the wolves, the vampires, and the fae. Neither a part of any of them, but not wholly separate either. It's a melting pot, a place where people of all kinds can meet and make a future for themselves. But it's also *constantly* under threat. There are those who seek to undermine us, to send assassins after myself or maneuver politically to cripple our economy. These people are our neighbors, and marrying into one of their families would be foolish. Maybe our progeny could begin to bridge that gap, but at this juncture, Father and I both agree a marriage free of politics would be good. It will allow us to strengthen our position, and for me to produce the heir we need. You're perfect for this. A virtual unknown, beautiful and mysterious..." Landon's eyes raked over me, seeing *everything*, "You'll do well."

Fire shot through me in the wake of his gaze, and I shifted under its heat.

Landon, oblivious, pulled at the cuffs of his jacket distractedly, "At the very least, you won't make our position worse, and Father and I can work on strengthening our economy. The dragon had been troublesome and damaging, but now we're finally free of the beast and can work on recovering from the damage it wrought."

I went ram-rod straight at the reminder of what Landon had done, and asked acidicly, "You see the dragon as a beast?"

Confused, he glanced at me, "Of course."

"Did you find no other solution to your problem than violence?"

"You speak of magic?" He asked. "Of course, we tried magic. But one cannot simply magic away a *dragon.*" Shaking his head, Landon declared, "There was nothing for it but to kill the beast. And now that the deed is done, it is time I turned my head to other matters."

I observed him carefully, and noted, unfortunately, that he seemed completely genuine.

Which meant I *had* to consider his words.

If he was being honest with me, then he really was offering everything I needed in one tidy bundle. Marry Landon, and then I'd be safe. I'd have a place I belonged in this world: at his side and as the mother of his children.

As a princess, I'd fully expected one day to need to bear kids and carry on my family's legacy, so this duty he spoke of was a familiar one. But I'd always hoped to do it from a place of love. My parents had filled Skyridge with laughter and good feelings, and I wanted that for my children as well.

Could I grow to love this man who slayed dragons? Was he capable of loving me?

I wasn't going to get any answers staring at him, as much as I wished for them, and every passing moment the omega wolf that lived inside of me was pounding at the doors of my heart, begging to be let free. She had a hundred things she wanted to do with the alpha across from me, with the musky scent that I knew would be even stronger at the base of his neck, and the strong lines of his jaw and his shoulders.

I stood there silent for too long, eyes locked on Landon's neck, and he didn't miss a single beat.

"Briar," he said, voice husky and deep. "Do you agree to be my wife? Will you agree to allow me to sow a child onto you?"

Taking a deep breath, I whispered, "Yes."

Immediately, the *second* the word left my mouth, Landon rushed across the room to me, hands flying to my jaw, and pulled me into a deep kiss. Immediately, my heat flared to full life, uncurling inside of me like a flower, reaching out to brush against Landon and finding sparks in return.

The part of myself that wanted to reason through things and question and sift through potential outcomes faded away to the back of my mind.

Instead, at the front of my mind, was my omega.

She was howling with joy, lunging to hold onto Landon with everything she could.

He was just as eager, hauling me close and slating his lips against mine, pressing roughly against me and pulling at the ties of my robe.

"Your heat," he muttered. "It ripens."

"Yes, yes, yes," I chanted. "Clothes off."

The heat was raging inside of me, blinding out all logic in a wave of lust and need and base instinct.

"Alright, darling, clothes off," he acquiesced. "I'll take care of you."

"Please," I breathed, tipping my head back to meet his eyes. "Please take care of me."

Landon moved quickly, peeled away my clothes, and took off his jacket, tossing both on a side chair. My hands flew to his shirt, tugging at the buttons, and pulled with him, fumbling through the process.

All I could think about was the skin that was waiting for me under his shirt and how it would feel under my hands. The warm expanse of it called out to me, and I barely heard it when the door opened, and Anita stepped inside and then stopped and gasped.

"O-oh my! Your Highness," she stuttered.

Landon pulled me against him and ordered her, "Leave the basket on the table, and then leave us. We're not to be disturbed unless I call for you."

"Of course!" she squeaked, scrambling to contain her surprise as she moved to quickly carry out his orders.

I barely glanced at her, catching a small smile on her lips, before she whisked herself out of the room, and Landon's hand was at my jaw again, turning me to look at him. He searched my gaze for a moment and then closed his eyes and kissed me deep.

Gasping softly, I leaned into his embrace, letting Landon take the weight of my body. He took full advantage of it, sweeping his tongue into my mouth and devouring the whimper that move elicited.

Everything about Landon, from the way he tasted, to the warmth of his body through his clothes, thrummed through me, getting me drunk off of him and the sensations he provided.

"Landon," I sighed, pulling at his shirt again.

I needed more. Kissing him was great, *beautiful,* but it wasn't enough to sate me. A deep emptiness was yawning inside of me, waiting to be filled. My sex was beginning to throb as blood rushed south, my heartbeat echoing in my chest and between my legs.

My heats had never become this intense, this fast, and whether it was because this was my first in a while or because Landon was so close to me, it was consuming me fast. Each kiss was an explosion of even more sensation that sizzled across my skin like sparks from a fire dancing along flagstone, creating little explosions of delight that shot directly to the center of my chest, and then radiated outward.

Heat gathered just under my skin, begging for relief, and I did what it took to satiate it.

His shirt fell from his shoulders, and then I yanked at the buttons on his trousers, making quick work of them too.

"Lay on the bed," Landon commanded me, hands catching my own. "I'll join you there."

"Okay," I said, immediately, turning and going to bed.

Under normal circumstances, I'd be ashamed of my blatant nudity, but I felt completely at ease there with Landon. This room had become my home over the last few days, and being there with the alpha that was Landon felt inevitable. Like I was always going to end up here, naked and at his mercy.

Maybe it was true. Maybe this was where I was meant to be.

I crawled onto the bed, one eye on Landon as he made quick work of his trousers and boots, and one eye to what I was doing myself. I settled myself on the bed on hands and knees, and then dropped down, chest to the bed, presenting myself to Landon. All the while, my heat was raging inside of me, crawling under my skin and making me yearn for more.

Emptiness was a yawning pit in my pelvis, and my sex was aching to be filled. Heat had never felt this intense before, never this demanding, but now it was consuming me. My skin was turning flushed and from head to toe it tingled with awareness, waiting for contact from the alpha across the room from me.

I was panting as I waited, looking over at him with avid fascination as he stripped down, revealing the perfect planes of his body. His chest was dotted with freckles and moles that I was desperate to map out, and a thatch of hair trailed down from his belly button into his trousers. Thick cords of muscles wrapped around his arms, bunching and relaxing as he stepped out of his boots and then his trousers.

Then, *finally* he looked up at me, and froze, chest heaving with deep breaths as he took me in.

"Briar," he rasped.

"Hurry," I begged him. "Landon, *please.*"

Tossing his clothes away, he did as I asked, coming over to the bed in two long strides, giving me a brief second to admire his body, the planes of his abdomen and thighs a beauty to behold. Between his legs, his cock bobbed with his steps, aroused and hard and ready for me. Then, before I could drink my fill, he crawled into bed behind me, spanned my hips with his hands, and pulled me into place.

The movement had me bending down even deeper, bowing down in front of him, giving Landon access to all of me.

He took advantage of that access, taking his cock in hand and then guiding it through my folds, gathering my moisture onto the tip. I was *sopping* wet, and all it took was one push and Landon was sliding inside of me, filling me and stretching me open.

"Ah!" I gasped. "*Yes.*"

I pushed back into him, trying to take as much of him as I could, immediately hungry for more, more, more. He wasn't all the way in yet, and I needed to feel the full length of him. I was coming apart at the seams with need, the omega inside of me whining and panting, needing more and more and more.

Landon growled, arching over me, "I'm in control here, omega. *Heel.*"

Whining, I froze, waiting for him to give me what I wanted. What I *needed.*

Slowly, he slid further and further into me, spearing me open and filling me whole. It took agonizingly too long, but once he was seated all the way inside of me, I arched my back and hissed, *"Yes."*

"You like my cock," Landon said, stating the fact plainly. "You'll take it and then you'll give me what I want. You'll let me come inside of you, stuff you with my knot, and seat you with my child. My *heir."*

My sex twitched, squeezing his cock, and Landon groaned.

"You like that," he growled, pulling out of me, and then slamming back into me, rocking me. "You want me to *breed* you."

My body squeezed around his again, and I knew I was going to have a heat that would stretch out and last a long time, because I was already so close to orgasm, and yet I knew it would never be enough. There would be no way to quench the thirst that I had for this, for *Landon.*

It was unbelievable, to think that I had briefly considered spending time with Elias. Landon was so responsive to every move I made, when I arched, he pressed in harder, and when I pressed back into him, his fingers dug into my hips, pulling me in close. We fell into sync so fast, and every little bit of it rushed through me in a blazing wave of beauty and lust and fire.

"Tell me you want this," he said roughly. "Give me words, Briar."

"I want this, I want you," I panted. "Yes, please. Be with me."

"I'm here," he promised me. "I'm here with you."

Fingertips dug even harder into me, as Landon yanked me back into him harder, my breasts swaying with the movement, and my skin dragging against the soft sheets, and then like a firework, I lit up. From the inside out, I exploded, clenching down around Landon with my first orgasm.

"That's it," Landon growled. "Come for me, Briar."

Ripples shivered up across my skin, and my omega immediately bowed to the command in his voice. I threw my head back, howling, losing myself completely as the orgasm made me tremble and quake before the prince. He never stopped fucking me, never stopped the steady push and pull of his cock, his tempo even and unwavering as I felt everything my body was giving me.

When I had mostly stopped shivering, and again began to pant and moan, Landon maneuvered us, turning me over so I was on my back, hips in his lap, and he was taking me slowly. With deliberate thrusts, he slowed down, hands sliding over my sides and then up to my breasts, squeezing them.

I'd never been well endowed, but Landon didn't seem displeased at all with my slight stature. In fact, his eyes seemed to flash with approval as he palmed me and then teased me. With rough pinches, he played with my nipples, drawing them to a point, and then palmed my ribs and ran his thumbs over those peaks.

"You're so beautiful," he said darkly. "So breakable in my hands."

"P-please," I begged, not even sure what I was begging for.

Landon took it how he would, driving into me even harder. That pace didn't let up, until I was shaking, poised on the edge of another orgasm that was set to roll into another huge wave of my heat.

This was just the beginning, but already the desire inside of me for him felt *huge.* I knew I could trust Landon with this part of myself, and when I fell apart after a few more hard, careful strokes, I fell apart in his hands.

"Perfect," he grunted, words breaking with his heavy breaths. "Fucking *perfect* for me."

With a rough, deep growl, he came inside of me, following me over the edge.

I knew this meant the heat would calm, for a moment, but already I could feel it building again inside of me, my instincts not satisfied with just one round of sex with Landon. I'd need him again, and *soon.*

It was more intense than my heats ever had been before, and all I could do was desperately hope Landon could keep up with me.

CHAPTER ELEVEN

As the first day of my heat calmed down into a warm night, I laid out on the bed, sated for now. I laid on my stomach, head turned to watch as Landon alighted from the bed and began to mill about the room. He gathered a loaf of bread and some cheese, wrapped them in a cloth, and placed them on the mattress next to me.

After I smiled at him gratefully, he nodded and turned away again, walking through the bedroom and into the washroom, unheeding of his nudity or the soft breeze.

I couldn't take my eyes off of him. I was now *intimately* familiar with what his body could do, and watching it move as he walked, casual and at ease, allowed me to admire all that power in his coiled muscles. He was every inch the warrior his kingdom hailed him as, with scars across his torso and arms telling stories of his exploits.

Landon wasn't just a slayer of dragons, that was obvious. He had seen battle and wore those scars proudly.

I could watch him move all day, but my view was cut off when he stepped into the washroom and the door was closed behind him.

Already, heat was building in my belly again, and I knew I'd be lost to passion again soon.

Better to eat now while I can.

Slowly sitting up, I pulled the cloth into my lap and used it to catch the crumbs from the bread and cheese. Hunched over, I devoured them both in record time, ravenous from all of the sex Landon and I had had.

I'd had heats before, of course, I'd even spent some of them with partners before, but none of them held a candle to Landon. *None of them.*

Which was a dangerous realization to come to.

Landon had not proposed to me marriage for love, or even for lust.

This was to ensure his lineage.

Nothing more.

But the omega inside of me thought the opposite. She was writhing in his attention, crooning about how Landon was her mate, *her* alpha. She was already in love with him, and she was stubborn.

This is not a romance, I told her firmly. *This is* survival.

He's perfect, she insisted. *Perfect alpha. Perfect, perfect.*

I rolled my eyes. *Sure. He's perfect.*

I could feel her rolling over in my head, belly up, wagging her tail.

Goodness. I knew she was going to be a handful with this.

For this to work, I needed to keep my heart out of it.

Landon didn't even know who I was, and he had no idea where I came from. He knew nothing of the real me, and honestly, I didn't think he cared. Not really.

If he did, he would have asked me by now. He wouldn't have proposed to me without looking into it, and he wouldn't spend my heat with me, surely, before he dug into my past. If he cared, that is.

Sighing, I looked into the fluffy interior of the bread, getting lost in it.

This was about survival. Nothing else.

There was no sense in tangling my feelings up in everything if all I'd get for it was heartbreak. I needed to safeguard both my body, my mind, and heart, making a new life for all parts of me. I wasn't going to sacrifice my peace in exchange for food, protection, and shelter.

No. I would get all three of those things, I'd give Landon the price he asked, and I'd make sure I was emotionally well while I did it too.

That was going to be that.

And I told my omega as such, as firmly as I could.

She didn't seem to really care, but I liked to think she at least listened to my proclamation.

I needed her on board with the plan, because if there was one person who could make it fail, it was her. She'd been waiting her whole life for this moment, to have an alpha take and seat her with a child. This was her cloud nine, and asking her not to get attached to the man making her dreams come true was likely futile.

But I did it anyway.

Before I could ask her again, just for good measure, Landon emerged from the washroom, having clearly wiped himself down, and came to me with a damp cloth in hand.

"Lay down," he told me.

In spite of my speech to myself, I did exactly as he asked as quickly as possible, eager to please.

Drat.

He noticed too, shooting me a small smile before he crawled onto the bed towards me, came to my side, and began to wipe my skin down with the cloth. The warm water felt *wonderful,* and it was glorious having the salt wiped away from me. It left a cool path in its wake, and I shivered a little.

"Poor thing," Landon cooed. "And we're not nearly done. Make sure you eat all of that."

Obediently, I lifted the bread to my lips and bit into it, chewing slowly.

He continued to clean me off, even taking his time to clean between my legs, clearing away the mess slowly leaking out of me there. I shivered again, this time not from the cold.

His curls bounced as he shook his head, "You're ravenous."

I shrugged, past being embarrassed about it. It was my heat, what else was I supposed to be?

"I've never heard of a heat like this before..." he said quietly to himself, continuing down my legs, eyes on the cloth. "I wonder why it's so strong."

Sighing I admitted, "I don't know. It's been a while since I had one..."

"You're overdue," he nodded. "That could be it. Your body is making up for lost time."

Finishing with the soles of my feet, he wiped them clean, even getting between my toes, and then tossed the cloth to the side, coming to lay down beside me. He took off a piece of cheese from the pile in my lap and popped it into his mouth.

"I suppose so," I agreed. "I don't know how long it will go for. Thank you for helping me through it."

Just having him near again was making heat build up in my chest, growing steadily with every breath. My core was growing damp and my senses muted. The only thing that mattered was Landon, and the ache in my sex.

"You're welcome."

I needed to get the words out while I could. I had questions for him, things I needed to make sure we sorted while I had the wherewithal to do it.

"What will we do when this is over? Will we remain here together or…?"

Would he send me away somewhere remote? Would he ignore me and treat me as if this never happened? Would I be alone? Safe, but alone?

No emotions, I reminded myself.

But still…

His eyes flashed, and he said curtly, "We'll discuss it when the time comes."

"Lan—"

He shook his head, and took the food from me, sweeping it away into a neat pile on the bedside table. Then he cupped my jaw and kissed me quiet.

Lost in the heat, I braced my hands on his chest to balance myself as I ground down into Landon's cock. He was looking up at me through hooded eyes, blue fire burning me as

I circled my hips, dragging my clit across the soft skin of his erection.

"Ah," I panted. "Landon..."

His hands bracketed my hips, holding me in place and pulling me down harder into him.

I went willingly, savoring the heat of his skin under my fingers, the soft touch of his chest hair, and the burning stretch of my body yielding to his. Landon's cock was hot inside of me, and the thickness of it drove me to the brink faster than seemed possible.

It shouldn't be this good, I knew that.

But there wasn't any time to wonder over *why* it felt like this, or why my omega was in raptures over being with him, or anything other than how close I could reach my next orgasm and have Landon's knot inside of me again.

I knew we were both close, his nose wrinkled as he snarled, harsh growls and low curses spilling from his mouth. His cock too was harder, the base of it swelling as his knot grew in anticipation of his release, and the additional fullness it gave me pushed me closer and closer. Soon, it was large enough that every rise and fall came with a pop as it pushed in and then pulled out of me, stretching me even further, my cunt aching and ravenous for more.

"Landon," I sighed, head falling back, chest pushing forward as I rode him harder still.

One of his hands came to my breast, squeezing the small mound, and then pinching my much-abused nipple. It was so sensitive, so overworked, it drove me *insane.*

"Oh gods," I moaned, arching into him, one of my hands coming to cover his.

I could feel him working me, the large span of his palm and the breadth of his fingers dexterous under mine. It was so close, intimate, and strange, to feel him giving to me as the fruits of his labor. Sensation shot through me from nipple to clit.

"Come, omega," he demanded, the words hardly audible; they were so surrounded by grunts and growls. "Come on my knot."

He drove up with no finesse, as hard as he could, locking his knot into me. It swelled, coming to its full overwhelming width, and then locked inside of me, pushing on my inner walls and against that rough, delectable spot inside of me.

It was that press, and the fullness he gave me, that did me in. As he came inside of me, I came around him, flexing around and gripping onto his cock, milking him of his spend and drawing it deep inside of me.

It wasn't the first load I'd taken from him, and I could feel how full I was of it. With a fluttering sigh, I looked down at Landon and found him staring up at me, sated and warm. I smiled at him, my free hand coming to my pelvis, pressing in where he was seated.

We both sighed. He was so big, and I was so slight, I could *feel* where he was inside of me, my body bulging to accommodate him and his seed.

"If you're not with child after this," Landon said, amused, "I don't know what we'll do."

Giggling, I admitted, "I don't know that we could have tried harder than this."

"Indeed." He rose up, pulled me down, and kissed me hard. "But still, we'll have to try again, to be sure."

"Right," I nodded. "We have to be sure."

He pulled me down, turning us both, and bore me down into the mattress, grinding his knot into me, his fingers playing with my sex as he did so.

And he didn't stop until I came yet again.

I lost track of how many times we came together. It was impossible to tell. I felt like I was floating as if gravity itself had ceased to matter, and all that was left was Landon and I. Even if there was a world beyond our bed, I didn't give a lick about it.

I especially stopped caring when Landon pulled me until my knees were on either side of his face, and my sex was hovering above his mouth. Quick as a flash, he wrapped his arms up and around my thighs, and then yanked me down, tongue making contact with my clit nearly immediately.

I nearly lost my balance and had to lean back and brace myself against the headboard to keep from falling to the side.

"You're so sweet," he murmured into me, speaking the words to the very heart of me. "And you're all mine."

"Yes, My Prince," I sighed, grinding into the flat expanse of his tongue, moving with him. "I'm yours."

"You're going to carry my child," he said, demanding it of me.

"I will," I promised. "I will."

I gasped, arching back as he rewarded me, sucking on my clit.

My inner omega was in fits, absolutely delighted with the attentions of the alpha.

My alpha, she was saying, over and over again. *Our mate.*

But that wasn't the agreement here, and I had to keep myself from calling out to him with her words. This was about *convenience.* Both Landon and myself.

There was nothing else to it.

"You're *mine,*" he said. "Mine."

Selfishly, I almost wished it was true.

Two or... maybe it was three more days passed in a haze, maybe four, and my heat wasn't letting up.

If anything, it was getting worse.

"Why are you so hot for me?" Landon asked once, slowly grinding into me from behind.

"I-I don't know," I gasped. "Just don't stop. *Please* don't stop."

"I won't," he promised. "I won't stop."

Whether it was how long I'd slept, or Landon's proximity to me, or whatever else, I had no control over it, so it hardly mattered. All I could do was helplessly ride the waves, and hope Landon didn't abandon me before it was through.

When two more days passed, Landon left me alone in our room.

I was asleep when it happened. I *immediately* felt the loss of his presence. Shooting up out of the bed, I began to pace around the room, heart racing, inner wolf crying out.

Where did he go? Why did he leave us? Were we not good enough? Is he tired of us?

"Oh no," I whispered, racing to the bathing room.

Searching frantically, I looked behind the privacy panel, hoping I'd been mistaken and he was just relieving himself. When that proved fruitless, I raced back to the main room, and then into the wardrobe room, searching among the carefully hung dresses for the prince.

Still nothing.

Sprinting back to the main room, I stood in the middle of it, breathing hard, panic welling in my chest.

What would I *do*?

Did I dress and try to find him?

What if he'd left me here alone again? Abandoned me for some errand the king needed done?

I wouldn't survive this alone. I *couldn't*.

My heat had not abated even slightly, and I knew soon I'd be ravenous again. And I *had* to have something to abate it. Otherwise, I'd go mad with the lust.

Perhaps I should find Elias, if for no other reason than to keep myself sane. To keep the heat from burning me right through.

No! My omega shouted, raging against the walls of my mind. *He's all wrong! He's not ours! We* need *our Alpha!*

"He's not here," I told her, glancing around to confirm. "He *left* us!"

No, no, no! She insisted. *He can't!*

Overwhelmed, I crouched down in the center of the room. It was all too much for me. My body was shaking with the heat and the stress and abandonment.

This isn't right! This isn't how it's supposed to be!

I stayed there, curled around myself, rocking gently as I tried to convince myself that this wasn't happening.

"He left us," I said. "He's gone. Gone. Gone. We're alone."

Minutes passed, though I couldn't keep track of how many, and I was still alone.

"Gone," I whispered. "All alone. He left."

Even his scent was beginning to fade from the room, and I wanted to *howl*. I hadn't transformed since I'd awoken, but I wanted to then. I wanted to change and to *run*. I wouldn't have to dress then. I would just have to *go*. Flee from the room that smelled of me and the Alpha who *left me*.

There was no rationale, no reason to my thoughts, but I was still so sure of them. Every part of me was *screaming*. How could those thoughts be wrong when they were so loud?

An aching, yawning pit of despair opened in my chest, and it was all I could do to lay down on the floor, curled up in a fetal position, and cry.

"Why?" I cried. *"Why?!"*

Irrationality seized me, and there was no wresting any logic back from it. The heat and my weeping omega were all I knew. Until, suddenly, warm hands were on my cheeks, and I inhaled and *finally* smelled the scent of Landon again. The musky scent on his skin was mixed with mine, which eased my mind slightly.

I turned, gasping, and clinging to him, wrapping my arms around his waist, *"Alpha."*

"Gods, Briar, what happened?"

"You left!" I cried, squeezing him tight. "You *left* me!"

"Shhh," he soothed me. "Briar, *shhh.* I'm here. I didn't leave you."

"You left the room," I accused him. "You *did.* You left me."

"I went to consult a healer," he said softly, running his hand over my hair.

I tensed, asking suspiciously, "A healer?"

"Your heat. It's running too long," he said gently. "I wanted to check with a healer to make sure it wouldn't harm you."

"I don't need a healer," I insisted. "It's fine."

I could just picture Eris intruding, posing as a healer, and taking advantage of us while we were distracted. She was powerful, powerful enough to do *anything* I could imagine, and I could imagine all kinds of horrors.

"She's concerned," he said. "This has been going on for nearly a week, and it shows no signs of slowing. Your body will wear itself out."

"I said I'm *fine.*" I crawled out of his grasp, getting as far as I could before my knees started to ache, and then turned, glaring at Landon.

"She gave me a potion—"

"No," I said swiftly. "I don't need it."

"You *do,*" he insisted. "It'll give you more strength, energy. Make sure your body is sound."

"My body *is* sound. I have no need for her brew."

"Briar, *please*—"

I stood, angry, and though I'd just been lamenting his absence, even my omega felt the urgent press for self-preservation. "I don't need it."

Carefully standing, he approached me, eyes concerned and bright in the dim moonlight, "Something is wrong, Briar. You need help."

"I *don't!*" I shouted. "I don't need help. Leave me be."

"Briar," he commanded. Landon's voice had shifted, becoming hard and dominant, a tinge of command creeping into it. "You will drink it."

"No," I said angrily. "I won't."

He advanced, taking long strides, "It's just a potion for strength, Briar. Drink it and then we'll go back to bed."

I did feel a twinge at the mention of a bed, my core clenching reflexively, but it wasn't enough to override the fear. I was operating on instinct alone, and I decided rather than risking drinking some poison Eris concocted, it was better to run.

In a flash, I ran, sprinting around the edge of the room, making for the door to the hallway. I didn't care if I was naked and a whole crowd was on the other side of the door, I was not drinking whatever the healer had given him.

"Fuck," Landon grunted, running after me. "Briar, *stop.*"

"I won't drink it," I insisted, making for the door.

I was closing in, bare feet pounding hard on the floor as I reached for the knob, just barely feeling it's cool metal against my fingertips… and felt Landon's iron strength wrap around my waist, pulling me back and into his hard unyielding body.

"Stop," he commanded the word firm and hard as nails.

I froze in the circle of his arms, both of us silent save for the heavy pull of our breathing.

"What on *earth* has seized you?" He asked, turning me roughly to face him. "Are you possessed?"

My mouth opened and closed around a hundred silent lies and the unbelievable truth.

What could I tell him? How could I explain to him the danger I could suddenly feel hovering above my shoulders. Though in reality, it wasn't hovering. It was hanging off of me, a sickening and heavy fog. I could hear Eris's laughter hanging in the air, echoing through my memories, and I *knew* she was watching me then.

As sure as I breathed, Eris was watching me, and she was *reveling* in my pain. In this turmoil, she'd created between me and Landon.

She's turned what should have been a time for bonding and mating into something filled with fear.

Landon must have smelled my fear, or seen it in my eyes because his face gentled, and he asked quietly, "Why are you so afraid, Briar?"

I glanced at him, begging, "Please don't make me drink it. I'll eat whatever food you want, but I will *not* drink that potion."

"Alright," he acquiesced quietly. "Come lay down."

With weary, wobbly steps, I followed him back to the bed, and slowly laid down, watching his every move.

He caught what I was doing, and sighed, muttering, "I created this conundrum."

I didn't answer him, because, on the one hand, he did, yes. But on the other, Eris was the true culprit here, though there was no way for me to reveal that fact to him.

There was nothing Landon could do about the powerful witch, and so there was no sense in saddling him with that knowledge. If he even believed me, that is. I hadn't heard anyone utter her name since I'd come here, so I had no idea if Landon even knew of her existence.

In my time, she was widely known, though not widely liked. She was mistrusted but seen as ultimately harmless. Though she was greedy for land and power, she never directly crossed Skyridge and its crown.

Until she cursed me.

All fae held magic, but the kind of magic Eris held was rare. So rare as to be mythological. How could Landon really believe I'd slept for five millennia?

I wouldn't believe me, were I him.

And so the sad truth was that still, even with him here in bed beside me, I was still alone with my secrets. With my past.

He knew I was lost in my thoughts, and didn't push me anymore. Instead, he drew me in close and held me against his chest. In the dark, we laid there together, breathing coming back to normal, hearts slowing, and soon, everything was quiet again.

And then I was asleep.

True to my word, I ate everything Landon put in front of me the following morning.

Heat still simmered in my veins and stirred in my pelvis, but I held it back long enough to eat an entire loaf of bread with cheese and honey, a large salad, and a ham and cheese croissant sandwich.

I was *stuffed* by the time I was done, but I couldn't deny that it was exactly what I needed. Once my belly was full, I slouched back in my chair and groaned, hand over my stomach. "Ahhh."

"I knew you needed food," Landon said, eyes narrowed on me.

"I did," I agreed. "All that... *well...*"

I trailed off, looking away from Landon.

Without the heat to dictate what we did and who we were to one another, I didn't know how to handle Landon.

I supposed, with his offer being what it was, us laying together meant we were... together?

"Are we going to be wed?" I asked him, the question popping out without any resistance.

"We will, yes," he said easily as if we'd been courting for years.

"Ah."

"Do you not wish to wed?"

I shook my head, "No, it's not that. I just want to, er, understand the state of play."

"The state is that, once this endless heat finally ends, we'll begin to prepare you to join the royal family."

"Huh."

"You will be queen one day."

"Right."

He chuckled, one brow raising with amusement, "Is that all?"

"I'm not... sure..." I frowned, eyeing Landon. If I was going to do this, I needed to trust him, right? Taking a deep breath, I decided to trust him, just a little. "I come from a noble family. It's not... entirely unfamiliar to me. But I never expected to, uh, join such a prestigious house."

His eyes narrowed, looking at me closely, "A noble house?"

I decided to stick with the same story I had told Elias. They were friends, and if they talked, I wanted them to be able to compare notes and find I'd told them the same thing.

"Not from Fenestral," I explained. "From the west. Past the mountains. I was born of an affair. My father took me into his home anyway after my mother passed. But when he passed..."

Landon winced, "I see."

"I came this way to start over, maybe find work as a lady's maid. That's why I was in those ruins. I was resting on my journey."

Sharp blue eyes roamed my face, looking for something. I wasn't sure what, but he looked... confused and somehow nostalgic.

"You were not dressed for travel, Briar."

I shrugged, "Step-mother was not keen on me taking things from her home."

"Hmm." He scratched at his chin, leaning back in his own chair.

The movement had his biceps flexing, and the heat that had taken a sleep while I ate flared to life again. My omega came roaring back in the recesses of my mind, demanding more. *We need more of him.*

I bit my lip, trying to tell her no, to command her to have patience. But Landon's nostrils flared, and his eyes came to me again, this time alight with knowing, his lips pulled into a smirk.

"You're ready."

I nodded.

"Then let me take care of you."

"Thank you, Landon," I said softly.

Standing, he came to me, slid his hand into my hair and pulled me to him for a kiss. All conversation ended.

We came together again, bodies tired but familiar with one another. Burning together slowly, we kissed and pressed against one another, falling to the floor before the fireplace and remaining there.

There, he entered me tenderly from behind, reaching around me to cup my jaw and gently pulled, forcing my back to arch and submit even further to him. He slid into me with languid, deep strokes, guiding me to the edge of my orgasm and then gently dropping me over it, allowing me to float off into the abyss.

I drifted there, aimless and outside of myself, my body hardly aware of itself. Instead, I was just nerve ending and lightning bouncing around in a glass bottle. Magic snapped in the atmosphere, thundering through me, and then Landon followed me. He met me where I was, our energies mixing together in the air around us.

I swear I could see it there, shimmering around us, clinging to our skin and lingering there until we were both sated and coming down from the peak, wrapped around one another on the rub before the fire.

"You will make me an excellent mate," he whispered into my skin. "And you'll make a wonderful queen."

My stomach filled with butterflies, my heart skipped a beat, and his words buried themselves deep in my brain where I knew they would linger forever more.

"How can you be sure?" I asked, nervous and afraid to trust them. They were so precious, I could hardly count on them.

Could he really mean that when he had no idea who I was? Could I *let* him say it when I knew how much I was hiding from him?

Landon looked at me quite seriously, "I can feel it. My wolf knows it. I know it. It is how it is meant to be."

"But—"

He put his hand over my mouth, keeping me quiet, "Trust me, Briar. I know."

"Ok," I whispered against his hand.

The hand dropped, and he whispered back, "Ok."

CHAPTER TWELVE

Landon

Rounding the mountain, Landon kept his eyes fixed on the horizon ahead, finding his way through the mountain pass. It was rough terrain, the granite rock of the mountain slick and icy. Spring hadn't reached this high up yet, and snow dotted the paths and coated the peaks of the mountains.

Everything smelled cold and sharp around him... except for that *one* scent. The one which was warm and bright, demanding his attention. It was the only thing keeping his body from flagging and collapsing on the spot.

Lifting his head, he inhaled deeply and followed his nose. It led him further down the pass, south from the dragon's den and then east, following the old trading route through the mountains, past an ancient spring with a crumbling ruin atop, and then through one final pass.

As he crested the rise, in front of him rose the crumbling ruins of a great castle. He didn't recognize its shape or the location, but it was clearly the remnants of a powerful city-state. Ruins of a town surrounded the main castle, and as he ascended, following his nose, he wondered just who had lived here.

He caught sight of buildings large enough to be warehouses, broken shards of greenhouses, and old stone signs carved with the names of shops. *Callaghan's Haberdashery. Smyth's General Store. Bar Llwyn.*

The eyes of their dead followed him, watching as he ascended slowly, following the road through the ghost town, and then arrived at the crumbling castle gates. The iron and wooden doors were rotted through, and after he dismounted his horse, it was easy enough for him to push open the doors. They gave way under his hands and swung with a great groan, revealing a once splendid great hall.

Stone blocks fell in on themselves along one wall, but along the others old, worn tapestries still hung, their threads faded and images almost lost to time. Landon could just make out a few old fables, and some dragons flying high in the sky.

"Hm," he grunted, eyeing them with confusion.

Dragons were destroyers. Why would they venerate them in their art?

It was a question he didn't see an answer to, and frankly didn't care to seek one out.

The wind blew through the pass, carrying to him another strong whiff of the scent he was chasing. It was here, somewhere, stronger than ever.

The prince was close to his prey.

Winding through the ruins, he came to a tower. Taking the stairs two at a time, he climbed, passing rotted planks and windows that had eroded with the wind and rain, widening their view of the mountains around him. Splendid vistas were just outside, and he heeded none of them as his mind began to race and his heart began to beat wildly with the thrill of the hunt.

Whatever this was, *whoever* it was, it was made for him.

His heart pounded with that certainty and his blood sang as his inner wolf howled, gnashing at the bit for the delicious, tempting scent.

It all drove him ever forward, culminating in the moment when he pushed open yet another dilapidated door and found a bedroom on the other side.

Bizarrely, in the middle of it was a perfectly preserved four-poster canopy bed, with gauzy white fabric hung from the top. In the middle of it was a woman, sleeping peacefully.

Her hair was a strawberry blonde so light, it shone almost pink in the sunlight streaming in through the crumbled room, and her matching pale lashes fanned out over freckled cheeks.

He couldn't stop staring at her. With hesitant steps he got even closer, inhaling deeper and noting how her slight form was deep in her dreams, her chest rising and falling with steady breaths, each inhale so far apart it made him hold his breath with her, waiting for the next draw.

Unable to help himself, he came to her side, sitting on the edge of the bed near her waist, turning deep so he could look down at her, taking in every constellation in her skin and the gentle slope of her pointed ears. So close, her scent invaded his mind as if he'd had too much wine. His whole mind was filled with her, and the world was fuzzy at its edges.

He'd forgotten all about his battle with the dragon and how he really should be on his way back home already. Neither of those things mattered when the most perfect omega he'd ever encountered was here, asleep.

She was supremely still. Like she was dead to the world, she slept so deep. It was odd, but he didn't count it for much. Some people simply slept deeply. His omega must be one of those people.

Leaning in close, he pressed his forehead to hers, breathing with her.

Then, as if it was the most natural thing in the world, he lightly brushed his lips against hers.

That slight taste, the smallest touch, and Landon knew with complete certainty that she was his. *His* mate. *His* omega.

CHAPTER THIRTEEN

Briar

Slowly, the waves of my heat grew further and further apart, until, two weeks after it had started, it ended, leaving me in a gentle rush all at once. Landon yet again made me come around him, buried himself inside of me, and with that final release, it left me.

My fingers and toes tingled as it seemed to drain out of me, and then I laid there, and promptly fell asleep, exhausted.

When I awoke again, Landon was settled there next to me in the bed, a sheaf of papers in his lap.

"You're awake," he noted, looking down at me.

I smiled up at him sheepishly, "I am. Hello, Landon."

He smiled back, quick and then gone as fast as it was there, "Hello, Briar."

"I think it's over," I whispered, blushing.

I really had *no* idea why it had taken that long to run its course, but now my head was clear, and for the first time in ages I could look at Landon and not immediately have my insides turn into a roiling pot of lust and need and all kinds of emotions I had no business feeling.

Though, complicating things, was the fact that the emotions *hadn't* gone away. Sure, they weren't bubbling up inside of me, demanding to be said aloud anymore, but they were there all the same.

That was not part of my plan.

And it felt dangerous.

But laying there looking up at Landon in the bed... it was a danger I was willing to accept, at least for now.

He was the first to leave my rooms, and five minutes after he was gone, my girls came rushing in, mischievous smiles barely contained.

"Well, someone took their sweet time," Anita chuffed, hands on her hips.

"She was having too much fun," Candela said, laughing.

My cheeks were on fire, but I managed to smile, "It wasn't a pain, at the very least."

Lily and Rose glanced at one another and then fell into a fit of giggles, which had all of us laughing.

"As long as you're not too worn out, we'll get you a bath," Anita said, taking stock of the room around her. "And the prince has asked we move your things to his rooms."

"Really?" I asked.

That seemed quick. Wouldn't doing that draw a lot of attention? We'd only just agreed to be together, to form some kind of alliance. Was he really going to make it so public so soon?

"Prince Landon is a decisive man," Candela said. "Must be from fighting all those dragons. He never wastes any time."

"He is very brave," Lily said quietly.

"He risks his life all the time," Rose continued for her.

"Prince Landon knows there's no time to waste," Candela finished.

"So we're moving your things," Anita announced. "Today. I imagine the prince will want you warming his own bed tonight."

"Well," I laughed. "When you all put it that way... How can I help?"

Anita looked aghast, "Help? No, My lady. You enjoy your bath, and we'll take care of the rest."

"I can do that," I promised her, smiling wide.

If this is what it meant to be with Landon, having this place and these girls forever, I could do that.

They weaved in and out of one another with perfect precision, packing my things and drawing me a bath. As I bathed, I heard them in the other room, chattering and laughing, handing trunks off to other people to carry over to the Prince's Suite.

I didn't even know what was in all the trunks, and when I tried to ask, Anita waved her hand, insisting, "The prince has taken care of everything."

It was all done before the afternoon was over, and just before tea, I walked into Landon's rooms for the first time.

They were equally as sumptuous as my own suite of rooms was, but even more so. The pink stone was complimented with deep navy tapestries in the main sitting room, with matching navy upholstered furniture and richly carved side tables. It was obviously the rooms of a prince, and no expense had been spared in making it look the part.

I ran my hands over the silken fabrics and the plush fibers of the tapestries, familiarizing myself with them and the space. This was to be my new home. A place I'd share with Landon. As his *mate*.

That word was the part that I couldn't reconcile. More than anything, mates were destiny. The person fate brought to you and insisted was the one for you.

Was Landon my mate?

I thought back to when he'd found me, waking up and finding him just... there. Patiently waiting.

Maybe that was fate?

I mused over it, until there was a soft knock at the door, and I whirled to find it already opening and Landon's father, the king, stepping into the room.

"Your Majesty," I said, surprised, dipping into a curtsey. "I wasn't expecting you. What a nice surprise."

He laughed, a rougher version of Landon's own laugh, "No need to bow to me, Lady Briar. I understand we're family now."

Hesitantly, I replied, "Yes. I suppose we are."

"Landon came to see me," he explained. "So I suppose congratulations are in order."

"Thank you," I demurred, unsure of the man before me.

We'd hardly interacted before today, and this conversation felt more like a test than anything. Like he was feeling me out, and I was on the defensive. In a way, I supposed I was. He was the king, and I was a strange woman who had swept into his lands and found her way into his son's bed. He had *every* right to be suspicious of me.

So I smiled and tried to summon every bit of poise my mother had given me, "I'm very grateful to you and to Landon for your kindness. I will do everything I can to be of use to you and to Fenestral."

His eyes narrowed, flicking over my face as he assessed me, "I have my doubts about you, Lady Briar. I sent some of my men digging into your past. They came up empty."

I flinched, "Did they, Your Majesty?"

"Indeed they did," he murmured, approaching me, the golden chains at his shoulder clinking softly. "You're a ghost. A specter haunting my castle."

"I know my background is… unusual," I admitted. "But I'm not here for malicious reasons. I genuinely have nowhere else to go."

"Then see to it you show us the proper gratitude. *And loyalty.*"

"I will, Your Majesty," I assured him, putting my whole chest behind the proclamation. "I will."

He dipped his head, "I look forward to seeing that." The king tapped his hand on the back of one of the couches, ending the interaction. "Good day, Lady Briar."

I curtseyed again, smaller than the first time, treading the middle ground between the respectful and familial, "Good day, Your Majesty."

King Eduard cast me one last look as he closed the door behind him, leaving me alone again in the beautiful navy and pale pink room. My shoulders slumped, and I put my head in my hand.

I had a place to stay now. This was true. Some security.

But I would be a fool to think this was the end of my woes.

Eris was still out there, and no one around me knew who I was. I was hiding from them, living a lie. There was no way to reveal the truth from them, so in the meantime, I needed to learn to lie better. To convince them that I was Briar Rhoswyn the Lost. And not Briar Rhoswyn, cursed woman and Princess of Skyridge.

I had a feeling my place here in Fleur depended on it.

Chapter Fourteen

Landon wasted no time installing me at his side. Though he apparently never made much of an effort to announce who I was to the court, word spread all the same the moment he had my things moved from my own room to his. Like wildfire, whispers of me and Landon spread, until everyone knew my name and was vying for my attention.

It was almost unnerving how quickly they all began to speak to me. If I hadn't already spent most of my life as a princess, I would have been drowning in court politics. As it was, I was hardly keeping my head above water.

From all angles, people tried to turn my ear to them, bemoaning some misfortune, or slyly marring the name of some other rival house. They begged me to weigh in on land disputes and inheritance squabbles.

The *only* person who didn't try to use me to their own ends was Elias.

I found him in the library two days after my heat ended, and he smiled at me with amusement.

"She emerges from the den," he teased.

I blushed and said, "Good gods, Elias. *Please.*"

"I'm not the one you should be begging, love," he laughed.

Blushing deeper, I sat on a chair across from him, rolling my eyes, "Glad to see your sense of humor didn't abandon you while I was gone."

"Indeed, it hasn't left me yet, though you certainly tried it with how long it dragged on." He looked me up and down, sobering up. "How are you? Is everything alright?"

"I'm okay," I promised him. "It went on longer than I thought it would, but I'm good now. I think Landon and I have come to an understanding."

"You're mated, I hear?"

"I... yes, I suppose," I admitted. "He offered me a place here. I know I asked you for help but..."

He shook his head, stopping my train of thought, "You don't owe me an explanation, Briar. I understand. You sought something platonic in me, and Landon has offered you a true partnership. A life together."

Smiling, I agreed, "He has."

"Then I am happy for you. And if you ever need me in the future, I will be here for you. As a friend. And not just because you are to be my queen, but because you are good and kind, and I am honored to count you among those I know." He chuckled. "Plus, your life seems to only be getting *more* interesting, Briar. You'll have to forgive me for wanting to witness it first hand. I'm too old to play the jilted suitor anyway."

Laughing, I teased, "You're just using me for entertainment."

"I'm an old man who bores easily," he sighed. "I cannot deny you're right."

We both laughed together, and it set my heart at ease. Elias was a friend, and you could never have too many of those. *Especially* where the court was concerned.

"I don't know what to do next," I admitted quietly. "This is not what I thought would happen here. Not in a thousand years."

"You keep your head up," he instructed me. "Don't let anyone take advantage of you, and keep smiling. The whole kingdom will be watching you."

Elias couldn't have been more correct. That night, Landon came to our rooms, and said, "We have a dinner. I've asked your girls to prepare you."

"A dinner?" I asked.

"With my father, some dignitaries and lords. We had negotiations this morning, and now we feast to signal their end," he explained. "I assume this won't be a problem? You are trained in etiquette, yes?"

He watched my response carefully, which made me uneasy. Did he not believe my story about my past? That would be problematic.

"I was," I nodded. Made sense. Business was done as much over a meal as it was in a meeting. "I'd love to attend dinner. Is there anything I should know about the attendees?"

Landon looked pleased, and came to my side, kissing the top of my head, "Know that hostilities will likely be high. Pretend you do not sense it. None of the negotiating parties were happy with my father's decision. They find him to be frustratingly centrist in his decision."

"Ah. I see."

My father had been the decisive type, which had its own pitfalls, but I was surprised to hear the king was more middle of the road here. Rarely did taking the center path make friends. Nobles especially liked to know when people were on their side, and there was no better way to determine who stood where than to involve them in business. The whey always separated from the curds where money was involved.

Though, begrudgingly, I had to admit that staying a middle course was shockingly difficult, and Landon's father must possess the significant inner strength to be able to do so in the face of angry noblemen.

"Dress," Landon commanded me. "I'll be back to get you."

He strode from our rooms, and two minutes later, my girls flooded in, huge smiles on their faces.

"Your first proper outing!" Candela cried.

"We must prepare you," Anita said seriously.

Lily softly admitted, "I already picked a dress."

"It's *gorgeous!*" Rose gushed. "Trust us, you'll love it."

"So is the underwear," Candela winked at me, flitting past me with a suspiciously small bundle of lace in her hands.

In no time, they had me dressed in a peach dress that clung to my waist and then flowed out in a huge skirt that swung and brushed across my legs in a delightful soft brush. The fabric was light and floaty, and embroidered with small little flowers in a peach that was barely a shade lighter than the base fabric.

The effect was striking, all the layers of it making my waist look small, and with the deep front scooped neckline, poofed sleeves, and ruffle at the bottom hem, it was a feast for the eyes. Underneath, Candela had pulled me into a matching pale peach corset that held my breasts up and on display, with small demi cups that barely covered my nipples, and a pair of matching open crotch lace panties that would make it easier for me to relieve myself, and... my imagination ran away with itself, picturing how it gave Landon equal access to the space between my legs.

Then, they curled my hair gently, placing little pins at my temples with rose gold butterflies on them, surrounding me with beauty. Lily gently brushed peachy sparkles across my cheekbones and eyelids, gloss on my lips, and then smiled at me, proclaiming me done.

Anita nodded thoughtfully, "I think she looks wonderful."

I turned, looking at myself in the mirror, tilting my head this way and that, admiring their work. "You guys are magicians."

"Oh, you're too kind," Anita said.

"Not nearly," I promised.

"It's our pleasure," Rose said, smiling at me. "You're to be our queen now. You're not just a nice lady we're happy to serve. It's our honor to tend to the future monarch."

I sat there, stunned. I hadn't heard such sentiment since I was princess, years and years ago from my own ladies in waiting who served me for most of my life.

To have that trust and devotion again touched me in a way that was hard to describe. Like the past leaking through the small cracks in my heart and bleeding into the here and now. Bleeding into the future.

There was no time to sort through those emotions because Landon came strolling in through the doors, already dressed for dinner.

"You're ready. Good," he said, looking me over. Then, he looked at Anita and said, "You did well. Thank you."

Anita flushed with pleasure, sputtering, "Y-Your Highness. Thank you."

She curtseyed low, as did all of my girls, and then they excused themselves from our rooms, leaving me alone with Landon.

"So... Dinner?" I asked lamely.

He looked me up and down but didn't respond.

"Ummm... Landon?"

His eyes snapped to me, but he still didn't say anything.

I looked down at myself and then met his eyes again, "Ummm... I thought you liked the dress?"

"I do," he said. "But if we spend too much time here, we'll miss dinner."

Realization dawned, and I said, "Ah. Then I suppose we should go."

One side of his mouth lifted in a smirk, "We should."

Holding out his elbow, he waited for me to come to him, and then together, we went to face the public.

Public may have been a strong word.

Though the dinner was packed with obviously important people, there was maximum of twenty-two people in the room. A mix of people, from wolves, fae, and vampires mingled in a small drawing room, and when Landon and I were announced, all eyes in the room swung to us.

"Prince Landon and Princess Briar," announced a squire.

Cold sadness washed over me, and if not for Landon, I would have frozen on the spot.

Princess Biar. Was that the first time those words were said in a millennium?

There was no time to ponder, because people were surrounding us, smiling and eyes shining bright.

"Prince, *Princess,*" one man with dark hair and a sickly smile said. "So good to see you here."

Landon inclined his head, a shallow acknowledgment, and looked to me, "Briar, please meet Marquis Du Met."

"Marquis," I said softly, dipping my chin at him. "A pleasure to meet you."

"The pleasure is all mine." His eyes flicked over me curiously, trying to figure me out. "I'm pleased to make your acquaintance. I've heard much about you since your arrival here."

Translation: *There are rumors about you, and I wish to know which are true.*

"I'm pleased you're able to satisfy your curiosity," I said between my teeth.

Translation: *I don't care. Decide who I am yourself.*

How I wished my mother was here to guide me through things. I would simply have to do my best to make her proud. Wherever she was, I knew she was looking down on me, cheering me on.

Du Met's smile grew, "I am as well, Princess."

I dismissed him, turning away, and another person took his place.

"Briar, this is Baroness Ferdinand," Landon offered, gesturing from me to the other woman.

"It is a pleasure to meet you, Princess Briar," the Baroness said, curtseying deeply. "Your beauty is uncompared."

I recognized the compliment for the political maneuvering it was, but I still smiled at her, "You're too kind, Baroness."

She spared me the half-truths and subtones Du Met had given me, dismissing herself and allowing a tall fae with arching horns to take her place. When they left, there was yet another, and then another, until every person in the room had come to speak with me and Landon, and only the king was left.

He came to us, smiling, "Briar, Landon, I'm glad you both could make it."

Together, we dipped our heads, showing him the respect that was due when interacting with him in public.

He got close, whispering, "Now, we can finally eat." Turning to the rest of the room, he called, "Come! Let us eat!"

The small crowd cheered, and a set of double doors on the other side of the room opened, revealing a small formal dining room on the other side. It wasn't a room I'd been in yet, and I couldn't help but crane my neck a little as we walked in.

The pale pink walls sparkled in candlelight, and lush displays of fresh flowers towered against it, springing out of white and gold porcelain vases. Paintings of the gardens hung above those, and tall windows looked out into the formal gardens beyond. The table was a pale wood that seemed to shimmer with a latent kind of magic, and it too was decorated with displays of flowers, and perfect place settings of golden plates and perfectly shined silverware. On top, there were napkins of fine pale pink silk held in shape by jeweled napkin holders.

Landon and I took our seats towards the head of the table, Landon to his father's right, and me to Landon's right. Around us, the nobles jostled for their seats, and when they were all settled, servers came from a door on the other side, one for each of us, and they pulled the napkins free from their rings, and settled them on our laps. Then, they left again, taking the rings away with them, and conversation sprung to life.

Landon and I shared a glance, and under the table, his foot tapped mine briefly.

Then, we dived right into it.

Across from us, there was a couple who, over the course of dinner, I realized had sat there *very* strategically. A lord and lady who had been a part of the disputes earlier in the day, and thought that, perhaps, they might be able to bend the ear of the new consort of the Prince.

They had *no* idea what they were getting into.

Throughout the night, I smiled politely at them as they tried to subtly relate to me their woes, while inwardly smiling and seeing directly through their scheme.

"Oh it's just terrible. Our tenants sacrifice so much," the Lady, Lady Delli said. "Would that we were able to prove them more pasture, I know it would improve their lives greatly."

And help her fill her vaults.

"It would," Lord Delli sighed. "'Tis a tragedy that our neighbors insist they will not sell to us, or relinquish the land which was rightfully my father's winnings."

"Indeed, if only they would acknowledge the validity of the bet from that night, we might be able to settle things amicably."

A bet for land? No wonder it was the point of such contention. There was no way the loser of said bet would want to honor it, and the winner would be forever bitter about it. It was a breeding ground for complaints.

So I nodded, smiling noncommittally, at the lord and lady, "I wish your tenants good fortune."

Because, really, I did. And the Lord and Lady Delli had plenty enough fortune already, if the rings on the Lady's fingers and the jewels at her throat were any indication.

I felt Landon's foot tap mine again, and I glanced at him, briefly, smiling at him. He nodded, and then looked back to his conversation partner. *He was checking on me.*

I slid a hand onto his thigh, careful to do it slowly so the lord and lady, who continued to complain, weren't distracted from their manufactured financial woes. His thigh tensed under my fingers, but then relaxed as I left it there, gently cupping his muscle.

His thighs were practically tree trunks. It was a wonder how they fit into his pants. I'm sure his tailors had to work hard to make sure they laid correctly over the width of them. If I didn't already know he was an accomplished soldier, I would be able to tell solely by his build.

Landon's legs were strong and well-defined, telling tales of miles hiked in armor and days spent hauling his weapons to where he was needed.

I shifted in my seat, stroking his thigh and savoring the feeling of it. Landon's foot tapped the side of mine, and I tapped back. But I didn't let go. I sat there for the rest of dinner, hand on his thigh, smiling politely at the Delli's, and made sure to use every lesson Mother had taught me.

I faced down the lords and ladies with my chin up, Landon at my side. And I made sure to do her proud.

Landon dragged me through the door, his impatience making his movements rough and demanding. He spun me and pressed me up against it, smashing our bodies together and holding my head in his hands. His blue eyes bore into me, and then his head descended, and Landon kissed me roughly.

His lips were warm and tasted of brandy and something sweet and smoky, his rough and invasive tongue giving me no choice but to taste and accept everything he had to give me. I folded instantly, relaxing in his arms and sighing.

"All mine," he ground out. "My mate."

"Mm," I murmured my agreement, sliding my hands under his shirt and splaying my hands out across his chest.

His skin was warm, and I could feel the rapid beat of his heart under my fingertips.

"You did well tonight," he praised me. "You made me proud. And you teased me *relentlessly*. My mate is a minx."

"Landon..." I sighed, melting even further into him.

The kind words and the desire in them went right to my heart, making it squeeze and thud unevenly. His praise lit me up like a firework, making heat bloom in my pelvis and my chest flush. I wanted more of it and more of him.

I'd thought I'd gotten enough of him during my heat, but now here the lust was again, coming to life inside of me and driving everything else away. Memories from dinner, from talking to Elias, and even from speaking to the king faded away, each of them being overwritten with the here and now.

"Now the whole kingdom can see why I chose you," he growled. "And they can smell me on you. And soon, they'll see your body change as you grow with my child. *Our* child."

I shivered with delight, nails digging into his skin. I wanted more words, but I also craved more of his kisses. I wanted to feel his skin grow damp under my fingertips as he worked his body into mine, working to make us both feel good.

I never knew sex could be so enrapturing. But with Landon, it was. It gripped me with a fierceness that seeped into my bones and left me feeling like a flower bending towards the sun or a river sliding across the terrain and finding its home in the ocean.

It was natural and hard to comprehend but *unbelievably* beautiful.

He kissed me, then slid his lips down the column of my neck, sending goosebumps all along my chest and arms. I was trembling, and Landon pulled me against him, supporting my weight. Eventually, when my knees became so weak I thought

I might fall, he scooped me up, wrapping my legs around his waist and supporting me with two large palms on my ass.

I wrapped my arms around his neck, clinging, and returned his attention. I bit his ear lobe, his neck, and his shoulders, sucking on his skin and leaving marks. I didn't care if he was a prince and the whole kingdom would see them, I *wanted* them to see them. Wanted them all to know it was me who left them there.

Landon shared my possessiveness, leaving his own marks at my collarbone and where the swell of my breasts peeked out of my dress. Then, he committed near blasphemy when he yanked at the fabric, making the seams groan. Everything slid or twisted out of his way, making some boning poke into my side, but I didn't care because the action had managed to pull the dress enough for him to scoop his fingers around my breasts and yank them free. They were high and exposed, resting on top of my bodice and perfectly placed for him to ravage.

His tongue circled my left nipple and then he took it into his mouth. He sucked on it, forcing my back to arch and my nipple to pebble under his touch.

"Landon," I cried, hands burying themselves in his blonde hair, holding him close.

He didn't answer me but instead pushed me harder against the door, keeping me pinned and suspended as he switched to my right breast, repeating the process there as his opposite hand came to the nipple he'd just tortured, twisting it roughly, keeping it hard and aching.

Sex throbbing, and heart racing wildly, I moaned, head thunking against the door as I writhed and withstood the exquisite torture. He bit into me, and then sucked, then licked, over and over in circles until my head spun.

I needed more but Landon seemed to be in no hurry to move on.

"Bed," I gasped. "Please, Lan—"

"No," he snapped. "You'll stay here."

"I can't—"

"You *can.*"

He looked me dead in the eyes, serious as anything, and then kissed me again, tongue sliding against mine. We kissed and we kissed, until I forgot all about the bed, and instead focused on Landon's hard body before mine.

Where he held me against his abdomen, I couldn't feel his cock, but if I tilted my hips and wiggled a little... *there.* My sex *finally* pressed into something hard, giving me the friction I needed.

Landon needed it too, because he hissed and then cursed, hips bucking up into me.

"Briar," he ground out. "Free me."

His fingers tensed where they were pressed into my ass, and together we shifted, creating enough space that I could untie the laces of his breeches and pull out his length. He was completely hard, the head of him dark and weeping a clear fluid that told me he was as ready as I was.

Thanking all the stars that I'd worn split panties, all I had to do was spread my legs, and I was bare and open for him. I was dripping, and when I pressed myself against his cock, Landon groaned.

"You're already prepared for me," he said, voice deep and strained. "Slide me inside of you, Briar. Let me fill you."

It was a pleading demand, silk laid over gravel, and I complied, needing it as much as he did. Carefully, I took him in my hand, squeezing him, and then tilted my hips, allowing the tip of him to run over my clit, and then to slot inside of me.

The second he felt it, he let his arms drop, allowing me to slide all the way down him in one fluid motion. Instantly, he filled me and stretched me wide open. Every bit of me was at his mercy, ready to be claimed, and he took it. His strength made it easy for him to manipulate me, taking my body weight and moving me over him, using me to find his pleasure, and feeding my own.

It was rough and fast and a little sloppy but undeniably delicious. The sound of our flesh meeting filled the air around us, and soon I could feel his knot swelling at the base of his cock, making the already tight fit even tighter.

It pushed into me easily and then popped out, adding to the rhythm Landon had established and pushing me so close to my orgasm I could taste it.

"L-Landon," I gasped. *"Please."*

I was sure there were a hundred other things I could say. Ways I could beg. But please was all I could manage, and it was enough for him.

He bit his lip, brows knitting together as he concentrated, angling his hips so the tip of his cock brushed against my inner walls *just* so, and it was like a match to tinder. Instantly my head flew back, curls flying everywhere as I surrendered.

"Fuck yes," Landon bit out as I moaned.

His hips stuttered, his knot swelling to its fullest before it seated itself inside of me, pressing against me and filling me, putting pressure on a sweet spot that restarted the whole process. I came again as Landon filled me, his warm spend kept inside of me by the knot. There was nowhere for it to go, and I savored the press of it inside of me. Savored the way his throat moved as he swallowed and ground out his pleasure with low groans and snarls.

It was carnal. Perfect. And it was all mine.

He pushed into me, pressing us flat against the door, keeping us connected as we breathed, coming down from our highs. I hummed with satisfaction, running my hands through Landon's hair and scratching at his scalp.

Rumbling happily, he tilted his head into my touch, and then took us away from the door. Walking carefully with our tangle of clothes still around us, Landon took us to the bedroom and then laid us out on the bed. With a few quick kicks, he had off his boots and breeches, and sighed happily, smothering me with his weight.

Together, we soaked in the contented silence, the evening air cool around us, the open windows letting in a breeze that danced gently over our damp skin.

Eyes fluttering closed, I hummed happily, wrapping my arms around Landon's waist and keeping him close. Not that he could get much closer. His entire weight was already bearing down into me. But he picked up on my intent and did the only thing he could, sliding his hands over my shoulders and then into my hair, pulling my face into his neck and keeping me there.

"I've got you, darling," he said gently.

"I know," I promised. "I have you too."

I squeezed as much of his huge, broad body as I could.

Landon chuckled, "I see that you do."

"You're a big man," I said. "I can only do so much."

"I know," he said, laughing outright. "I appreciate the effort."

"You're welcome," I chirped. "Anytime you need me, I'm there."

Shaking his head, he kissed my temple, "I'll keep that in mind."

I was *glowing*.

With each day that passed, each soft moment with Landon, I was reassured that I'd made the right decision. I belonged here with him. I truly did.

CHAPTER FIFTEEN

One Week Later

When I wasn't attending functions with Landon, I'd taken to sitting out on the balconies of Fleur. There weren't many of them, but along the back walls of the castle, a few had been built in recent years. Sturdy enough to withstand the winds coming in off the mountain, and made with the same strong pink stone as the rest of the castle.

Landon had his own work to attend to, so I was often left to my own devices.

I sat out, a book in my lap, and enjoyed the sun.

To my delight, Elias had taken to sitting with me, looking elegant in his standard all-black, his own book held in one hand, propped up on one of his crooked knees.

"Thank you," I said softly, smiling at my friend.

"Whatever for?" He asked, brows knit.

"For not abandoning me."

He scoffed, "This again? Briar, come now. What true friend would abandon someone just because they'd found their mate and canceled their plans together? It's to be expected among you wolves. Even aside from that, I could not begrudge your happiness. All I ask is that you come visit me with your prince once all is settled."

"I'm sure that can be arranged," I said, believing it with all my heart.

Since speaking with the king and living in Fleur as Landon's betrothed, life had settled down in a way I could never have imagined. I spent my nights with Landon in bed, the fires between us not having settled even slightly.

Though he'd said he was only interested in me as a mother to an heir, Landon spent a lot of time with me, even outside of bed play. He listened to me when I spoke, and I told him the few stories I could of my family. Innocuous things like when I'd learned to ride from my father or the first time I'd turned into a wolf and went running with my family.

And with Elias's understanding of my change in plans, and his steady unyielding friendship, I was forging a new life for myself.

It was easy, and it felt right.

Settling back, smiling to myself, I concentrated again on my book. It was another history book I'd taken from the library, this one covering more recent topics. I was still determined to learn about these modern times, and it was easy to wave away questions over my book choice by stating I hadn't learned about Eastern politics and history on the other side of the mountains in my fake past life.

I was reading about Landon's great-grandfather, when a familiar sound I hadn't heard in a long *long* time began to ring out through the hills.

Confused, I set the book aside and looked towards the distant mountain range. Snow-capped peaks lined the horizon, and from that same direction, a steady *thud thud* sounded like great huge drums.

I couldn't place the sound, and narrowed my eyes, trying to see further. Surely such a loud noise would have an obvious source. A rockslide, maybe?

"What is that sound?" Elias asked, head turning to look the same direction as me.

"I don't see anything," I told him. "Perhaps—"

Rounding one of the mountain tops, a huge dark shape with wings was approaching. It was so far away the sound of its wing beats was out of time with what we could see.

As it approached, the sound began to match the visual, and I realized what we saw was an enormous blue dragon, with glittering scales and strong wings and claws I knew were larger than a bear.

"A dragon," I whispered, frozen with shock.

"Oh gods, hells, and damn it all," Elias said, standing from his seat. "Get inside, Briar!"

"It's a dragon," I repeated, eyes locked on the rapidly approaching beast.

It was just as beautiful as I remembered. Dragons were the pinnacle of nature and terror and strength and majesty. They were awesome, truly, but they also belonged in the mountains.

Why would one be this far from its home?

"Briar," Elias repeated, pulling at my hand. "We must take cover and raise the alarm. *Come."*

He pulled at me again, practically yanking me from my stunned stupor. Stumbling, I followed him inside. Immediately, Elias began to shout, raising the alarm.

"A dragon approaches!" He announced, turning to the closest guardsman. "Alert the king and the prince. We need to prepare."

"A dragon?!" The guard asked. "Approaching Fleur?"

"They never come this far from the range!" Another said, shocked.

"Alert the king," Elias said again, leaning in close, snarling the words.

Even I could feel the power rolling off of the older fae, and the guards immediately sprung into action. They sprinted back down the hall, armor clanking as they went.

"Come, Briar, we must get you somewhere safe," Elias insisted, pulling me further into the castle.

"W-wait," I stuttered. "They can't really be attacking us, can they?"

"Dragons are *dangerous* and unpredictable," Elias said. "Do they not attack on the other side of the mountains?"

"N-not as such," I stammered. "We live in peace, mostly."

"Strange," he muttered, eyes forward and strides long as he pulled me into Fleur.

We fell into silence as we wound through the halls, activity springing up all around us as we advanced. I realized after Elias had us turn down one of the longer, taller halls in the castle, that he was taking me to Landon's office.

Throwing the door open without prompting, Elias pulled me inside, announcing, "I've brought her."

Landon was standing with his father, their heads bowed together as they spoke in low voices. Their heads rose to take in Elias and I.

"Good," the king said, nodding. "Accompany her to the safe room."

"Yes, Your Majesty," Elias agreed without questioning.

Landon bowed to his father, "I'll escort them and then return."

"Very well."

Landon left his father's side, taking quick strides toward me, "You'll remain there until I come to get you. Understand?"

I looked up at him with huge, uncomprehending eyes, "Is the dragon really going to attack the castle?"

Landon's blonde curls shook as he nodded, "It seems so. Come. It's approaching rapidly. I need you—"

The stone shook and shouts rang up through the castle as something hit one of the walls.

"It's throwing boulders!" Landon shouted. "Elias, take her to the safe room. The lever to open it is under my desk. *Protect her with your life.*"

Elias nodded, "I will."

The king came to his son's side, and together, they rushed from the room, running right into gods knew what.

"Dragons aren't evil," I said to no one and everyone.

But my words were drowned out as another rumble shook the castle, and screams echoed as the clear sound of dragon fire came all too close.

Elias left me standing there and rushed to Landon's desk, ducking under it and looking up. He grabbed around and, a moment later, cried out with success as he yanked on something, and a great groan came from one of the bookshelves along the wall.

"Come," Elias said, grabbing my arm again. "We must keep you safe."

"This cannot be real," I said to him, looking up into his eyes and begging for an answer.

"This is real, my lady," he promised. "Real and *deadly*. You may carry with you our future. The future of Fenestral. We *must* keep you safe."

The unfair reality did not wait for me to come to terms with it. Instead, it trundled forward, bringing with it another great boom and more screaming, men beginning to shout as they mounted their defenses.

Elias didn't wait for me to unstick myself. He swept me up into his arms and carried me behind the bookcase. On the other side, there was another lever which he yanked on, closing the doors behind us.

Then he descended down a set of stone steps, going carefully and by feel as the stairwell was *completely* dark.

He didn't stumble once, and after going down nearly three flights of steps, we came to a small, comfortable room. Elias was able to find some tinder and a torch near the doorway and after setting me down on a settee, went about lighting the first torch, which he then carried with him as he lit the rest.

Once the space was filled with warm light, he stood in front of me, head tilted back so he could look up at the ceiling.

"What is happening?" I asked him quietly.

His chin dropped, and Elias looked at me sympathetically, "I wish I could tell you, love."

"You don't know?"

"The dragons have never come this far out before," he explained. "There's no telling what damage they may wrought."

"This is... all wrong..."

Elias kneeled in front of me, one hand settling on top of my knee, "I know this is upsetting, Briar. But we need to wait here. We won't know anything until it's all done."

"That's not it," I insisted, shaking my head. "Dragons don't *do* this."

"They haven't attacked the castle before," Elias nodded.

"No! I mean—" I huffed, caught between my mind railing against reality and wanting to tell Elias the truth.

"Briar, there's no sense in trying to understand the actions of beats."

"Are you sure they're beasts?" I asked desperately.

Elias was taken aback, brows knitting. I didn't know if it was because of surprise or if he was confused and concerned. I didn't seem to understand dragons were *bad,* but he didn't have the chance to question me.

Another huge rumble shook the castle, dust and small chunks of rocks crumbling onto us from the ceiling.

"Oh gods," I whispered. "How can this be real?"

Elias gathered me into his arms, holding me tight, "This will pass, poppet. It will."

I clung to him, my mind warring and horrible reality dawning.

My new life was nothing like my old one.

Nothing.

CHAPTER SIXTEEN

I stood next to my father, my younger siblings to my left, as we watched the scene before us. Our huge, majestic protectors, the dragons, were scattered among the mountain tops, clinging to the sheer faces of rock with their massive claws, iridescent wings folded close to their sides.

They glittered like jewels among the gray rock, the last vestiges of snow in small piles around them, shining like silver. It amazed me this year, as it had every year before. It seemed impossible that we shared the mountains with such great creatures. The power in their limbs and in their wings was truly awe-inspiring, especially when they launched themselves away from the rocks and into the air.

A symphony of wing beats sounded like drums around us, pounding into our bones as one by one, the dragons swooped down and took their prizes. An assemblage of offerings were laid out in the field before us, donated by farmers and from the crown. Older livestock whose time was done gently laid to rest and then put out into the field to serve our protectors.

The dragons kept us free from invading armies, free from malicious magic, and free from the huge predacious beasts that roamed the higher altitudes.

And in exchange, we gave them this offering.

One by one, they came down, took their prize, and then disappeared into the mountains again. They flew away, high up and north, where we could not go until there was but one dragon left.

He was larger than the rest and older, with lines around his eyes where his scales creased. Deep red scales shimmered in the sun as he came down, took two offerings, and then flew away, signaling the end.

"It is done," Father announced, voice booming.

We all cheered.

CHAPTER SEVENTEEN

Hours later, Elias and I sat, waiting.

Our stomachs churned, but there was no appetite to be found in either of us. The safe room had been stocked with food and water, but we left it untouched. No way would be able to settle in for a meal and pretend like we hadn't both listened to dragons ravaging the castle with fire and claw.

But we couldn't leave either. There was no telling what was on the other side of the door if we did try to open it, so he and I remained in place, sitting close to one another, hands in our laps, waiting in the torchlight for news.

It came in the form of a door opening suddenly somewhere above us and a heavy pair of feet pounding down the flights of stone stairs.

At the landing, Landon appeared, dressed in the same full set of armor he'd been wearing the day we met.

I stood, "Landon!"

He rushed to me, hands immediately brushing over my hair, then coming to cup my jaw, turning it this way and that. And then he dipped his head down, kissing me hard, his tongue coming into my mouth to touch mine and drink me in.

"You're safe," he murmured there, kissing me over and over. "You're safe."

"I am," I assured him, leaning in, planting my palms on the cool metal of his breastplate. "I'm okay."

Our lips separated, and then he dragged me into his arms, pulling me tight against him. I didn't even care about the hard edges of his armor, it was *wonderful* to be in his arms again, to have my alpha's scent in my nose and his strength surrounding me.

Mostly, it was wonderful to know that we'd both *lived*.

"How did the castle fare?" Elias asked after a moment, the words quiet.

"Fleur stands," Landon told him over the top of my head, his arms still tight as iron around me. "There were three of them, all coming down from the range."

"Gods above," Elias gasped. "Three dragons?"

Sighing heavily, Landon admitted, "It was a tough battle. We would have lost it but... they left."

"They *left?*"

"Mm. Out of nowhere. Flew back to the range as if they'd never been there at all." Landon sounded frustrated, and confused.

I couldn't understand why. What would compel them to attack in the first place? And then why would they leave just as quickly as they'd come?

"That sounds like a warning shot." Elias noted, sounding unsettled.

"Were dragons capable of such cunning, I'd agree," Landon said.

"Three dragons..." I whispered into his chest.

I could scarcely imagine one dragon attacking but *three.*

This was more than just one lone dragon acting out of its nature. *All* dragons were changed from the gentle beasts I knew.

How was that even possible?

Landon squeezed me even tighter, "Worry not, my rose. All is well again."

"For now, anyway," Elias muttered.

Landon must have glared at him, because the fae sighed and then changed the subject.

"Let's exit this dreary hole, hm? Find some hot food. Briar and I have not eaten, and I imagine our hero prince here hasn't either."

"I have not," Landon admitted, reluctantly letting me go.

Together, the men put out the torches, and then we ascended the stairs, coming back up into the castle proper.

All the while, Landon kept my hand tucked into his arm, keeping me close. We streamed through people as they rushed back and forth, making our way back to our rooms, and breathed a sigh of relief.

CHAPTER EIGHTEEN

After the attack, Landon doubled his training. During the day, I hung out with Elias and his friends, wandering around Fleur, reading history books, before we all went to dinner. Landon would join us there, hair damp from a fresh bath, taking away the sweat from his training.

But I could still smell the exertion on his body, making me squirm in my chair.

It was impossible for my omega to ignore how obviously strong and virile Landon was. It came off of him in waves, how confident he was, how in control he was of his body, how easily he commanded those around him.

As soon as dinner was over, he'd shoot me a look, and then take my hand, excusing us both from after-dinner retreats. Then he'd take me back to our room and keep me up *far* too late.

But then one day... the routine changed.

I decided, instead of idly wandering, I'd find where Landon was training and watch.

Honestly, I had half a mind of going out there and asking to join him. I'd never felt so helpless as I had when I'd been in the bunker with Elias, waiting for it all to be over. I wanted to be able to do more, to wield at least a knife when I fought.

Elias gave me instructions to where they trained, waving me off to go on my own.

"I've no interest in their war games and training," he said loftily. "I have magic if I need it. But you go enjoy yourself, poppet."

"Will do," I promised, waving goodbye to him.

The directions were easy to follow, and took me to a balcony overlooking one of the inner courtyards of Fleur. Huge diamond-paned double doors opened out onto the pink stone balcony, appointed with plush chairs, a small wooden side table carved with flowers, topped with a glass vase filled with fresh flowers, and a plus wool rug to cushion my footfalls.

Clearly, it was a favorite look out for castle occupants, and I immediately saw why when I settled into one of the chairs. I had a *perfect* view of the courtyard below.

There were dark scorch marks from where the dragons had descended, but otherwise, the shimmering pink stone was *perfect*. It sparkled in the sun, pearlescent and beautiful, reflecting gentle light onto the figures below.

In the courtyard, a small squad of soldiers were gathered. Among them were a few fae with horns over their heads, their points tipped in gold or silver and sharpened to be deadly, wolves who were half-transformed and outfitted with special armor, and vampires who had their claws and fangs extended, their speed allowing them to dart around so quickly they were nearly invisible.

All of them were clashing with one another, wielding dulled blades that were clearly still made of very heavy steel that whooshed as they swung through the air. I noted immediately that none of them wielded knives, and each of them were *very* comfortable with their swords. It looked dangerous, even without the blades being sharpened.

It dawned on me that Landon, somehow, hadn't been coming home covered in bruises.

Which meant none of these men had managed to hit him.

Wow.

When I looked a little closer at the wolves down below, I was able to quickly parse out which one was Landon. Largely, because he was the fastest among them, moving with light feet and swirling and dodging the others' attacks.

I couldn't take my eyes away from him. I'd never seen Landon transform before, and seeing him even halfway there, it was obvious he was an *enormous* wolf. He was nearly golden, his fur was so shiny and a pale gold, making him stand out from the others where it was sprouting on his arms and legs. When he was fully wolf, he must have shone like the sun when he ran.

I hoped I'd be able to see it sooner than later.

The armor he wore over his larger half-wolf-form was clearly custom-made for him. A matte black helmet framed his slightly elongated face, covering his snout but leaving his fangs out to be used. It was covered with golden metalwork, flowers, and thorns forming a crown around his head.

The other pieces of his armor were similarly colored, with a huge chest plate, and no metal on his arms, leaving him mobile and with easy access to his claws. Black chainmail covered the fronts of his thighs, attached to his chest plate, and loosely held around his thighs with leather cords. His feet were as free as his claws were, shaped into huge paws, with claws at the tips, which gleamed pearly white when I caught sight of them.

All over, it was as if he was a dark prince, emerging golden from the blackness, here to save his people. His half-transformed face was even more appealing than I'd have imagined too. Even under the armor, I could see how his eyes were still just as blue, but now larger, with slit pupils and a harsher brow. I wanted to touch him and pull him in for a kiss.

His control was, frankly, impressive.

Holding such a defined half-form was no easy feat. Few people could manage it, and fewer still could hold themselves in that shape for extended periods of time. I myself could only manage half of an hour, max. Our bodies longed to be in one form or another, and it took years of training to overcome that instinct and stay only half transformed.

Lan, clearly, had mastered that instinct.

As fully in control of that as he was his body.

I couldn't stop staring as they all sparred, sparing no blows and going full tilt at one another. Their grunts of exertion and battle-shouts rang through the open space, and I took it all in, entranced.

Mostly, I watched Landon, squirming in my seat, unable to help how my body was reacting to his obvious display of mastery.

He was *perfect.* In every possible way.

After some time, Landon glanced up at me, smirked, and then turned back to his battle with renewed vigor.

"Caught," I muttered to myself.

I didn't think he minded though. If I thought he was fighting full-tilt before, he was going *full-out* now. An alpha displaying his strength for his mate.

That too got to me, my cheeks warming and a helpless smile pasting itself onto my face. In my core, heat pooled, and my stomach filled with butterflies. In my mind, the images of Landon moving above me merged with the movements he made on the field of battle, drawing my attention to all of his many, *many* attractive points. The way his stomach and abdomen flexed, how his biceps bulged and strained his shirts, the glint of golden fur that was just as beautiful as the dusky blonde of his human hair.

All of it was enticing beyond belief, and soon I was squirming in my seat, core damp and heart pounding with desire.

It was a show just for me, I knew it, and that was confirmed when his spar ended, and he looked back up at me again and winked.

Winked!

I had no idea he possessed such a playful side, and I couldn't help but laugh.

This drew the attention of all of the fighters below, all of whom glanced between me and Landon with open curiosity. Landon ignored them, and I tried to remain poised in the face of their curiosity. Mother had taught me that enduring other people's gazes was a skill, and though I was a little out of practice, I still fared well enough. Their eyes turned away from me when Landon clapped, and they all gathered around him.

The end of their practice, apparently. The soldiers began to clap one another on their backs and disperse from the courtyard.

Landon didn't leave with them. In fact, he stayed rooted to where he was, nostrils flaring. Then, he glanced up at me, eyes narrowed. Hesitantly, I waved at him.

He smirked a decidedly very wolfish smirk, and not just because of his snout, and held up one finger, pointed at me, held the same finger up, and then drove it down towards the ground.

You. Wait. There.

Well then. I could do that.

I nodded down at him, and he smiled back up at me and walked out of the courtyard.

Anxiously, I squirmed again in my seat, trying to have patience and relieve the pressure in my core.

Sooner than I thought he would, Landon was opening the door behind me and stepping onto the balcony and closing the door behind him. To my delight, he was still half-transformed, and his eyes were hooded.

"Hello, Landon," I squeaked out, standing from the chair. "I... er... you were very impressive down there."

"Indeed?" He asked, voice rougher than I was used to, and deeper.

"Yup," I basically gasped.

Why was that deep voice making my insides turn to liquid and my heart race harder than it ever had before? I swore even when I was in heat, my heart hadn't pounded this hard.

Landon stepped even closer, taking off his helmet and setting it on the chair I'd vacated so I could see the full glory of his golden mane and the blue of his eyes against it. I was nearly blinded by the beauty of it all.

For his part, he seemed *amazingly* amused by my reaction to him. He leaned down, dwarfing me with his *giant* form. He had to be at least a head taller than he'd been before. And he was *already* tall before.

"You must realize I can smell quite well in this form, my rose," he growled.

"C-can you?"

"Mmm."

That wasn't really a confirmation, but the twinkle in his eyes was nearly as good as words spoken out loud. Clearly, Landon knew how he was affecting me, and he was delighting in it.

"Well," I said, turning my face away, trying to hide how I blushed, "I suppose I'm not used to you looking like this."

A huge, clawed hand gripped my jaw, my whole face really, and turned it back so I was looking up at Landon. The sharp tips of his pearly white claws just barely dug into my skin, making me keenly aware of the power and strength in his grip.

"Look at me, Briar," he rumbled.

I was *looking.* Though it made my heart stutter, with his permission, I drank him in, noting every little detail of this new side of Landon.

All of it pleased me, and that pleased Landon.

With a growl, his head descended, and he took me in a savage kiss. It was hard and rough, with his fangs pushing against my lips and his long tongue found its way into my mouth.

He invaded me. There was no other way to describe it. My whole being surrendered to his, and he took it, plundered me with tooth and tongue, practically devouring me as his jaw opened and he drove his tongue in deeper. It wasn't even a kiss anymore. Landon was just conquering me, pulling me into him as his tongue touched the very recesses of my throat, almost uncomfortably deep.

I moaned, tilting my head and pressing myself closer to his chest plate, the golden metal work warm from his body under my fingers, the fine lines delicate and soft against my touch.

Landon growled, the low rumble reverberating through the metal, as one of his paws came up to roughly grope at my chest, the claws on his fingers digging into the linen of my day dress and through my shift so I could feel their tips against my skin.

"Landon," I sighed, knees growing weaker with every moment. "We should find our rooms."

"Hmph." He grunted and then reluctantly stepped back from me.

I mourned the loss of his touch, but then he swung me up into his arm, just one arm, and carried me away from the balcony, stopping only to dip a little to grab his helmet in his free hand. With casual grace, he carried me cradled in his arm and pressed against his chest.

We passed several people in the halls as we wound our way back to our rooms, and they all stared at us, some smirking and some with confusion. But none of them attempted to stop us, and we were quickly closed back behind the doors.

Landon immediately set me on the bed roughly, allowing me to fall back to the sheets, and then tore at the ties on his armor. Not wanting to be useless and wanting him naked as soon as possible, I launched myself at him, pulling at as many leather ties as I could locate and throwing open the few latches that held his chest plate and chainmail to his body. Under the armor, he had on a black linen shirt that was sleeveless, and a cloth loosely wrapped around his waist and then passed through his legs to tie at the back. It did little to hide how aroused he was.

Landon's cock was different too from normal. While his normal form was outfitted as many others were, save for the addition of his knot, which swelled to life at the base, this half-form was undeniably *huge*. He hadn't been small before, but now his cock was impossible to hold in one hand. I had to use both hands to fully wrap around his base, and it was only then that I could truly comprehend just what I was in for.

My whole body clenched, and I was *excited* for the challenge. The length of him was longer too, and his knot was *already* swollen at the base, and all of him was a purple-red color that was demanding and eye-catching.

There was absolutely no denying his desire for me. It was right there, and I couldn't help but stroke him, observing the thick veins that moved beneath the surface and how he pulsed gently at my touch.

"Ah, Briar," he sighed, one huge hand coming to my shoulder, holding me close.

"This is *beautiful*," I breathed.

Which was no lie. It was the essence of his power, his strength, curving beautifully and heavy in my hands.

He laughed, "Thank you, my rose."

I stroked him carefully, familiarizing myself with him for another moment, before gently dropping his and sliding my hands up his newly exposed torso.

The longer fur trailed down his chest, coming to a long point where his chest hair normally ended, and then thickened and lengthened again just under his belly button, and then down where a thick thatch of it nestled the root of his cock.

It was addicting, sliding my hands up his abdomen, mapping out the new ridges and the softness of the short fur that now covered him. Landon sighed, leaning in closer, allowing me to take in more and more. I scratched my fingers through the fur between his pecs, and then finally did the thing I'd been dreaming about. I slid my hand into the fur at the sides of his jaw, and pulled him down for a kiss.

Languid and slow, the kiss was nearly tender, his tongue less invading me and more exploring, as if he was experiencing me anew as much as I was him.

Then, his hands came to my clothes and began to tug. I helped him, yanking at laces and sliding off the layers of my outfit. Once I was *finally* bare to the warm afternoon air, Landon's hands came right to me, digging into my hips roughly and pulling me to my knees at the edge of the bed. Even with the added height, I was nowhere near tall enough to reach his face, so Landon had to lean down to meet me where I was.

His jaw opened, fangs coming to either of my cheeks and then his tongue slid into my mouth in a wolfish form of a kiss. He devoured me again and didn't pull away until I was panting, breath stolen away by his passion.

"Lay down," he commanded me, pushing at my shoulders.

I did as he asked, settling back. Before I had really laid all the way down, he grabbed my hips, lifting me high up into the air until only my shoulders were on the bed, and he held my ass in his palms. He tilted me, bringing me to his mouth like he was drinking from a cup.

And then he did drink.

His tongue lashed against me, so big it covered all of me, from my clit, down the length of my sex, and then even further, tickling at my rear entrance, sending unexpected sparks up my spine. Writhing in his grasp, I twisted, not sure if I was trying to get closer or to push further away.

Sex with Landon was often overwhelming, so many stimuli assaulting my senses at once, but this was... beyond what he'd given me before.

He could manipulate so much of me, toss me around me, maneuver me however he wanted with so little effort. There was no resisting him. With long laps, he licked at my pussy, tasting all of me at once and then flicking the tip of his tongue against my clit.

"Oh, *Landon*," I gasped, writhing, definitely trying to get closer. *"Yes."*

A fire built inside of me, my liquid core coming to a roiling boil, spilling out of me in roiling clouds of passion and loud moans and needy whines.

He gave me no break, continuing to feast on my sex, using the full length of his tongue. Then, he slid it inside of me. It wasn't as firm or hard as his cock was, but *gods*. The wet silky length of it filled me, and I lost all composure. An orgasm rocketed through me, blazing a fierce trail through my nerves, frying them, and making me go limp in his huge palms.

Landon growled, pleased with my response, and carefully lowered me to the bed. Then, he yanked at my hips, turning me over so I was on my belly, and then pulled at them. I caught on, gaining control of my arms as my body still trembled, and I assumed the position before him. My shoulders to the bed, and my hips in the air, presenting my sex to him.

He rumbled, "All mine."

And before the orgasm fully left me, Landon entered me again.

It was a slow, arduous push, the much larger size of him not what I was used to. But my body did give way to his, stretching to its limit until as much of him as I could take was seated inside of me.

Behind me, Landon growled, and pulled on my hips, inching in even further.

I whined, "Landon, it's too much."

"No, omega," he rumbled. "You were made for me. Made for *this.*"

He pulled out, and then pushed back in slowly... and he was right. Something deep inside of me, in the same place where my omega lived, surged, and he slid in another few inches.

"That's it," he encouraged me. "Take all of me."

It felt like shifting, in a way. Like my body was turning into something else. My vision grew hazy and then sharpened as he pulled out again and then pushed in even further. Then on the next stroke, I could feel my canines elongating, and my fingernails shaping into claws. And then on the next, I could feel the thick, warm base of his knot against me.

I was *transforming*, I realized. But not all the way. I was holding myself somewhere in between, just as Landon was, allowing my body to take more of him, matching him where he was.

"Perfect," he rumbled, drawing out again and then pushing fast until the knot pushed again... and then slipped inside of me.

The knot filled me, making me fuller than I could have imagined, and then it popped out of me as Landon drew back again. I didn't even have the chance to whine because now that I could accommodate him, he didn't hold back.

With rough, hard strokes, Landon fucked me, the knot at the base of him sliding in and out of me with every stroke, accompanied by a soft sound and my chest filling near to burst with pleasure. It was *perfect*. In every way, this was Landon *really* possessing me.

Somewhere between both of our forms, our wolves so close to the surface they were bursting through, we were both Landon and Briar, alpha and omega, and together we were *beautiful*.

"You're *mine*," he growled in my ear. "Mine to breed, mine to fuck, mine to *possess*. Tell me, omega. Tell me you're mine."

"I am," I gasped. "I'm yours, alpha. Everything. Yours."

He rumbled with pleasure, clearly approving of my words. "You are. You're *mine.*"

Driven forward by our words, he powered into me fiercely with a steady rhythm, and my knees began to shake and my thighs tense as I felt another orgasm begin to build inside of me.

He, as always, could sense it.

"You're gripping me so tightly," he growled. "Are you going to come, omega? Come on my cock? Let me fill you with me seed and knot you? To *breed* you?"

Fire shot through me, and my body tensed around him. Then, he drove me over the edge with one final push as his knot filled me again, forcing itself inside of me and filling me to the brink.

"Ah, gods," I groaned, head flying back. *"Alpha.* Landon, yes. *"*

He bit into my shoulder, holding onto me, as he kept himself buried inside of me, and released.

Warmth flooded me as Landon himself filled me with his spend.

I collapsed to the bed, and he came with me, teeth still digging into my shoulder, his body trembling as he felt the full effects of his release.

We stayed like that, breathing together, my sex still pulsing around his cock, which itself was still twitching inside of me gently.

All of it was beautiful, and all of it was good.

CHAPTER NINETEEN

"I will see you, my rose," Landon said, kissing my cheeks.

"Bye," I whispered back, smiling up at him.

He gave me one last kiss, and then swept from the room, leaving me to my own devices. As the prince, he was busier now than ever, working closely with his father and coordinating with endless leagues of scouts as they tracked dragon movements and worked on repairs to Fleur.

It kept him away from me, but it also made me proud to be his mate. He worked so hard to keep his people safe, to keep *me* safe, it warmed my heart.

I sat back in the plush chaise, basking in the glow of being mated and the possibility that maybe we were starting a family. It made my heart flutter and my stomach filled with butterflies.

My life was turning for the better. In spite of everything, it was turning into something *beautiful.*

I could never have imagined I'd end up here the day I'd woken up from the curse. At first, I thought my life would never know any kind of normal again. That all happiness had been taken from me and would never be returned.

But then Landon came back to me, accepted me as his mate, and now…

I sighed, smiling to myself. There were no words for the feelings I felt now. Though the shadow of dragons and witches and my past were still there, they were far from my mind. I had my mate and my baby to think about. Those were what mattered to me.

Out of nowhere, red smoke began to fill the room, and Eris's evil laugh rang out.

"No," I gasped, standing, pressing my back against the wall, and glancing about for an escape.

But before I could flee, the witch was standing before me, black hair and a cape of stars fluttering in an invisible wind.

"So, did you like my little show?" She asked me, smiling a feline smile. "I thought it was impressive, all things considered. A fine taste of things yet to come."

"Things to come?" I asked, confused and terror clawing its way up my throat.

"Yes! I'm delighted you asked," she laughed, rich and full of malicious delight. "I'd love to tell you the full details, but that would ruin the surprise. We can talk about it all afterward when it's done."

"I don't understand why you're doing this," I said, shaking my head. "Don't you have enough? Can't you be done?"

"A woman's work is never done," she said smoothly. "There's always some new horizon to cross, a new skill to master. You must understand this, you're a *princess*. I doubt you were ever idle."

"You're mad," I accused. "Using such justification to take lives and sow discord."

"I'm not mad," Eris's eyes rolled. "I'm old, and I'm bored. You live as long as me, dear Briar, I have no doubt you'll come to understand that sometimes the only thing that will slake your thirst is *blood*." She thought for a moment, "And perhaps a fine wine."

Then, she smiled and stood, her cloak whirling and shimmering with its stars around her, "I must bid you farewell, your mate approaches, and I don't feel like dealing with him."

"Wait, Er—"

She was gone in a flash of red smoke and glowing ruby light before I could get her name out.

I wanted to beg her to stop her madness, to have mercy on Fenestral and leave her feud with me in the past, but she was gone, and the door was opening, and Landon was approaching me, brows knit together in worry.

"Briar?" Looking me up and down, he glanced between me and the window, and then around the room, searching.

I forced myself to smile, eyes focusing on him, "Lan! Hello."

He glanced around the room again, "Were you talking to someone?"

The room was painfully empty, and there was not even the faintest trace of Eris and her magic left.

I didn't want him to grow any more suspicious of me than he already looked, so I said the first thing I thought of. "Oh, no. Just aloud to myself, I'm sorry."

"Okay," he said, eyes narrowed, watching me closely. "Then, we must discuss our wedding. With the attack—"

In a flash, Eris appeared again between us, a wicked smile splitting her face nearly in two, it was so big, "Oh my dear Briar, I nearly forgot something!"

Landon jumped back,   and he began to shift, nails elongating into claws, holding himself halfway between human and wolf as he demanded, "Who goes there?"

"Oh you are just as dashing in person as I'd hoped you would be," she gushed, walking directly for him, squeezing his biceps. "Oh, Briar, why didn't you *tell* me?"

She looked him up and down, taking in his breeches, leather armor, and dagger at his side. Landon looked between her and me, unsure, his hands held into claws, ready to strike.

I desperately wished he and I were closer, that I could signal to him with a glance alone that he should strike at her, or that he *shouldn't*. I couldn't decide either way, she was so powerful, it seemed unlikely she could be felled so easily... but on the other hand, a slice to the throat proved fatal more often than it didn't.

"Briar?" Landon asked me, glancing between me and Eris.

The witch didn't let me respond, "Oh, Briar and I are *old* friends. I simply *had* to visit her when I heard about the dragons. What a *shame* about that. And if there's to be a *wedding*, then I simply must insist on an invitation!"

"Who are you?" He asked, increasingly suspicious, hand reaching for the sword at his hip. "Briar, how do you know this woman?"

"I'm Eris, Mistress of the Dragons. Witch of the Mountains. Lady of the Springs. Whatever you wish to call me is just fine, young man."

He reared back, "Excuse me? Mistress of—"

"Of course! You don't know yet, do you?" She asked, filled with glee. "Oh, Briar, why didn't you *tell him* you and I were friends? He might have been less surprised by the dragons then, surely."

"We're not friends," I said to her. "Landon, this woman is not a friend."

"Nonsense!" She declared. "I brought you here! You'd never have met the fine prince here if not for me, *princess.*"

Landon's expression grew stony and guarded, trying to make sense of everything unfolding in front of him. "What is the meaning of all of this? Why are you here?"

"I thought I made it clear. I'm visiting my good friend, Briar, to speak to her about the dragons," she chirped. "It's really an absolute pleasure to have met you, Prince Landon. I wasn't expecting to be able to. I'm sure we'll see one another *real* soon."

Leaving us stunned and confused, the witch disappeared again in another puff of smoke and light.

Landon looked at me with a stony expression of mistrust, and I held up my hands, trying to explain, "She is *not* my friend. Eris is an evil, conniving witch."

"She called you princess," he pointed out.

"R-right, she did," I admitted.

He walked towards me until we were practically pressed together, his chin dipped practically to his chest to look down at me, assessing me. "Is that all you have to say? Who was she? How does she know you?"

"It's complicated, Landon."

"I never implied it was otherwise," he said flatly. "But you need to tell me. Now."

"R-right."

His eyes were as flat as his voice, the blue of his irises like an eerily calm sea. The calm before the storm.

"I am waiting, Briar," he prompted me.

"I don't know what to say," I admitted. "Eris is *not* my friend. She is… she's *evil.*"

"So I'm to set aside all the things she said? Treat them as lies?" He shook his head. "Briar, you're my betrothed. I need to know I can trust you. I need you to tell me *the truth.*"

"I am," I insisted.

"No." He said, flat out. "Do better. Give me more. I *need* an explanation. I *deserve* one. She seemed to imply she knows more about the dragons than we do. I need to know who she is and what she knows, and I need to know how she relates to *you.* I need to know what you know."

"I don't know how to tell you," I admitted. "But I swear, Landon, she is *not* my friend, and I know not what she schemes."

Tentatively, I put a hand on his chest, stepping closer.

He closed his hand around my wrist, pulling it away, "Answers, Briar. Now." His words weren't just flat now. They were hard, anger beginning to seep into them. "If you refuse, there will be problems."

"Problems?"

"You'll be deemed a security risk. I have no other choice than to treat you with suspicion."

My mind reeled. His decision-making was sound, of course. I'd deem myself a risk too, were I in his shoes. But since I was me, and not him, I knew the truth, and I *hurt*. I hurt because he looked at me with such suspicion. I hurt because we'd fallen in together so easily, and in that time he hadn't grown to trust me any more than a stranger.

If he did, he would at least listen to what I *could* say, wouldn't he?

"Landon, I-I understand," I tried to explain. "I do. I know this looks bad, but it isn't what it seems. Eris came here of her own accord to gloat. I think she is scheming. I don't know *how* she could possibly have enough power but... I swear, dragons aren't *like* this. They don't attack castles. They don't leave the mountains. Eris *must* have something to do with it."

"Nonsense," he scoffed. "Dragons have *always* been dangerous, unpredictable beasts."

"They haven't!" I insisted. "There's more going on here, Landon. I don't know what it is, but there's *something.*"

"You seem to be sure of a lot of things," Landon said, words laced with sarcasm. "Tell me more, Briar. What truths bring you across the mountains?"

"I'm being serious!" I insisted.

"You are not." He snarled, finally snapping. "You are telling tales. Weaving fiction. My kingdom is in danger, all of our lives are on the line, and you're inventing stories. Are you trying to distract me on purpose? Keep my attention away from defending the kingdom and turning my mind to solving your nonsense dragon mystery?"

"No!" I nearly shouted. "I just don't know how to explain all of this to you. I can't even begin. I don't even know if you'd believe me!"

"Try me."

"W-well," I stuttered, wringing my hands.

I needed space from Landon and stepped back, turning away from him and pacing around the room. I waved my hands around my head, gesturing and trying to make Lan see how serious I was.

"Eris is *not* my friend," I said. "She isn't."

"Hm."

"And where I come from, er... Where I grew up, dragons *are* different there."

The *second* the words came out of my mouth, his shoulders slumped, and Landon looked away from me.

"The same again," Landon sighed, looking... broken. Disappointed. Like he really had been prepared to believe me but just couldn't. "I've had enough. You'll remain here. I'll come visit you later, and when I do, I expect you to tell me the truth. The *real* truth."

Distrust simmered just beneath the surface of his disappointment. It was right there in his narrowed eyes and how he looked at me as if he didn't even know me. He'd spent all this time with me, shared my bed and my heat, and yet he looked at me as if I was a stranger.

"Lan—"

"No," he snapped, turning away from me and making for the door. "I've had enough for now. I don't even know who you are, Briar."

"You do!" I insisted, unable to stop myself.

I wanted to beg, to get on my knees and plead, but I didn't think that would help my case.

"I don't," he insisted. "I don't know you, Briar. How can I possibly believe you when a *strange woman* spirits herself in and out of Fleur and you can't even provide me with an explanation? That's not *normal.* It's dangerous. And I can't afford danger, Briar. Not as prince."

"I'm not dangerous," I swore. "I'm not!"

"Then *why was she here?*"

I debated telling him the truth, admitting that she had cursed me, but he already looked so suspicious. How could he believe she had settled me with such a powerful enchantment?

"She wants to cause trouble," I finally settled on.

"And she wants this why?" He asked, pressing.

"She's evil," I repeated.

"How do you know that?"

"I... I just know," I said lamely.

Landon sighed, dropping his head and propping his hands on his hips, "Briar, this isn't good enough. This isn't enough."

"I don't know what you want from me," I said, desperation making the words harsh.

"The truth."

"This is the truth!" I insisted.

There was a pause, where Landon lifted his head, eyeing me, assessing me. I squirmed under his gaze, nervous and hoping he'd believe me.

He saw right through me. I knew he did. It was almost immediate. The bond we shared was strong enough he could sense it. I was his mate, it wasn't difficult for him to see when I was lying. His eyes shimmered with disappointment and regret.

My stomach dropped and heart clenched when I realized tears were gathering in his eyes. He blinked hard, holding them back, but didn't break eye contact.

Not until the door slammed shut behind him.

The glow of the morning seemed so long ago.

Another lifetime.

In the empty rooms, I sat alone, tears marking a familiar path down my face.

Eris had finally broken me. Truly broke me down and took the single small bit of happiness and contentment I'd managed to carve out for myself. She'd shoved me into this unfamiliar world, leaving me alone and with no choice but to fend for myself, and now she was determined to make sure I never succeeded in anything.

I wasn't to have any happiness.

This new life I had, the one I'd just begun to hope could be beautiful, was a sham.

I'd never had a new life. *Never.* It was just another one of the witch's illusions.

CHAPTER TWENTY

Landon didn't return to see me for four days. In those days, he didn't leave me a note or send any kind of word through Anita. I was left in the complete dark, with Anita, Lily, Rose, and Candela fussing over me and shooting me sympathetic looks when they thought I couldn't see.

When he did come to me, it was in the middle of an afternoon, completely unannounced. I was sitting on the chaise lounge with a book in my lap, not reading any of the words before, when the door opened and Landon stepped into the room.

"Landon!" I exclaimed, coming to my feet. "Hello."

"Lady Briar," he greeted me.

The 'Lady' part stung, but I was still just happy to see him and would take what he was willing to give to me.

"Sit, please," I gestured to the couches, manners kicking in automatically.

These were his rooms too still, of course, so he didn't need the invite. Landon took it anyway, settling on a couch and draping one arm along the back of it.

I sat across from Landon, hands folded in my lap and fidgeting nervously. His gaze was stony and guarded like he didn't know who I was or how to handle me.

It hurt, I had to admit. I didn't like the way he was looking at me, and I didn't like what it meant.

Landon had lost all trust in me. He thought I was a liar.

In a way, there was no refuting that. I had lied about my past, who I was, and where I came from. But it had never been with the intent to hurt him.

Unfortunately, the consequences appeared to be the same regardless.

"Lan—"

"Silence," he snapped, glaring at me.

I did as he asked, mouth snapping shut.

"I will give you one chance to explain. *One.*" He ground out words forced through clenched teeth. "Then I will deal with you as I see fit. If I'm unsatisfied with your explanation, you'll be sequestered immediately until the danger is dealt with."

I nodded, not yet speaking.

"Begin," he bit.

"Okay," I whispered, shifting awkwardly in my seat. "I don't know where to start."

"Start."

"When you found me, that was the first time I'd awoken in five thousand years."

His eyes flashed with something, perhaps disbelief, but he didn't stop me from continuing.

"At first, I didn't know what happened. I woke up, and the castle had crumbled and aged around me. I had no idea how it was possible, but I tried to keep my silence. To go with the flow. I didn't know who you were, be you friend or foe, so I observed. I noticed the rivers had moved, trees had fallen, and all of Skyridge were ruins covered in moss and lichen. Everything I knew had changed. The only thing that remained were the mountains around me." I looked to the opposite wall, remembering vividly how confused and fearful I had been. "I thought at first you'd been part of what happened. But you disappeared so fast after leaving me at Fleur, I couldn't see how you'd benefit from confusing me so."

Landon's eyes narrowed, and his nostrils flared like he was holding back a protest.

"The first night I was here, a healer came to visit me," I revealed, the memory sour in my mouth. "She gave me a potion and then revealed her true nature. She was the witch, Eris."

"Eris," Landon repeated, frowning.

Nodding, I continued, "The witch came to me to gloat. To bask in the completion of her plan. Five thousand years ago, she had forced me to sleep. For generations, she had tried to convince my family to give her control of a sacred spring in the mountains. We had always denied her, not knowing why she wanted it. The waters were said to be healing and were a boon to the whole kingdom. It was not meant to be held by only one person. When I denied her request as the future Queen of Skyridge, she cursed me."

I shivered, remembering the magical words she'd spoken, the circle of red malicious magic in her hands. "I went to sleep that evening and woke up five thousand years later."

"How is that possible?" He asked, watching me closely.

Honestly, I admitted, "I don't know much about magic, but Eris is powerful. My family had always shown her respect because of her power, but it wasn't enough for her. She wanted more. And so she took it." My throat closed, and I had to force out the next words. "I woke up to everyone I knew dead. My kingdom gone. And my family line in ruins."

For the first time since I started speaking, a flash of sympathy stirred deep in Landon's eyes.

I held onto that flash, rushing to say, "I tried to find them in history books. I wanted to know what became of my siblings, of my parents, but the books don't speak of them. They're so far gone, even their names are lost to history. All that remains is a mention of a castle in the mountains. But Skyridge was so much more than that. Skyridge was my *home*. It was where my family lived and breathed. It was where I always knew I'd rule and build a family of my own. And now it's all gone."

"I didn't know how to tell you any of this. Surely, you'd think I was lying. After all, who can sleep for that long? How can one witch be so powerful? I had no answers for you then, and I don't have them now either. All I can tell you is what little I do know. And it is this: Eris is evil. She has already come to me twice now and has admitted to influencing the dragons. I don't know how even she could be powerful enough to do that, but she has claimed it all the same."

"Dragons have always been this way," Landon insisted, speaking finally with rough words. "They are evil."

"They are *not*," I insisted. "We lived with them peacefully for millennia. They protected us from foreign armies, smiting them when they tried to cross into our land, and kept the beasts in the heights at bay, hunting them and preventing them from descending down to Skyridge. We never worried about bears or wolves or giants. They're *sacred* and in exchange for all they did for us, we gave them tribute. Animals whose lives were at their end laid out as a meal for the dragons, a peace offering. Every year they took it without fail, and every year we lived in harmony. They didn't need to attack our lands because we shared with them. Worked with them so we may both thrive."

"Impossible."

"It *was*." I said, as true and as firm as I could. It was *vital* he understood this. "It was *beautiful*. They came to us in peace year after year. I am telling you, Landon, I saw it. I saw it not just once but *many* times. I stood beside my father and my family, watching as the dragons took their due and then left us in peace. It was a kind of magic, perhaps. But it *worked.*"

"Dragons are incapable of peace," Landon said, eyes haunted. "They are *beasts."*

"They are not!" I cried, standing. "Landon, please. You must understand. Something here is terribly wrong. Eris is scheming, and we're—"

"Enough," he declared, standing and glaring at me. "Enough, Briar."

I closed my mouth, looking up at Landon with pleading eyes.

There was no persuading the prince. His glare remained firmly in place as he issued his commands.

"You'll remain here, sequestered, until I can speak to my father," he declared. "He and I will discuss what to do with you. If I've somehow seated you with a child, you'll be sent to a country home to live out the pregnancy and birth. If not, you'll be sent to asylum."

"Asylum?"

He sneered, "Be glad it's an asylum and not prison for lying to your prince and bringing a disturbance upon the kingdom."

"A disturbance? I didn't ask to be brought here, Landon! That was *you."*

"Indeed," he agreed. "And what did you do with that opportunity? You squandered it. Used it for ill and misled me.

Misleading the crown is akin to betraying your country. We do not look upon such things kindly."

"This is insane," I said, sitting back. "I don't know how this happened."

"Your plans have failed, whatever they were," Landon told me, voice as cold as the northern seas. "Goodbye, Briar."

He turned from me, and I watched helplessly as he opened the door and left.

Never once looking back at me.

Chapter Twenty-One

My options were limited.

I could either wait here and be sent away, try to talk to Landon again and somehow change his mind, or I could escape.

Each option had its own strengths and weaknesses, and each one was final in its own way. Completing one plan precluded the ability to complete another.

So I decided to work on all three at once.

I'd wait here patiently, pretending for all who cared to look that I was an obedient mate who was submitting to her alpha's commands. Though, truthfully, no one was looking at me. Not even my girls came to tend to me. Landon had taken them from me too, likely concerned that I'd use them somehow. Either involve them in my 'plot' or otherwise expose them to danger.

Somehow, I knew I had to send a letter to Elias.

It was a long shot, but it was possible the fae would be willing to help me escape. He was crafty enough and well-traveled enough to know the ins and outs of wherever it was Landon planned to send me.

While I waited for his reply, I'd work on Landon.

There had to be a way to convince him of the truth. There *must.*

I wasn't willing to give up on him yet.

As much as his words hurt, he was *mine.* My mate, my Alpha, the one who my heart ached for and my omega yearned for.

It wasn't even a choice.

It simply *was.*

Landon was meant for me, and when I sat down and considered his reaction to my truth… I could hardly blame him. What happened to me was unprecedented and unbelievable. I hardly believed it when I awoke. It took Eris's evil glee when she revealed herself to me to really make it sink in.

Though my heart bled, and I wished he had trusted me enough to believe in me… I couldn't blame him. It truly was unbelievable and fantastical.

It didn't help that their history books were woefully lacking in their knowledge of the past too. I was his only window into what life was life before we turned against the dragons, and that reality, that *world,* was so far from the one he knew and ruled.

I started first with my letter to Elias, writing it out as plainly but discreetly as I could, inviting him to visit me soon, and hinting that I may not be in Fleur for long.

Then, I began to write down other things. Memories of my family, chats I'd had with my father, fights with my sisters, or battles of wits with my brothers. My mother's lessons.

I wrote sheets and sheets of memories. How we made offerings to dragons, and how we danced and celebrated them. Of my nighttime meeting with Eris, and her demands for the spring. Each story I labeled and placed together, wiling away the days with my work.

It was all I could think to do. Landon may think I'm being fanciful, making these things up as I go along, but every word I wrote was true. They were all a part of me, and I could only hope they would be enough for him.

There could be no questioning my dedication as the sheafs of paper multiplied. I hoped to prove that no one could make up this much. Could create so much mundane fiction. I wrote even of our feasts and what we ate. Etiquette lessons and diplomacy meetings.

Every last little detail of my old life logged until I had nearly six hundred sheets of paper.

It took me weeks, and I dedicated myself to it entirely.

Meals were sent to my rooms, and my sheets and clothes were checked thoroughly for blood.

None came, and once eight weeks had passed from my heat, a healer was sent to my rooms.

It was the same woman from my first night at Fleur.

The moment she stepped into my rooms I stood and backed away from her, eyes narrowed on her suspiciously.

"My lady," she said, bowing slightly at me. "Pardon my intrusion, Prince Landon has sent me to check on you."

"Did he?"

"Mmm." She approached me, unbothered by my clear distrust of her, and said, "May I?"

One of her gnarled hands was extended towards me, palm up, and I warily placed my own hand within hers. Quick as a whip, she gripped it hard, pulling me towards her, head bent to look at my palm.

"Hmmm, I see," she murmured. The healer pressed her thumb into my pulse, counting the beats. "You're cold and slow for a wolf."

"Am I?"

"Almost as if you're just woken," she said, mostly to herself.

The ghost of Eris's laughter rang in my ears, but the healer remained as she was, turning my hand this way and that before settling it down, and peering up into my face.

"Look at me," she commanded. "Let me see into your eyes."

Obeying, I looked down into her wizened gaze, and allowed her to make of me what she could.

"I see," she murmured, stepping in closer, inhaling deeply. "Yes, you have the scent on you. The spark."

Nodding to herself, she seemed quite satisfied, "For now, I am comfortable declaring you carrying. Though it is early yet, you appear healthy enough, despite your cold energy."

Stepping back, she continued, "You'll need a warming tea, to balance, and give you strength for the baby. I'll also send along some potions and herbs for nausea. You may need them in the coming weeks."

The woman didn't appear to need an answer from me, but I still replied with a polite, "Thank you."

Her eyes narrowed on me, and she said, "Congratulations, my lady. You carry our future with you."

The proclamation hung heavily in the air between us, and as I watched her, too stunned to be wary anymore, she walked out of the room and closed the door behind her, leaving me to ponder my future.

Landon did not come to see me, even after the healer returned to me, giving me potions and herbs and strict instructions on when and how to prepare and consume them.

Without my girls there, it was all left to me, and I carefully followed her instructions, drinking my first batch of nausea tea that night, laying in bed, and considering what came next.

I was not to be sent to asylum if Landon's words could still be trusted.

I'd be sent to a secluded home in the country, presumably to be watched and guarded until I gave birth.

Inside of me, my omega ran through the implications and arrived at a conclusion she did *not* like. That once I gave birth, Landon would take my child away, and I would be kept silent and away, helpless and separated from my new family.

I growled to the empty room, holding the cup close to my chest and my other hand curled protectively around my middle.

That was not going to happen.

I was going to escape. Elias or no, I would get to that country home, and then I would find a way out of it, no matter the cost.

Settling back, I curled into myself to sleep, mindset and heart determined.

This was the end of Landon's punishment. The end of his control over me.

I was going to do whatever it took.

Chapter Twenty-Two

Landon

The prince paced his room, listening to the healer's words.

As if she'd just woken from a deep sleep, she'd said.

"Hm," he grunted, eyes narrowed on the walls as he turned and made another lap around his room.

Nothing made sense since the dragons had attacked the castle. Not a word out of Briar's mouth, and not the circumstances around her pregnancy either.

Deep in his heart, his alpha wolf was howling with delight, insisting that he and Landon had done a good job, saddling Briar with their child.

We need to see her, he insisted. *Go to our mate.*

"No," Landon told him. "We don't need to see her."

We do. She carries our child.

Sighing, Landon glanced out the window, noting the late hour. The moonlight streamed in through the window, turning dust into fireflies drifting lazily in a slight breeze. It was late enough that Briar would likely be asleep.

Perhaps... perhaps she wouldn't even notice if he went to her rooms.

He didn't need to speak to her. Just to see her.

Make sure she was okay.

"Fuck," he muttered. "Hells and damnation."

The walk to her room was short, though it was still too long for the alpha who was railing inside of his mind, ecstatic at the thought of seeing her again. *Finally.*

It'd been *weeks*. Far too long to go without seeing his mate.

But who *was* his mate?

That question kept him from her.

She was too much of a mystery. Too much of a risk.

Of course, his alpha didn't care about that. He knew who she was in all the ways he cared about. He wasn't political or scheming, and he couldn't imagine a world where anyone else was either. Wolves don't scheme or plot. They said as they meant, and that was it, according to him.

Or at least, they should. And he had no patience for anyone who did otherwise.

It was maddening.

The anger was easily forgotten though, the second he turned down the hallway where Briar resided. The whole space smelled of her, and immediately he was thrown back to when he first found her. The first moment he had smelled her.

When he had kissed her.

Her scent was the same now as it was back then, but deeper, clearly ripened with the onset of her pregnancy. It flooded his mind with sweetness and drew him in without even trying. The prince followed his nose right to her door, and then inside, opening and closing the door as quietly as he could.

Just as he'd suspected, his mate was inside, asleep in their bed, curled in on her side and under the covers.

The vision of her there, the first time he had seen her in weeks, quiet and beautiful, struck him dead square in his heart.

It was so much like when he'd first found her, and yet everything was so different now than it had been then.

Unable to help himself, he reached out a hand to stroke her cheek.

On instinct, she turned into his touch, sighing in her sleep.

She's still our mate, his wolf told him.

Landon sighed, unable to refute the fact. She was still their mate, even if she was a liar. Even if she was a danger to his kingdom.

This fact proved to be complicated to acknowledge, so Landon shoved it aside and enjoyed the feel of her skin under his fingertips. The softness of her cheek. The curve of her shoulder. All of it perfect and temping, now even more than the first time he'd laid eyes on her.

When he first saw her lying there, he'd wanted to flee; he'd been so overwhelmed with feeling. Now, he wanted to run towards those feelings, to fall into the fires of passion with her, and to build a life that would make them both happy.

Withdrawing his hand, he had to admit that for now, he couldn't do that.

For now, he needed to watch her, to arrange to have her sent away, and for healers and spies to closely guard her with a retinue of his most trusted soldiers.

He wasn't sure what he'd do with her once their child was born, and he wasn't sure what to make of her fanciful stories.

Were they fact, then the witch Eris was a new enemy for them to deal with. If Briar spoke true, she would be the most powerful witch in the world. There was no other fae or witch or fairy with the power to do what Eris had supposedly done to Briar.

But if they were true, then his mate was not a liar or a loon.

Then she was a poor woman who had been the victim of a curse, and he had punished her for it.

Landon slipped quietly out of the room, leaving a sleeping Briar behind.

Such thoughts were not suited for the middle of the night. They would serve only to keep him awake and feed self-doubt, neither of which were good things for the prince to bear.

Though try as he might, he couldn't turn his head away from thoughts of Briar.

And so Landon had another sleepless night.

CHAPTER TWENTY-THREE

Landon

Without warning a sudden, shuddering quake rocked the castle, a huge *boom* coming from across the building. It vibrated through the walls and echoed in the great ballroom, causing all of its inhabitants to freeze.

Prince Landon, who had been hearing petitions with his father, rose to his feet and immediately began to run towards the sound.

"Landon," his father called. "Rouse the men!"

Landon waved his hand, a plan already front and foremost in his mind.

His father might be king, but Landon had spent his whole life training to fight and then fighting dragons. He knew the sound of dragon fire when it roared over his head and the sick *zing* as claws swiped for his middle, aiming to disembowel him.

He knew what he needed to do.

He left the throne room and took a left, heading towards the outer walls, shouting at guards as he went.

"You! Sound the alarm. Rouse the men." He commanded.

Guards scrambled at his words, and Landon took the stairs two at a time, descending into the depths of the castle as another *boom* echoed. His heart sank as he heard a loud clatter and heavy thuds like stones were collapsing in on themselves.

"Hells," he cursed, running faster for the armory.

His second hand, Harold, was already there, door flung open, passing out swords and spears to men as they ran past. Landon ran past him and made his way inside to where his half-form armor was stored, and began to yank it on.

Around him, the other wolves he'd trained with were doing the same. All elite soldiers, and all beginning to shift, holding themselves between forms and sliding on their armor.

Hopefully, the battle would be short. None of them could hold this form forever. When he went abroad to hunt, he did so as a normal man, human-sized, because it could take days or weeks to hunt down a beast.

Now, with this battle, they had max four hours before they would inevitably give in to the shift and become full wolves.

It would have to be enough.

With well-practiced moves, they were dressed in minutes and then running again, making their way back up the stairs and to the west side of the castle, following Landon. Their prince led them to the outer walls, their swords already in their hands, and then, as one, they fell into action.

The walls had been breached. Crumbling pink stone littered the ground around them, the huge chunks of granite heartbreaking in their broken beauty. The stones belonged together, shielding the inhabitants of Fleur and standing tall as a symbol of the strength of Fenestral.

Instead, they were laid low by the biggest dragon they had ever seen.

The shimmering white beast had pale blue eyes and wings that were so thin the sun practically shone through them. He left no shadow as he swooped and laid down a line of fire, charring pink stone, trying to engulf soldiers in his fire.

Men shouted and lifted their shields, trying to hold back the assault.

"Line!" Landon called, and his soldiers fell in beside him, shields lifted. "Spears!"

As one, the elite phalanx tore spears from their back, and with the enhanced strength given by their half forms, hurled them at the dragon as it swapped past again, circling to blaze another path of fire.

Landon ignored the cries of pain and shouts of surprise around him and focused only on the heft of his spear and the sharpened point where it glistened in the sunlight. With a mighty heave, he tossed it, praying to the gods it would find its home.

The gods did not answer his prayer.

The dragon tucked his wings to his sides, falling suddenly, losing altitude, and bringing him free of the spears. He threw his wings open again and then opened his mouth, aiming directly for Landon.

Landon tucked and rolled away, his phalanx doing the same, all of them scattering to miss the wide swath of fire trying to incinerate them. It was hot on his back, and Lan knew he'd just barely missed the attack.

Coming to his feet again, he whirled, eyes searching the sky for the great pale beast.

It was hard to see it with the sun at its full brightness, but eventually, he caught sight of it and realized it was circling, preparing to attack the other side of Fleur.

"Fuck!" He shouted. "Move! It's gone east!"

With horror, he realized *east* meant the family wings. It meant Briar's rooms.

"Fuck, fuck, *fuck*," he chanted as he ran, feet pounding in time with his curses.

Halfway there, his lungs aching with his effort, the castle shook, knocking him off of his feet.

Shit.

He scrambled upright again, and then kept running, making his way as quickly as he could for his mate's rooms. He hadn't seen her in days, but she was all he could think of now. Visions of her flooded his mind, Briar under him sighing, how she laughed with her girls, how she danced with grace.

All of it a vision of the girl who'd captivated him from the first moment he laid eyes on her.

Hell, even before then. From the first second, he'd caught her scent, she had him in her grasp.

And he'd *foolishly* held her at arm's length, refusing to trust her, refusing to let her in.

Now he regretted all of that as he ran towards her and imagined he'd already seen her for the last time. Imagined he'd lost her. Lost their child.

His heart beat fiercely in his chest, and his throat went bone dry as he took the stars two at a time, the heavy steps of his fellows around him a small comfort compared to the dread that weighed on his bones.

"Find the dragon, go to the top!" He commanded. "I'll meet you there later."

"Aye!" They called, peeling away from Lan, heading up another flight of stairs as he turned down the hallway and made for Briar's rooms.

"Briar!" He called panic leaching into the name. *"Briar!"*

He called out in hopes she was already running out of her rooms and making her way to safety.

He got no reply, and as he barreled into her suite, he saw immediately why.

The wall on this side had been breached, just as the other side had. Huge heavy granite blocks had been pushed inwards, collapsing in part of the outer wall of her bedroom, crushing part of her bed and covering the space with debris.

"Briar!" He called again, searching the rubble for her, panicking in earnest now. "Briar, my rose, where are you?"

A weak, sad cough came from the corner, and Landon practically flew towards it, his sword and shield clattering to the ground as he threw them down and began to claw his way through the stone.

"Briar?" He asked. "Say something, let me hear you."

"I'm down here," she said weakly, so weak it was barely audible even with his wolf ears. "I think I'm okay."

"Don't try to move," he commanded. "I'll get you out of there, just hang on."

"Okay," she agreed, coughing again.

With single-minded panic, he clawed through stone and the remains of her bed, tossing them all to the side or over his shoulder, until he got through the small pile, and found his mate underneath it.

"Briar," he breathed, pulling her gently up and into his arms, holding her tight.

"I'm okay..." she gasped, clinging to him. "I think."

Concerned, he lifted her up and into his arms, and carried her away from the outer walls, and then descended back into the depths of his castle.

He was the commander of their army, the leader of Fleur's forces, and he abandoned that duty to tend to his mate. The castle shook around them as more dragon fire assaulted the castle, and Landon ignored it. Stones crumbled, and small pieces fell from the ceiling, but his mind remained fixed on the woman in his arms. Nothing would tear him away from making sure she was safe and whole.

Together they descended further and further until they were once again in his office, and he yanked on the hidden lever that disguised the stairwell into the safe room. He closed it behind them, and, using his wolf eyes, descended into the darkness, easily able to see the stairs in the darkness.

Briar clung to him, the darkness impenetrable to her in her current form, and Landon responded, arms closing even tighter around her.

At the bottom, he laid her down carefully on a sofa and then made quick work of striking flint to the torches, lighting the space in a dim, flickering amber glow.

"Landon," Briar called softly. "Are you okay?"

"I will be," he snarled, "once I know you are okay."

Obediently, she settled back into the couch, sensing he was not to be bartered with.

With quick, efficient motions, he patted her down, cataloging every bruise and scrape, checking her for broken bones or gashes.

He looked into her eyes deeply, assessing their clarity, and checked over his hands to see if he'd found any blood on her.

When he'd checked her head to toe, he took her head gently into his hands and pressed their foreheads together, breathing a sigh of relief.

"I'm okay, right?" She asked quietly.

"You are."

"Does... does this mean you're talking to me again?"

Pressing a kiss to her forehead, he told her, "Yes, my rose. I'm done running."

CHAPTER TWENTY-FOUR

Briar

Landon waited on me hand and foot. We weren't the same as we had been before Eris's first visit, but it was nice to have him there and close. I was sure that it was a side effect of the dragon attack, but I would take what I could get.

Even if I could tell his heart was still conflicted.

Even if he hadn't kissed me once since the attack.

Even if it did nothing to alleviate the suspicion I harbored deep inside, it was nice.

The problem was, Landon hadn't believed me when I tried to open up to him. To tell him about myself. The issue was that while, intellectually, I could hardly blame him, my heart held grudges right alongside my pride.

And I could *tell* he *still* didn't believe me.

It was in the way he refused to talk to me about the dragons. It was how he side stepped my questions about how castle repairs were going.

Could I forgive him for his disbelief? Could I accept him back into my life, into my bed? As my mate?

All those questions swirled around my mind, but whenever he touched my hand to help me down stairs, or brought me a goblet of juice, suddenly, I knew the answer.

Yes. Yes, I could.

I could do all of those things and live a happy life with Landon... as long as he believed in me *now*. I needed to talk with him one more time, tell him *everything,* show him all the stories I'd written, and see how he reacted.

Then I could commit to him fully. Body, mind, and heart.

One more chance.

I decided, four days after the attack, when the castle had settled into repairing the damage from the dragons and Landon showed no signs of stopping his overprotective behavior, it was time.

After lunch, which Landon had once again fed to me by hand, I asked him, "Landon, may we talk?"

"Of course," he said, serious eyes finding mine. "What about?"

"Hang on." I turned and pulled out the sheafs of paper I was hiding behind my pillow. I'd put them there that morning, hoping I'd get this chance.

"What is this?" He asked, taking them from me and examining them.

"They're my memories," I explained. "After... well... our discussion, which did not end so well, I spent some time writing."

His eyes widened just slightly, but that was all the reaction he gave me.

"I wrote down everything I could remember about my life, about the world as I knew it. It took me a long time to do, but I hope... Well, I hope you'll read it."

"Your life," he mused, opening the first page, eyes scanning my words.

"Yes," I said nervously. "It's not perfect, obviously. I don't have a perfect memory after all, but it's a lot. Everything I could remember of my mother, my family, Skyridge, all of it."

"Skyridge?"

"The ruins you found me in," I explained. "They were a castle, once. A great fortress in the mountains, guardians of the pass, friend of the dragons. Skyridge."

His eyes cut to mine, narrowing slightly, "I see."

"Not that we were some great world power," I hastened to say. "But we were known, and we were proud of what we were known for. My father, the king, worked hard to make sure he was fair and just, passing along those same values to me."

"You," he repeated. "Princess Briar."

"Princess Briar Rhoswen," I said proudly, squaring my shoulders. "Heir to the throne of Skyridge."

"Very regal," he noted, turning his eyes back to my writing. "Would you allow me time to read this before we… discuss this matter further?"

I could *feel* how careful he was trying to be, trying to give me a chance, and I latched onto that care like a woman who'd never known it before.

"Of course," I rushed. "There's no need to, well, rush things. I'm not going anywhere."

He didn't respond, and in the absence of words, I laughed awkwardly and rambled onward, unable to stop myself.

"I mean, not that I want to go anywhere," I assured him. "Just that, I feel like you'd notice if I tried, and I'm not exactly prepared or skilled enough to make an attempt anyway. I was raised a princess, not an outdoors person or a soldier or something. You found me in a tower, still in my nightclothes, for goodness' sake."

"I did," he confirmed, amused.

I did not stop rambling.

"Not the most practical clothes for adventuring, and since I got here, it's not like Anita has been supplying me with leather breeches and linen shirts. It's all silk and lace and pretty things. Hardly suited for horseback riding or venturing through the countryside."

"Indeed."

"So, really, even if it took you an age to read it all, I'll probably still be here, lounging away and reading more history books. I can't seem to stop myself from devouring as many of them as I could find. I missed so much while I was asleep. Whole *wars* and kingdoms falling and such. I was horrified to read of the vampire-wolf war. Or of the plague among the fae. Oh, and that one king, the nasty one. What was his name…"

"There's been plenty of those in a millennium, Briar," he pointed out.

"That's fair," I sighed. "I was actually quite surprised by how many. It seems most in power these days are quite alright, though. I've been trying to read about them, but the pickings in the main library were scarce on the subject of current events."

"I can have my secretary fill you in," Landon offered. "Princess lessons, for the princess."

Smiling, I said, "That would be *wonderful.*"

Lifting my papers, he asked, "Are these all of your papers?"

I nodded, suddenly shy again, "Yes, they are. Try not to judge them too harshly, please. I'm no author."

"I shan't," he promised.

Then, he removed any further chance of my rambling and stood, making his way towards a chair by the window, and settled in.

Blinking, I watched him.

I hadn't expected him to start *now,* and I'd hardly expected him to read them right where I could watch all of his reactions, but there he was, right there, reading my writing.

I forced my eyes away from him, and took in Landon's rooms, not for the first time.

With the old suite a pile of rubble, and with the fact that I was still, technically, Landon's mate and the bearer of his child, me and all of my things were moved into a new set of rooms.

There was a the bedroom, where I had been confined since the attack to rest, with a small seating area at the end of the bed, a pair of massive wardrobes to one side containing spare bedding, a vanity, and lush rugs all over the floor. Everything was colored either in a soft cream or a rich navy blue, all of which complimented very well the pink stone walls.

On either side of the headboard were two doorways. One led to the closet space, where my dresses now lived, and the other led to a washroom even bigger than the old one I'd had.

Outside, through a door on the opposite wall, there was a sitting room with huge blue velvet couches, plush ottomans, and a small private dining area nestled before huge windows and a door that let out onto a private balcony.

Attached to that room was another, smaller office, should Landon have use of it, and a drawing room, where he could host a smaller, private group of people instead of using the main seating area and lounge.

It reminded me of the suite my parents had occupied at Skyridge, both in size and functionality. It gave Landon everything he needed at the tips of his fingers, should be need it.

Thinking about it made me homesick... but also comforted me, somehow.

Like no matter how far removed I was from my own time and my own family, royalty was still royalty, and the things people needed never changed. Life was life, no matter the time it lived in.

After pursuing the space, my eyes drifted back to Landon again, scanning his whole body for reactions or clues to his thoughts. His eyes were cast down, hiding the blue from me, but it was clear he was a quick reader, eyes scanning the pages efficiently and then flipping them with care, missing nothing.

His blonde hair was pulled back neatly at the nape of his neck, tied with a black satin ribbon that contrasted beautifully with the strands. He was dressed in all black as well, with black knee high boots, leather breeches, and a black linen shirt which he hadn't tied shut at the neck.

It dipped down into a deep vee, showing me a brush of chest hair, and the softness of his skin.

Then, he laughed, chuffing at something I'd written, and I was distracted by that, too.

His laugh was nice, and it was that laugh, the soft timbre of it, the deep richness of its ring, that had me hoping beyond hope that this time... this time he would believe me.

Because the truth was that Landon had wormed his way into my heart. He felt like a part of me, like someone I'd been waiting for my entire life without me knowing.

I'd always thought one day I'd marry for politics, to form an alliance or strengthen our position somehow. I'd never considered anything else.

But now that I was here with Landon, it seemed like a foregone conclusion.

Of course, I belonged here with him. Of course, he was my mate.

It was all meant to be.

Feeling too much, and tense with waiting for his next laugh or sigh or confused look, I took my current book from my nightstand and began to do my own reading. This was an exercise in patience, so I did as my mother taught me, and I waited out my time with as much grace and dignity as I could.

I barely read a word.

Everything was a blur before my eyes, and none of them made sense or had any meaning.

Names I *knew* I'd read about before became unfamiliar, and locations and cities were just abstract concepts without any real geographical meaning or significance.

So I gave up and set the book to the side with a huff.

"Boring book?" he asked me, eyes still on my writing.

"I can't concentrate."

His eyes lifted to me as he frowned, "Are you unwell?"

"I want to know what you're thinking," I admitted. "I'm nervous."

"Why?"

"Why?"

"Mm."

"Isn't it obvious?'"

Landon shrugged, "I'd rather not assume."

"Assume," I encouraged. "Tell me why you think I'm nervous."

"Are you sure?"

I nodded.

"Very well."

He marked his place carefully, sliding a free sheaf of paper between the pages to save his space, and then looked me over. The bright blue of his eyes was really a physical thing, brushing over me and taking in everything, leaving nothing unnoted.

Then, he spoke.

"I think, Briar, that there is a part of you that's lost and looking for someone or someplace to belong with. Whatever is on these pages won't fix that. I think everything you've done, all of the stories you've told, tell me that. I can see it in your eyes how much you want to belong. And I don't want to give you false hope." He ran a hand through his hair. "I'd like for you to belong here, Briar. But I can't do what *I* want. My life has never been about that. I need to do what's best for my people and for Fleur. I've told you this before, and that has not changed. It never will."

I sat frozen, listening, holding on desperately to my composure. I wanted Landon to talk, and I didn't want him to think I was putting on a show for him, crying for sympathy or begging for him to believe me.

He sighed deeply, "If I was being honest, though, I want this all to be true. My wolf is telling me it is, and my heart is telling me the same, but my mind... my mind is too logical to accept it. And I think you're nervous because it'd be easy for you to belong here with me. We're *both* feeling that pull towards one another."

"Yes," I whispered.

He was right. However convenient it was for me to be here, however safe and comfortable it would be, it was more than that. I *belonged* here. With Landon.

And I was terrified he wouldn't have me.

CHAPTER TWENTY-FIVE

The aftermath of the second attack was *wildly* different from the first.

When the dragon came down from the mountains the first time, it was seen as a fluke. Something that would never happen again. Landon and the entire kingdom were convinced that dragons were just beasts, following their instincts and attacking at random.

But *two* attacks? So far from where they lived?

No one could ignore that.

I might be the only person in all of Fenestral who knew dragons were more than they gave them credit for. That they were kind, intelligent, and protective. But now the whole kingdom knew, at the very least, that there was something wrong with the dragons.

These weren't the actions of a mindless beast. This was something more sinister. Why else would they stray so far from their home? They *never* left the range. And now they had, and so they were deemed a constant and emerging threat.

And while they all wondered what had changed, why the dragons were behaving so, Landon continued to read.

He diligently sat down with my book daily in our rooms, taking in as much as he could. Then, when he was done, he'd set the papers aside and climb into bed with me, holding me close. His palm would come and press into my stomach, caressing the spot where our child grew.

But he did not call me *his* rose.

And he did not kiss me.

Those two things hurt me more than I thought they would.

It wasn't like I hadn't been living without them for a while now, but the fact that he continued to withhold them made me think what I wrote wasn't working. None of it was working.

I was still an ill woman to him. Or a liar. Not someone to take seriously in the least. Or to be treated with any kind of closeness. I was a stranger who he happened to share space with. Who he was kind to.

But that was it.

Nothing more.

It hurt even more than I could have imagined.

Telling myself to be patient, I took what he gave me. As he went through pages and the kingdom tried to understand the danger it faced, I waited, savoring the small touches he gave me.

With each day, the fact that I was pregnant became more apparent as well, and that knowledge was the only thing strong enough to distract me from the pins and needles I was on. I woke in the mornings with my stomach churning and my head foggy.

Thankfully, breakfast cleared up most of those symptoms, and by noon, I was functioning mostly at full steam. Anita and the girls fussed over me, bringing me tea from the healers and plates of fruits and vegetables to keep my energy up.

"You're taking care of our little princeling in there," she said, boisterous and overjoyed with the news still. "We need to make sure your energy is up!"

Lily and Rose were at my feet, giving me an unneeded but still very nice foot and calf massage.

"You need to rest," Lily said gently.

"No more pacing with worry," Rose said, less gently.

Candela was flitting back and forth, arms full of soft textiles for my approval, meant to outfit me with some maternity wear, "And you need to decide what colors to wear. Pink would be very fetching on you. Really send the message you're a lady of the castle!"

"Imagine, Briar the Pink Lady of Fleur," Anita said grandly. "The title would suit you."

I smiled between them all, grateful as ever for their companionship and care. Without them, I'd be lost and alone, floundering.

"Thank you, Anita," I said. "I hope to make you all proud."

Landon returned that evening, found me lounging, and nodded in my direction.

"Landon," I greeted him. "Welcome back."

He came to me, pressed a kiss to my forehead, and said, "Hello, Briar."

The greeting was distant, but I would take what I could get, "How was today? Is all well within the realm?"

"No one's seen a dragon since the last attack," he said, absent-mindedly milling about the space, collecting my writings, and finding his way to his chair. "We're at a standstill until we get more information."

I *burned* to say that the information was *right there in his hands!* That this was all Eris, *it was!* But I bit back the words I knew he wouldn't hear and smiled instead. "I'm sure you'll figure things out soon."

He grunted, non-committal, and turned to my writing, picking up where he'd left off the previous night.

We sat there. Silently.

Landon seemed entirely unbothered by the silence, but it made me antsy.

It stretched long and lean between us, with Landon's eyes set on the words I'd written and me sitting on my chair, foot bobbing up and down with my nerves.

"So," I said, "which part are you reading now?"

His eyes flicked to me briefly, "I believe you're 18 here, readying for your debut."

"Ah."

He didn't expand, didn't share his thoughts.

Carefully, I ventured out again, "I remember that day. I was very excited. And very nervous."

"Mmm." He grunted, turning a page and crossing his legs. He balanced all my words on his knee and carefully turned the page.

"My mother gave me so many lessons and warnings beforehand." I imitated her voice, *"Back straight! Keep your eyes up, Briar. People are watching!"*

"Ah," he said again, not even meeting my eyes.

I deflated. I thought perhaps today might be the day we finally spoke, *really* spoke, but I was wrong. Again.

How long could I keep this hope? How long could I wait for him to open up to me again?

Every day where he was emotionally distant from me was painful. As if there was some connection between Landon and I, and him pulling away was affecting it. It was a sharp pain in the back of my mind, and it hurt more when he was closer to me.

So close, just out of touch, but not even in the same realm as me emotionally.

Embarrassingly, I felt my nose begin to itch as tears sprung to my eyes, making Landon a vision in watercolor. The bright gold of his hair a splash next to the navy blue of the seats and the ever-present pale pink of the stone around us.

He must have smelt the salt because he looked up and asked me, "Briar?"

I shook my head, plastering on a smile, "I'm fine, Landon."

I heard him shuffle the papers, setting them aside, as he yanked a handkerchief from his pocket and handed it to me.

"Thank you," I sniffed, dabbing at my eyes. "I'm sorry, I don't mean to cry."

"Why are you crying?" He asked, voice completely flat and devoid of emotion.

God. It *hurt*.

"Does it not hurt you, too?" I asked, looking at him desperately.

He looked sad but distant, "Of course it does."

"Then… why?" I asked or really begged. "Why can't we be how we were?"

"Because, Briar, I don't *know* you."

"You didn't know me before!" I insisted. "You had no idea who I was when you came to me for my heat!"

"I didn't," he agreed. "But at the time, you and your past were a blank slate. Not to be trusted, but not distrusted either. Now? You've admitted yourself to lying to me. Making up stories. I have all the reason in the world to distrust you."

And that distrust shone clearly in his eyes now. If I'd thought the distant looks had hurt, they were nothing compared to what I saw now before me.

"Has what you've read made no difference?" I finally asked the question that burned at the back of my mind. "Have all my efforts been in vain?"

Shaking his head, Landon admitted, "I don't know, Briar. I can't tell you yet, because I'm not done. But it's possible. You should prepare yourself for that reality."

"Please, it *can't* be this way," I insisted. "I couldn't handle it."

"You think this is *easy* for me?" He asked, brows heavy over his forehead. "I found you in that tower and *knew* to the depths of my soul that you were meant for me. You were *made* to be mine. And when I saw you and I kissed you, you woke up and *looked* at me with those *eyes.*" He sighed. "This is *far* from easy for me, Briar. How am I supposed to know if my *mate* is a lie? How can I let my heart and my wolf tell me you are when my *entire* kingdom is on the line!"

"You could *trust* me," I cried. "Give me some room to prove to you I am who I say."

"I can't do that, Briar," he said, shaking his head.

"You don't understand," I despaired. "You've read enough to know I was a *princess*. You *know* that. I'm not some naive little lady who doesn't understand the courts and how they work. I trained my entire life to one day rule a nation. *Same as you.* And I had the *best* teacher. *The best.* My mother was a woman who knew exactly what to say and when, how to handle even the worst of situations. Your history books may have forgotten her, *but I haven't!* Every day I'm here, I'm working hard to make her proud, to remember her teachings and keep them alive how I know she'd want me to. By *using them.*"

I was breathing hard, and my head swam with anger and upset, but did it even matter?

"I could be an asset to you, someone to stand at your side, strong and proud and knowledgeable! But instead, I remain here, enduring people's pitying looks and waiting desperately for you to *see me!*"

None of this seemed to. *None of it.* It was all bullshit. I'd always imagined the future to be this place where peace swept across the land and everyone learned how to get along. Where innovation and humanitarianism became our priorities.

And now, here I was in the future, and it was none of those things. People's priorities hadn't changed. Not one bit. They were still as stubborn, selfish, and short-sighted as they'd always been.

Even Landon. My prince. *My mate.*

He wasn't any better than them.

For days now, he'd been reading the very contents of my soul, and it'd had no effect on him. Perhaps what was really what despaired me. More than anything. It was laying myself out to be judged and being found wanting. Not even worthy of a reaction.

It was this that made my voice grow louder, borderline hysterical, "I just don't understand *why* it has to be this way! Why can't you people *listen* to me!? It's *painful.* Especially you."

Landon's head jerked, just a small fraction, but he didn't refute what I said.

"You're here, but you're *not.*" I told him. "And what's the point in that? You'll hold me and sleep in my bed, but we hardly speak. Even when what I have to say is *vital,* you won't listen to me. How is that right? I'm supposed to be your *mate.* But this doesn't feel like mating. It doesn't feel like love or even affection. It feels like you're humoring me until you have your heir, and then you can send me away to that country home, never to be seen or heard from again."

"You think I'm using you?" He asked softly.

"What else am I to think?" I threw my hands up. "What do I have to gain, Landon? How do my stories, the stories of *my life,* benefit me to tell? *Unless they're true?* Surely if they were lies, I would have abandoned them by now! Given up on the tales and done whatever you asked me. Made you sure I was sane and rational. But that's not what I want! I want to be known for who I am, regardless of how you think of me. Regardless of how it makes you feel!"

"Briar," he said gently. "Let me speak."

"Why?" I cried, pacing the floor in front of him. "So you can tell me to calm down? Insist I sit down and think of the baby?" I laughed bitterly. "I've had enough sitting and minding and thinking for a lifetime! I want to be *heard!*"

"Briar, I do believe you," he said, sliding the words in as I took a breath and prepared to pace another lap.

I froze and looked at him suspiciously, "What?"

"I haven't said anything because I wanted to finish all of it before I did," Landon explained, gesturing to the tome to his side. "I finished it today."

"And?"

"And it was lengthy. And detailed." He looked at me. "Too detailed to be made up. Too consistent. And the size..." His head shook. "It would take a novelist months and months to think of all of it and then jot it down. You wrote this all on your own with such speed. They must be memories."

Standing, he came to me, taking both of my hands into his, bending down to look my dead in the eyes. "I believe you, Briar. Your words have convinced me."

I felt my lips part as I gasped, unable to truly believe his words. Not at first.

Was that what it took? Laying my heart out on parchment for him to pour over and judge?

I didn't know how to feel about that idea, so I set it aside for now and focused on the positive.

He believed me.

For the first time in weeks, my inner wolf roused from her depressed slumber, interested in what this might mean. She had been just as dejected as I when Landon had first tossed us aside. Her Alpha abandoned her as much as my mate had abandoned me. And she was just as suspicious as I was.

"Prove it," I demanded.

He frowned, "How?"

"Tell me something. Anything."

"Something about..."

"About me," I clarified. "From my writing. Tell me what you thought."

"Hmm..." he mused. "The passages about your lessons. Etiquette with your mother. Diplomacy with your father. The things you learned felt so familiar, similar to the lessons I also took as a young man. No one could make up the sheer monotony of them. The nuance of the subject matter. Truly, somehow, it always comes back to horses and cows. And I thought... perhaps... that saying, that joke among nobles, must have survived all this time. Passing from your parents' generation all the way to mine."

He squeezed my hands, "It wasn't the parts about the dragons or your offerings to them. It was the small things. Those lessons. Your siblings. The staff. All of them painted a life that I found myself picturing easily. Believing in."

I looked down at my feet, absorbing his words, and weighing them.

Part of me was elated. More than just a small part. I had to reign in the parts of me that wanted to throw myself at him and cling to him because the other parts of me were still nursing their hurt. Their suspicion.

"Landon," I whispered, "I don't know..."

"I know," he said, stepping closer, pressing his forehead to mine. "I have work to do. I understand, my rose."

My heart squeezed, and the elation I felt began to win.

"I'm sorry," he continues. "I couldn't understand what you were trying to tell me. Couldn't comprehend that kind of magic—"

Red smoke that I recognized began to fill the room, rolling past our ankles and shins, lazy billows that I *knew* meant Eris was near.

"Eris," I gasped, pressing closer to Landon. "Landon, she's here!"

Feminine laughter filled the room, and then she was standing there, clapping slowly.

"Awww, look at this *touching* scene," Eris drawled.

I glared at her, and Landon wrapped me close, glaring at the witch, "Eris."

"Leave us be," I told her. "Please. You've done enough already."

"Have I?" She asked, tapping her chin. "I'm afraid I have to disagree, dear Briar. I mean, really. Who are you to decide anyway? If anyone can declare me done, it's *me*. Not you."

"You're not welcome here," Landon declared, glaring at her. "Leave. Now."

She laughed again, and the red smoke that heralded her arrival became so thick it was hard to breathe. I coughed, bending over as Landon tried to hold me close.

"I won't be listening to either of you," Eris informed us. "I find it to be quite insulting that you even considered ordering me around."

Her head shook, her dark hair brushing over her shoulders, and her ever-present cape of stars began to fly in a violent, invisible wind. The red smoke around us rose, fogging our vision, and Eris's voice, normally silky and deadly, boomed with her power.

"There's nothing I hate more than mice who try to move beyond their means," she sneered. "For years, I told your family *exactly* what I wanted, and they thought themselves prudent to deny me. And now here you are again. The same *fucking* girl, thousands of years later. Instead of being a good little pup and being miserable, you just had to go and try to be *happy*." Her eyes rolled, like somehow the idea of being happy to her was lowly and unfathomable. "Ridiculous. So now, instead of tending to my dragons or ordering around my castle servants, I have to come and make sure my revenge is complete. I have to make sure *you* are *miserable*."

The witch raised a finger and pointed directly at me.

"Why?" I asked, hand to my heart, squinting through the smoke to try and sight the witch. "Why does my happiness matter to you?"

"You cannot possibly imagine," she declared, "the timeline I live by. I don't take revenge on insignificant little people. I take it from their families. Their towns. Their lineage. I wipe out everything they know and love. Everything they *could* love. It is the only way to make a lasting mark. And *your* family, you stupid bitch, deserves all of the revenge I can give to them. For denying me the power that was *always* destined to be mine."

Landon pushed me behind him, putting himself between me and Eris. "Back, *witch*." He spat. "Leave us, now. Or I will slay you where you stand."

Smirking, Eris stepped closer, and I felt a malicious, cold hand grip my ankle, and I knew it was a curse. I knew Eris was planning to make good on her threats, and that began now.

She wasn't satisfied with the havoc she had already wrought on my life. She was determined to *break* me. To make me bow to her, to crawl on hands and knees for forgiveness just so she could deny me.

Sickly fingers crawled up my calf, like rotten, fettered bugs that made flesh freeze. They wormed their way inside of me as I gritted my teeth against the horrific sensation. I tried to move my leg, but it was stuck in place, and the mere act of attempting to move shot pain up my leg and then forced my back to curl and cramp. My bones cracked, and I *screamed.*

The curse continued to move as Landon glanced between me and Eris and made a quick decision. In the blink of an eye, he went from being the tall, handsome prince I'd first laid eyes on after waking to a half man half wolf, with an elongated face, fur that shined in the red light of her magic, and claws that were wicked sharp. He aimed right at Eris, lunging with a ferocious howl.

Eris laughed. "Oh, has the puppy come to play?"

Her eyes rolled, and she twirled one of her fingers, sending small spheres of bright red magic flying right at Landon.

I would have screamed if I wasn't already screaming. It was all I could do with the curse making its way up my body, forcing my muscles to contract painfully, cramping and pulling me into myself. I arched and then curled, over and over, my arms coming against my chest as if I could hold myself together.

But there was no fighting it. Every cell of my body was being taken over by the curse, and no amount of my screaming, begging, or willing it away would slow its advance.

Though, when Landon turned, launching himself off a wall and directly at Eris, the curse did stutter.

It was *working.* If you distracted the witch, you slowed her work.

He hit her dead on, colliding with a smack that would have made my chest hurt if it wasn't already aching. The collision gave me just enough freedom to take a step, calling out, "Landon!"

"Stay there," he growled, landing on top of Eris with a heavy thud, both of them tossed to the ground.

But the witch didn't stay down for long. She rose up, bringing them both off the floor and then pushed, flinging Landon with such strength that he cracked completely through one of the pink stone walls and out into the larger room beyond.

With the additional space, Landon managed to turn and land on all fours, nails piercing the expensive carpet and scraping against stone as he slid to a stop. His head lifted, and his eyes locked onto Eris, immediately beginning to calculate his next move.

Eris yawned, feigning boredom, "I thought you'd be better than this, *dragon slayer.*"

Growling, Landon flew at her again, and Eris did little more than lift a hand, a magical circle forming in front of her. Landon hit the circle as if it was another stone wall, falling on his knees to the floor.

He recovered quickly, and leapt to her side, and then at her again. It was so quick I could hardly track his movements, and Eris was caught by surprise. With a grunt, he hit her, sending the pair of them flying against a wall. Landon let his fist fly, meeting her jaw. Her head flew back, and when it came forward again there was a trickle of blood at the corner of her mouth.

"Fucking *brute!*" She cried, sending Landon flying back with a push of red magic.

It sparked in the air, and with her anger, the curse had hold of me again, like it was feeding her magic. It slid up my legs and thighs so quickly it made my skin crawl, the pain following right behind it as it began to circle my hips.

I cried out in agony, falling to the floor, unable to watch as Landon snarled Eris's name. Claws against stone, the grating sound of her magic, and grunts of effort filled the air as I screamed. It was a cacophony of agony, and it only ended when I heard Eris gasp and then grunt as Landon again made impact.

I fell to the ground, breathing hard, and out of the corner of my eye, I saw the red splash of blood, followed by Eris screaming with rage.

"*You dare!*" She shrieked. "You know not whose blood you spill, you *animal!*"

Laughing, Landon asked, "Do you think I care?"

Then they met again, Landon's claws aimed for her throat. Eris scrambled back, throwing up shielding circles as she moved, but Landon was *fast* and Eris was having a hard time keeping up with him. Eventually, she missed one of her shields just by a few inches, and his claws met her flesh again.

He tore open her bicep, and Eris's displeasure was clear when the walls around us began to shake. Before my eyes, her form seemed to shimmer, moving between Eris and something more sinister. Something bigger.

Landon caught sight of it too and grabbed Eris around the waist. Hauling her up, he sprinted to the window, holding her tight, and without a second thought, launched them both out of it.

The curse lost its hold on me, though my legs still ached with phantom pain, and I quickly scrambled to the window, looking out into the gardens below.

Tumbling, they fell down the cobbles away, and then both of them stood again. Eris was floating off the ground, hands held out to her side, red and black smoke swirling under her. Across from her, Landon stood ready, claws out and eyes focused on the witch.

Suddenly, the doors below me flew open, and Landon's elite squad of half-wolves came running out to join their leader.

"Prince Landon!" One of them shouted, tossing a huge sword to Landon.

He caught it easily and then lifted it to the sky. With a flourish, he pointed it at Eris, daring her silently.

Eris seemed to take a moment to consider her options... and then laughed again. That sickly laugh that haunted my dreams and always heralded something dire.

"Oh, prince, we're not done here," Eris crooned. Turning, she looked up at me and then waved. I glared back, making her laugh, "Oh, sweet thing. Your time is limited."

Then, in a flash, she flew into the air, retreating back to her mountains.

I watched the red dot head west and then fade, and finally, when she was out of my sight, I fell to the ground. My legs *screamed,* and every muscle in my body was tight and tense from how cramped the curse had made them.

It was as if she was turning me to iron and then forcing me to rust. Like my bones were crumbling from within as my muscles refused to obey me.

I laid there, breathing hard, and then, shortly after, passed out, dead asleep.

Chapter Twenty-Six

When I again awoke, it was Landon who I saw first.

There was no escaping the parallels to the first time he and I had met. Sunlight streamed in through the window, catching on his hair in the most fetching way, and lighting his blue eyes so they were as clear as the clearest waters and shimmering with deep emotion.

"Briar," he whispered.

I tried to smile up at him, but it hurt. Even my face was sore from screaming. "Landon," I whispered back.

"Thank all that's good you're awake," he breathed, leaning in to press his forehead against my own. "I thought you'd never wake again."

Laughing gently, I admitted, "I wondered about that myself. She was… not easy on us."

Landon had a bruise blooming on his cheek and several cuts and bruises on his arms. I had no doubt his chest, back, and legs were in similar condition.

"She was not," he agreed. "Eris is… who you say she is."

The words were careful, and I was able to read between them. Eris was as I described. He had seen her with his own two eyes, and Eris herself had confirmed some of the things in my writings.

If she was as I'd said, and she herself didn't dispute me, then the rest of it was true, too.

I was telling him the truth. And now he had his proof.

"My rose," he said, voice husky with emotion, almost choked. "I'm *sorry.*"

"Lan—"

He sat back in his seat, taking hold of my hand, "Let me speak, please."

I nodded carefully.

The emotion in his voice, his eyes, it was unsettling, and it pained me to see him displaying such obvious guilt, but if he wanted to apologize to me, then I could listen. It was the least I could do for him, especially since he'd saved me a second time from Eris's clutches.

"From the moment I first laid eyes on you, from the moment I first *scented* you on those mountain winds, I knew you were my mate, Briar. I knew you were meant to be mine. Made for me. And then I went up into your tower, and you were laid there so peacefully. It was like a dream." He shook his head. "*You* were a dream. When you came here, I left but the *whole time* I was gone I thought of you. I sent you dresses to wear and jewels and anything else I thought you'd like because I had no idea how to deal with your presence."

"That was you?" I asked. "You gave me all those dresses the girls brought? I thought they'd just... found them somewhere..."

Obviously, in hindsight, there was no way they could have found such fine gowns just laying around for them to purloin. They had to come from *somewhere*.

"It was me," he admitted. "When your heat came, I knew I couldn't run anymore. I vowed to myself that I would stay there with you. But then Eris and..." He ran a hand through his hair. "I didn't believe you, *couldn't* believe you. It was outlandish, the things you said, the things you *wrote*. But you stuck by them so fiercely, I couldn't make heads or tails of it. I thought you might be mad, that I had lain with someone who was unwell and saddled her with a child she wasn't fit to bear. I thought it would strain you, break an already fragile mind." He sighed, squeezing my fingers tightly. "Then I considered you a liar. Whether you wanted my attention and invented stories to get it or were working for some other purpose, I thought you might be maligned. Looking to gain my favor so you could lead me astray. A spy or a cultist of some kind. Someone tempting and placed in my path so perfectly... it seemed manufactured. How could I find you, *you,* of all people, in those ruins of all places. But from the moment I scented you, I *knew* you were meant to be mine. Meant to be my mate. And so I struggled. I struggled to consolidate what my heart and my wolf knew with what I was witnessing before me. I failed to have faith. I failed to believe in you, and for that, I put us all in danger. Had I known the truth, had I seen the light, I might have prepared better. I might have seen her coming for us."

"You couldn't have known," I assured him.

"I could have," he insisted stubbornly. "You're my *mate.* It's my duty to protect you. What worth am I as a prince if I cannot protect even my own mate? And here I was doubting you when I should have been busying myself with ensuring your safety. The safety of the life you carry within you. *Our child.* I put my entire future, my *family,* at risk because I could not believe in you. There is no excuse for it, and I am *sorry,* Briar. Sorry for all of it."

I sat up from the bed, and then leaned in close, trying to emphasize my words, "There is *nothing* to forgive, Lan. *Nothing.* Had I been you, I would have doubted too. Who could believe such outlandish things? For weeks after I awoke, I didn't believe them myself." I touched his cheek, forcing him to look at me. "I will admit, it hurt to not have your faith. But I have it now, and that is all that matters. We can forge forward together, making a new and better life. One with trust. One with love. Though you have done nothing to forgive, I forgive you anyway, Landon. I swear it."

"Can you truly forgive me?" He asked. "So easily?"

His eyes were filled with uncertainty, and I ached to quash it.

"I can. I can, and I do. Please, don't trouble yourself over it any longer. Though..." I laughed. "If you insist on trying to win me over again, I'll accept some gifts. If it will please you."

That made him smile, "My rose, I didn't know you to be so scheming."

"There's no scheming about it," I said. "It's simply what I am due. As a princess and as your mate."

His eyes softened, and he stood, captured my jaw with his hands, and kissed me, murmuring there, "My mate."

Now that Landon knew everything, and had seen Eris firsthand, things moved *fast*.

There was no time for Fenestral to wait, not if they wanted to be able to best the witch. And Landon was not a man to allow his chance to pass.

Scouts were sent to the mountains to watch the dragon's movements and attempt to locate where Eris was operating from, if anywhere. Landon met with some of the best warriors he had, his half-wolf squadron, as well as older fae and vampires who had battle experience. Elias was among them and smiled at me cheekily when he saw me after.

"Looks like the fair damsel princess has need of my magic," he said, eyebrows wiggling.

I laughed, "Well. Not me specifically, but thank you for lending your magic, Elias."

He shrugged, "It's about time we had a battle that wasn't driven by hatred. This is about protecting what we love, about keeping Fenestral safe. This place is unique, it means a lot to all of us. It's the only place where we may co-mingle without a second look or thought. It's normal here. If we go elsewhere..." He sighed. "It's different."

I nodded, understanding.

He was right. Here, I saw more fae and vampires than I ever had in my life before. People mixing and mingling without care and without judgment. A lot had changed in a millennium, but people's prejudices proved to be lasting. Many vampires still did not like werewolves, and vice versa, and fae people in general tended to be reclusive, mysterious, and mistrusted by others.

But not here. Here everyone was equal, and Elias was right. We had to fight to keep Fenestral safe. It was the window to the North and a beacon of peace and prosperity for other kingdoms.

And now that I thought about it... it was time I told Elias the truth. He was my friend, one I'd lied to at that, and he deserved better than that.

"Elias, can we speak for a moment?" I asked.

His forehead creased, and his eyes swept over me, "Is this about your pregnancy? It's the worst kept secret in the castle, love. You don't need to fuss over telling me. Besides that, even *I* can smell it on you. The vamps and wolves will have clocked it weeks ago."

I winced, I hadn't realized word had spread so far yet. But still, that wasn't what I was aiming for anyway.

"N-no. It's not that. Though, I am pregnant, it's about something else. Come with me to my rooms, I can explain there."

With a curious look, Elias followed me from the hall where we'd crossed paths, down the pink halls and into the suite of rooms I shared with Landon. Though the space was still mangled from his fight with Eris, it had been tidied enough to be used, and guards kept anyone from coming down the halls so it was as private as if the walls still stood.

I sat, and he mirrored me, watching me with his eyes narrowed.

"Are you dying, Briar?"

I laughed, "No. I'm not. I just have to clarify a few things. You're my friend, and I don't want any... well... lies between us."

I watched his reaction carefully, but like the long-lived noble he was, he kept his expression cool and politely curious.

"I lied to you about my background, and I am sorry for it. The reality of who I am is just so strange. I didn't know how to approach you about it."

A small smile lifted one side of his mouth. "Oh? You have me interested, Lady Briar. Do tell. You never cease to keep things engaging around here."

"Well. It's complicated. But I assume Landon has spoken to you about Eris, the witch?"

His smirk disappeared, replaced by a small frown, "Eris. He did mention a witch but didn't use her name. But it sounds familiar..."

"Perhaps you've crossed paths with her before? She is a fae. My family always called her a witch due to her less-than-savory actions, but at her heart, she's just a very old and powerful fae."

"Perhaps we've met, then. Did this Eris do something to you?"

Nodding, I admitted, "She cursed me. To sleep for five thousand years."

Elias didn't say anything for a beat, just carefully observed me, processing and absorbing what I'd said. I tried to wait patiently as he did so, but I couldn't help but squirm a little under his gaze.

"Do you not believe me?" I asked. "I don't have proof, but... I did write some things down. I gave it to Landon, but you're welcome to read it too."

Lifting one hand, Elias shook his head, "Landon believes you, yes?"

"He does now, yes. He met Eris. She confirmed what I had told him."

"Before that?"

"Before that, he didn't believe me, no. Which is when I wrote to you. Asking you to rescue me, basically."

"Because you were afraid?"

I shrugged, "In a way. Not of Landon. But of my future with him where he was convinced I was lying to him. He has a kingdom to protect, and I don't think he saw a way to do that and have someone who 'lies' at his side."

Elias looked... irritated. "That was the meaning of your absence? The questions and the letters? You were... looking for a safe haven?"

"Yes. Not just a new life *beyond the mountains,* like I'd told you. That whole story was a lie. The reality is that I am a princess. Princess Briar Rhoswen of Skyridge. Heir to the throne. An omega, but no less capable than any alpha. With a family and parents who meant the world to me. One night I went to sleep, and when I awoke, everything I knew was gone. Everyone was dead, and even the very landscape had moved. Rivers flowed down a different path. Once proud trees were reduced to stumps. And my home was a ruin."

"The ruins where he found you," Elias surmised correctly. "Five thousand years... I can see how he found this story to be *fanciful.* That is quite the tale, Briar. But if Landon believes you, I do as well. Plus, there's..." He hummed to himself, considering me. "There's some ring of truth to it all.

Your words match something about you. How lost you looked when we first met. It's as if this was etched into your very aura. Your story. Your truth."

Laughing, he snickered, "You have always lived up to my expectations of you, Briar. You really are the most fascinating woman. I'm glad to call you my friend."

"You don't mind that I lied, then?"

"Gods no," he said. "I thought you were about to tell me you were a shapeshifter or some other wild tale. This is unbelievable, but so was the thought of the dragons coming down from the mountains."

"That's the other thing!" I said quickly, jumping on the topic. "Something is wrong with the dragons!"

"Yes, they're attacking us. Very problematic if you ask me."

"Not just that," I insisted, shaking my head vigorously, the silver ornaments my girls had put into my hair that morning clinking gently. "They *never* attacked in my time. They were our *friends*. And I know Eris is behind it. She implied that she had *control* over them."

"Over the dragons?"

I shook my head vigorously again, this time in the affirmative.

"Yes."

"Hmm…" His eyes narrowed on the hole in the wall behind me as if he could gaze into the past and judge Eris for himself. "She kept you asleep for millenia. Such power is already hardly comprehensible. But if she can do that, perhaps dragons are not outside the realm of her control."

Elias stood and began to pace around the room, hands on his hips as he thought aloud.

"She'd need some sort of conduit... A way to spread her power. Or amplify it far enough to take hold."

"Is that..." I had no magic to call my own. I had no idea how it worked. "Is that really possible for someone to do?"

Shrugging, he admitted, "I don't know. But I'll meet with Landon and discuss it further. There must be a solution here. Something we're missing. But maybe..."

"If we find out how, we can stop her?"

He nodded, "Ideally, yes. If we can release her hold over the dragons, she becomes significantly less dangerous. She'd still be a powerful fae, but better to fight that than a powerful fae *with* control of dragons."

"Yes," I nodded. "The dragons aren't *like* this. I swear to you. They were our friends. Guardians. We sacrificed livestock to them yearly, and then they left us in peace. They kept bears away from the castle and village and helped protect us from unsavory bandits and ill actors. They were *allies.*"

"Do you think they would be again?" A deep, familiar voice asked from the doorway.

Landon stepped into the room, nodding to Elias and me in greeting.

"I was wondering the very same," Elias said, smiling at his friend. "You're no fool, my prince."

Landon sighed, "You're learning of this now?"

"One is never too old to learn new things," Elias quipped.

They eyed one another and then chuckled. Landon shook his head, and they made me smile too.

Sure, Eris was afoot, dragons were attacking, and a war between Fenestral and the witch was about to break out.

But friendship still thrived here. Love. Determination.

Eris might have crushed some of the stones of Fleur and dented our pride, but none of us would allow her to dim our spirits.

It would have to be good enough.

CHAPTER TWENTY-SEVEN

Landon and I reconnecting lit up something inside of me like a fire coming to life. It burned bright and hot in my chest, and that night when I climbed into bed, a huge smile made my cheeks ache and warm.

Finally. Although none of this had gone the way I'd wanted it to, in the end, we'd gotten here. We'd gotten to the place where I'd always wanted to be.

With it, Landon had *proof,* too. Although I wish he could have believed me on my own merits, my own words, I had to concede that he was a man of honor. Duty. As much as he was my mate, he was a prince.

His dedication to that role was something I understood all too well and I *admired.*

He'd done something incredibly difficult. He'd put his mate at a distance to protect his people, and all the while, he'd still spent time with me and listened to what I said. He'd taken time from his schedule to read my words and give them consideration.

It was more than I could say I'd have given him were our roles reversed.

I would have been aghast and stuck to my duty regardless of my own feelings. My own mate.

I would have pushed it all aside and concentrated on what I knew.

Landon hadn't done that. He'd kept his heart open to me while doing his best to protect his people at the same time.

Softly, the door opened, and Landon joined me in the bedroom, "My rose, do you sleep?"

"No," I answered. "I'm still awake."

"I see." Walking to the bed and sitting on the edge of the mattress, he leaned down and kissed me gently. "You should sleep. You need your energy."

"I know… I'm just thinking."

"About what?"

"You."

"Ah," he smiled. "All good things, I hope?"

"The best," I said, sliding one hand up his thigh, savoring the strong muscle under my fingers.

He rumbled happily, watching with keen eyes as I explored his upper thigh and abdomen. His strong form was well-defined, even at rest here in our rooms. At any moment, I knew he could spring into action, and the gently sloping muscles under my fingertips would turn hard and flex and turn with his movements.

I vividly remembered him training and fighting. Maybe if I asked nicely, he'd let me watch him again. In a more private setting this time, perhaps.

I sighed, sliding my hand higher, cupping his pecs and then the side of his neck, pulling him down for a kiss. He came easily, meeting my kiss and melting down into me. His chest met mine as he twisted to cup my cheek, keeping us close without putting his boots on the bed.

Each kiss was leisurely and soft, the brushes of our lips almost chaste.

It drove me *crazy*. I wanted him closer than he already was, to feel his weight on top of me and mould my body to his. That closeness felt more important now than ever. I was *keenly* aware of the fact that I could have lost Landon.

If it wasn't for Eris appearing right before our eyes, I might never have gotten this chance ever again.

And I *missed* him. Missed his body and the way he made me feel.

So I pressed myself against him tighter, writhing under him and putting as much of myself against him as I could.

"I got you," he promised me.

A second later, I heard his boots hit the floor, and Landon was in the bed with me, slotting his hips between my legs and coming down on top of me with his full weight. He was dressed more casually today, in a cream linen shirt and dark brown leather pants with a deep green velvet jacket on top. I pushed the jacket off of him and tossed it to the side, letting it slump in a heap on the floor.

Sighing happily, I wrapped my arms around his shoulders, enjoying how the fewer layers allowed me to map out the muscles shifting over his shoulder blades. I could feel his prowess as a swordsman there and just faintly feel some of his larger scars and burns from encounters with dragons and enemy soldiers.

"You want me to fuck you?" Landon asked, husky, and whispered.

"Yes," I panted. "Please. Yes. I need to feel you."

He moved swiftly, pulling my nightgown over my head and then rose off of me, pulling his shirt off with one hand. It left his hair a tousled mess that I itched to rake through and pull at. When he lowered himself onto me, I did just that. I ran my hands through his hair as we kissed, nails scraping along his scalp and sliding along the shell of his ear.

Shivering under my touch, Landon signed my name, hips moving, pressing into me so I could feel his arousal. I arched up into it, savoring the hard press of his length against my sex. Teasing him and myself at the same time. Only the fabric of his trousers separated us, and it was both soft and textured against my bare skin.

Growling, Landon leaned into it, finding a rhythm with me. We kissed, and we ground into one another, taking our time and allowing the heat to build between us. It had my heart pounding and breath hitching with every press and every slide.

"Lan," I sighed. "More, *please.*"

"I know," he breathed. "I know, my rose. I know."

The words were reverent and deep and had me shivering in his arms. Landon slid his hands up my thighs and then worked at the laces of his trousers between us. In a few quick motions, he freed himself and was pressing into me, slow and relentless. My body had no choice but to give in to him, and Landon slid inside of me easily, my own slick easing his way and allowing him to seat himself completely inside.

"Fuck," he growled. "I missed this."

"I did, too," I admitted. "I missed you so much."

Heavy inside of me, he stretched my walls and made space for himself there, and then pulled out halfway before pushing forward again. I sighed, kissed the side of his neck, and lifted my hips, encouraging him to do it again.

Not willing to disappoint, Landon repeated the process, sliding halfway out of me and then in again, a smooth and relentless glide that built up into a rhythm that made my toes curl. Normally, I'd begin to float away, basking in the feelings and sensations Landon gave me.

But this time, tonight, I was grounded here. Eyes riveted to Landon as he moved above me, keenly aware of every shift in his expression, the bulging of muscles, the strain in his neck, and the heaviness of his breath.

All of it was like a symphony around me, a beautiful dance that made me fall all the more in love with my mate. Our bond was healing; the parts of myself that had ached and hurt when he pulled away strengthened again, binding us together the way we were meant to be.

Landon felt it too. I knew he did because his eyes were locked onto mine, and swimming in their depths was understanding and tenderness. The blue of his irises bright and unwilling to let me go.

"My omega," he growled. "You'll never be parted from me again. *Not ever.* By my hand or anyone else's."

"Yes, alpha," I agreed, arching my pelvis, allowing him to sink even deeper into me.

"You and our child are *mine,*" he said, growling. "I'll protect you both."

The words were heavy with promise and unspoken meaning, but I knew what he meant. He was done with Eris. Done with how she was disrupting our lives and threatening his family and his kingdom.

The soldier in him, the protector and the prince, was determined, and I could feel that determination in every stroke.

It was intoxicating, having him pour all of that power and focus into me. It took what was already good to a whole new height, bringing me closer to Landon... and closer to my orgasm.

"I know you will," I assured him. "Landon, *I know.*"

He nodded, satisfied, and then lowered his head to kiss me. Our eyes fluttered shut, and in the darkness, we gave ourselves over to our bodies and to our bond.

It didn't take long for us to find our orgasms. With the steady strokes of his thick length and how deeply inside of me he reached, we came together.

CHAPTER TWENTY-EIGHT

The answer came to me a week later.

Letters from scouts piled up on Landon's desk, and he sorted through and read each one diligently, sorting through them for useful information. At night, he'd discuss the findings with me, laying aside me in bed and sharing his day.

Together we'd muse over the meaning of every little thing, searching for the missing puzzle piece.

"She can be anywhere," Landon sighed. "At any time. Tracking her down will be difficult. And there's no sign of any base of operations. Not even a home or a shack where she might be sleeping at night. Does she not sleep?"

I shrugged, "Honestly, she may not. We used to speak of her after she'd come to us with her demands, and none of us knew very much about her except that she was old, powerful, and demanding."

"Sounds like she earned her title of witch," Landon mused.

"She did."

We both sat in silence, turning the problem of Eris over and over in our minds. She was a threat, too dangerous to allow free, and too crafty to try to trick or trap.

Landon made the decision for the both of us to take a break. He pressed a kiss to the top of my head, "Come, my rose, for now, we sleep. In the morning, we'll scheme again."

We slept, and with the dawn, the answers came.

Eris had called herself Lady of the Springs.

The springs were magical. With rivers running through and under stone deep into the mountains.

In the clarity of the morning, it all came into focus. Eris used the springs and the magic contained in the waters to control the dragons. Spread her influence somehow and control the dragons. That had to be it. That was why she had asked so often after the springs, insisting me and my family had them over to her. And when she finally grew tired of waiting, she had taken them by force and destroyed my entire family in the process.

The answer had been there all along. In my memory and on the pages of my writings. Eris's lust for the springs had no other explanation.

I sat up in bed, and shook Landon, "Landon, I know what we have to do."

Groggily, he turned over and blinked up at me, "Briar, what do you mean?"

I leaned in and kissed his cheek, "I know how she's controlling the dragons. Her base has to be there too. It's the springs. It was always the springs."

"What springs?"

"The land Eris wanted. The day before she cursed me she came to see me. In the past, she had demanded it from both me and my father and my grandfather. A spring near Skyridge. It was old and renowned for its healing abilities. The waters poured from a tree in the center of a cave, and people traveled to from far and wide to lay in it or drink from it."

"Why would she have interest in a spring?"

"No idea," I admitted. "I don't think she wanted us to know. If she tilted her hand to us, we might be less inclined to give in to her demands."

"She valued it highly, then, to try and conceal how badly she wanted it."

"I didn't realize myself until she came to visit me that night. My final night in my own time. I never imagined she'd wanted it *that* badly. I refused her, as had all my predecessors. But…"

"She coveted them badly enough to curse you," he surmised. "When you denied her, she decided to take them by force. Eris was done waiting."

I nodded, cheek sliding against his chest, and then shared the real crux of my thoughts, "Springs travel deep under mountains, and if they really were magical then..."

"Perhaps she's using them, somehow," he continued. "Using it as a way to amplify her own powers. Spread her influence so far even the dragons could not deny her."

"Eris is powerful. With such a focus for her magic, there's no telling what she can do."

"She is a powerful foe," Landon said quietly, his hand sliding over my hip, pulling me to his side. "We will need to approach her carefully. What else do you know of her?"

"Not much," I admitted. "She was always on the outskirts of Skyridge. Showing up at castle events uninvited, offended whether we included her in festivities or not. There was no pleasing her. My great-great-great-grandmother had tried to befriend her, but all she got for her efforts was one of Eris's lesser curses. The witch made it so she could never smile again. She lived her life looking dour and angry, regardless of how she felt. The people gave her the nickname the Dour Duchess."

"Vindictive witch," Landon cursed, squeezing me closer. "I don't want her anywhere near you."

"Landon," I sighed, relaxing into him. "I have to see this through."

"No, you don't." He said firmly. "You're with child, Briar. You don't need to go anywhere near Eris."

"I'm not an invalid," I protested, detangling myself from him and sitting up in the bed. "This is my responsibility, Lan. I denied her the spring, made her this angry, and brought her attention to Fleur. And she *cursed* me. I deserve my revenge."

It was the first time in my life that I'd felt this way, and the power of it shocked me. My heart burned with a sudden flashfire of anger and determination. I was going to watch Eris's destruction with my own two eyes. I was going to play a part in her demise.

She had taken so much from me, and orchestrated carefully the disruption of my life. And I was going to see that she paid.

Landon sighed, looking me over, taking in my knit brows and burning eyes.

"You're not about to listen to me, are you? But Briar, we're talking about dragons and an angry, old fae witch. It's *dangerous.*"

"She is my responsibility, my problem." I insisted. "It's me she wants. I can be bait, draw her to the springs."

Landon bit out a quick, "No. No, Briar."

"There's no other option," I insisted.

"There *is.* There are a hundred other options."

"Landon—" I tried to press the issue, but he covered my mouth with his hand.

"I'll go over it with my people," he said. "And I will tell them you offered to be bait. But Briar, I don't like the idea. Not at all. You're *my mate.* You're carrying our child. There is nothing I hate more than the idea of you facing down Eris again. Once was already enough for me."

"I know it's dangerous," I promised. "But I *have* to do this."

Gently, Landon took my hand and squeezed it, "Briar. For me, *please.* Let me sort this out."

"I can't let you do this alone."

"I won't be alone." He promised me. "I have men. I have Elias. A whole army to help me. I have *never* known fear like I felt when Eris had you in her grasp. *Never.* Do you understand?"

His eyes swam with emotion, and I nodded, heart twisting with guilt.

"I know you want your just revenge, and it truly is just. You deserve that, I believe it wholeheartedly. But whatever it is you're due, it is *not* worth the price of your life. It is not worth putting yourself and our child in danger. Allow me to get revenge for you. *Trust me* enough to do this for you."

"I do trust you," I promised. "But this isn't about trust, Landon. This is about justice."

He closed his eyes and bowed his head, exhaling deeply, "Very well, my rose. We'll find a way to make it work."

"I don't intend to fight her," I promised him. "But I must bear witness to her end. I *must.* For my family. For Skyridge."

Landon didn't protest me this time, and I considered that his assent. After a moment, he shifted us, pulling me into his lap and gathering me close.

"Promise me," he said hoarsely. "Promise me you'll be careful. And that you will *listen* to me. Take no risks."

"I will," I promised him easily. "I will."

Leaving me to doze, Landon took my information to his war council, assembling everyone as soon as he could get the word out.

I nearly asked to go with him, to be a part of the planning, but the words of my mother rang in my ears.

Be not where you're unneeded, Briar. There's a time and a place for your opinions, and you must learn to discern when that is.

I was no warmonger, nor was I a tactician. Landon was both of those, so I took a deep breath and let go of my own ideas, choosing instead to trust him. He would allow me to go with him to the springs to witness the end of Eris.

That was enough for me.

He remained in council for the majority of the day, and I took all of my meals alone, waiting for him to return.

When he did, he came with Elias at his side.

"My lady," Elias bowed, greeting me.

"Elias," I smiled. "It's good to see you."

"We have a plan," Landon announced, coming to my side and kissing my temple before he took a seat next to me.

Elias took a seat across from us both, curious eyes flicking from Landon to me, observing us.

"We depart for the springs tomorrow," Landon continued, ignoring Elias's stare.

"Tomorrow?" I asked, whirling to look at Landon. "So soon?"

"There's no sense in delaying it," Elias shrugged, answering for the prince. "The longer we wait, the longer Eris has to draft her own schemes."

"We need to catch her off guard. The element of surprise."

"Surely she'll be able to see your approach from the mountains?" I asked.

"She would if we were idiots," Elias said, scoffing. "But we're not idiots, love."

I shook my head at him but waited for their answer. If they were so smart, then I wanted to hear their intended plan in its fullest.

"We'll approach in disguise," Landon told me. "A small elite team hidden in some wagons. One of my men will pose as a trader taking goods through the pass."

"Okay," I nodded. "The spring is just off the pass. That will work."

Remembering something, Landon stood and paced to his desk, unearthing something from the pile, and brought it to me.

"Mark where the spring is exactly," he instructed. "It'll help us plan our exact approach."

I took in the familiar landscape, marking the places that were unchanged from five thousand years ago and the ones that were. Formerly small towns were now cities, borders moved along with rivers, but the mountain ridges still trod the same path. Lakes still filled the same basins. And the ruins of Skyridge remained where they always had.

I marked first Skyridge, circling it and labeling it. Then I went northeast, following the mountain pass, and marked off where the spring was just past the next mountain.

"Hmm," Elias mused, watching me place down the ink. "I've heard talk of springs there, but not in hundreds of years at least."

"The witch is likely keeping people away, allowing the memory of it to fade," Landon said. "Clever. It's easier to guard something no one knows exists. If word got out, she'd have to turn away leagues of curious explorers."

"And weary travelers," I supplied. "That's who visited the spring in the past. Travelers and those looking for healing."

"I imagine Eris would find such intrusions to be tedious and unwelcome," Elias deadpanned. "Having her evil plans and spells interrupted by the sickly and weary."

"She would, yes," I agreed.

"So she allowed the memory of the spring to fade." Landon finished.

"Unluckily for her, she didn't wipe my memory," I said, frowning down at the map. Then, I looked between Elias and Landon. "We'll make sure it means her doom."

CHAPTER TWENTY-NINE

That night I laid awake in bed alone, mind focused on the day before us.

Landon left with Elias again after they both took dinner with me in our rooms, taking the map I'd marked up with them. Landon promised to be back soon, but now it was well past the eleventh bell, and I was still here alone.

I couldn't stop thinking about the future. About what would happen tomorrow.

What if Eris saw us coming and sent a dragon to greet us? What if her spring was guarded by dragons?

Sure, Landon was a revered and successful dragon slayer, but the thought of him having to fight more of them, to *slay* them, made my stomach churn. Nausea crawled its way up my throat, and I sprung from the bed, running for the bathing room.

I barely made it to a bucket in the corner before I properly lost my dinner. Pregnancy and nerves were not a good combination.

"Ugh," I groaned, leaning over the edge of the bucket, hoping this was the last of it. I'd managed to avoid many of the symptoms so far by taking it easy and religiously drinking ginger tea and taking the healer's anti-nausea herbs.

But there was no helping this kind of nausea. It was born of something deeper than my body adjusting to growing a new life. It was born of fear.

Chilling, encompassing *fear.*

Eris was not to be messed with. I knew this first hand. What if she put me to sleep again? What if she put Landon to sleep?

Worse yet, what if people died on this campaign? What if they died because of a witch I'd brought into their lives?

If I'd stayed asleep, would Eris have bothered to attack Fleur?

I didn't think so. She was doing this because she hated that I was awake. Hated that I was living a life that I could be happy with. She wanted me to suffer, and there was no collateral damage she considered to be unacceptable in that pursuit. She would kill man, woman, and child in her quest.

I pictured Landon lying lifeless before me, and my stomach turned again, making me vomit once more into the bucket.

"Enough of those thoughts," I told myself. *"Enough."*

Standing, I grabbed a sprig of fresh mint from where my girls had hung it on the wall and chewed, banishing the taste of bile from my mouth.

Now was not the time to be losing my composure. So I gripped my dignity with both hands and pulled it around myself like a cloak. I would get through this. I *would*.

Stepping into the main suite of rooms, I found Landon there, lounging on the couch, a glass of amber liquid in one hand.

"Landon," I said, surprised. "You're back."

Wearily, he smiled at me, "I'm sorry I was away so long. Are you alright?"

His eyes flitted up and down my body, taking in my flushed cheeks, pale green nightgown, and bare feet. His eyes softened, and he leaned forward to put down his glass. Then he gestured me forward, opening his arms and making room for me next to him on the couch.

I went to him, sliding into the space he'd made for me in the crook of his lap, and then settled into his arms. He wrapped me close, burying his nose in my hair and breathing deep.

"I wish you would stay here," he admitted quietly.

"I can't, Lan," I whispered back.

"I know."

His arms squeezed, drawing me further onto the couch so he was wrapped around me from behind, and I was lying in front of him, soaking up everything.

In the silence, we basked in one another. My eyes fluttered closed, and Landon's hands softly moved over me. Sliding up and down my sides, savoring each curve and dip before coming to gently cup my slight breasts over my nightgown. The fabric was a soft barrier between his touch and my skin, but it wasn't nearly enough to keep me from gasping when his thumb brushed over my nipple.

"Landon," I sighed.

"We leave in the morning," he reminded me, as if he was trying to convince the both of us to sleep instead of having sex.

"I know," I replied, arching into his touch, pushing my breast into his hands and my bottom into the hard length of his cock.

"We don't have time for this," he whispered into my neck, kissing me and biting my earlobe.

"I know," I repeated, sighing and sliding my hand back to grip his strong thigh.

Together we ignored responsibility, Landon's hands finding their way under my nightgown, and my own hands caressing his cheek, his neck, his chest, his length. Feeling out as much of him as I could while his hands laid siege to my body.

He pinched my nipples, trading one for the other until they were aching and hard. They were already sensitive from carrying the baby, but Landon's ministrations pushed them nearly to breaking, the tender peaks making me want to sob. Or to beg for more.

Then his hands dipped between my legs, finding me uncovered and already damp from his play.

"No panties," he breathed, sliding his fingers through my wet folds, gathering the silken slick there before he pushed inside of me, testing me.

"No," I gasped, words catching. "I... No."

"Were you hoping I'd lay with you tonight?" He rumbled. "Hoping I'd fuck you and stuff you with my knot and my cum? Make you ride all the way to the springs tomorrow with my spend leaking out of you?"

"Y-yes," I admitted, a rush of heat diving straight for my sex, making me even wetter. "I was hoping for that."

"Would that that witch knew," he said, withdrawing his fingers and circling them around my clit, "that though she may have cursed you, she ensured you and I would meet. That I would find my mate. That you would find yours. Or perhaps she does know, and she can't stand it. She knows how well I fuck you, and she can't stand it. She knows I've already planted the future of my country deep inside of you."

"M-maybe," I stammered, head swimming with his words and the heat from his ministrations.

Chuckling, Landon pulled my nightgown high over my hips and then pulled at my top knee, bringing it up and back so I was forced to tilt my pelvis, leaving my legs spread and sex bare to the air. Bare to him.

He took advantage of it, circling his fingers over my clit in deliberate strokes. It made me squirm. It was so much, and yet not enough to satisfy me. Each stroke dove heat into my core and sparks up my spine, like a blacksmith's strokes against hot iron, but he kept it so slow and deliberate it would never make me orgasm.

"Landon," I begged. "Faster, please."

"No," he answered. "Tonight, you'll come with me inside of you, and only then."

"Then fuck me, *please*. I want you inside of me."

He bit into my neck, "No."

Groaning, I tried to wiggle and arch to force myself closer to his fingers and increase the pressure. But Lan was wise to my tricks and took his hand away from me entirely, leaving me bereft.

"Landon," I begged. "Please. Don't stop."

Suddenly, this hand came down onto me, slapping my cunt.

"Ah!" I gasped, more surprised than anything.

The heat from his strike perfectly complemented the heat of my lust, and I could feel a rush of wetness pour out of me, making my thighs wet.

"I'll do as I like," he growled into my ears. "I'll fuck you in my time. And you'll be happy to wait for it, won't you?"

"Yes," I rushed to say, wanting him to touch me again, now more than ever. "Yes, please. Alpha, *touch me.* Please. I'll wait. I'll behave."

"Good girl," he whispered. "So good for me. You're such a good omega."

The deep timber of his words and the growling edge to them told me he was as affected as I was. But that was all the gratification I was going to get because instead of touching me where I wanted, he slid his hands over my thighs, coming close to my cunt, but not close enough. Over and over, he circled down my inner thighs, then up my hamstrings and over my knees, and then back down.

Each stroke made my stomach dip, wondering if this was the time. If this was when he would finally touch me again. But he didn't.

I had to bite back on my whines and complaints, wanting to be good for him. Wanting to behave and prove I could be patient.

After five... six circles, his fingers finally found my clit again and slowly circled it.

"Good girl," he praised me again.

My heart skipped a beat. My mate praising me was the ultimate aphrodisiac, gripping me firmly and causing me to squirm in his grasp.

"I know how bad you want me, but you have to wait. You'll wait for me, won't you?" He asked. "You'll wait until I say so."

"I will," I promised. "I'll wait, alpha. I'll wait as long as you want."

In answer, he slid one finger inside of me, a cruel tease. It wasn't nearly enough to satisfy me, but it was just enough to drive me crazy thinking about *more*. About how much better his cock would feel. About how much thicker it was. About his knot and how it would fill me.

"That's it," he encouraged me. "Take my fingers. Let me stretch you. Prepare you for my knot."

"Yes," I gasped. "Please, Landon. *I want your knot.*"

"I know," he assured me. "I know, my rose."

But, cruelly, he did nothing to make that a reality. He kept sliding that single digit in and out of me, until my thighs were more than a little damp. Then he added a second finger, stretching me wider, starting the process over again.

Then a third finger joined, and I was *panting* in his grasp, barely holding in my pleas.

"You're doing so well," Landon told me. "Look at how good you are, taking three fingers in your pretty, swollen cunt. You were built to take me, weren't you? Built for me to fuck and claim."

"Yes," I panted. "Yes, I was."

"A breedable, fuckable omega," he practically purred. "All mine. Mine to breed and fuck however I please."

Squirming, a fire burning in my chest, I began to beg. "Please, alpha. I need you."

"I know," he assured me. "I know, my rose. Let me have you."

With deft movements, he pulled open his pants, undoing the buttons with one hand, and then pulled himself free. The heat of his cock was a firm press at the small of my back. Landon pulled me close, one hand fisted in my nightgown to keep it up, his knee lifting to keep my legs spread open, and his right hand guiding his cock between my legs.

With careful movements, he pressed against my opening, and then slowly slid inside of me.

"Ah," I gasped, head pressing back into his chest. "Landon."

"My rose," he growled, pressing further and further, an unrelenting pressure that filled and stretched me. "You're so tight. So hot around me."

"More," I begged. "I want all of you."

"You'll get it," he promised. "I'll make sure you're full."

On and on he pushed until the root of him was pressed flush against me, his chest warm against my back. One of his hands still held my nightgown, while the other came to press in against my lower stomach, creating more pressure.

It was *beyond* filling. Even without his knot being swollen, he was thick inside of me, easing the ache. Starting slow, he pumped in and out of me, hips flexing and thighs tensing under my fingers. Landon was in complete control of his body and never changed his pace from slow and torturous.

It was maddening, and I made sure he knew it.

"More, *please*, alpha," I begged. "You're going too slow."

"No, I'm not," he insisted, chucking. "I'm going as fast as I want to go."

You're going too slow *for me,*" I clarified, trying to arch back into him to get more of him faster.

Clicking his tongue, he admonished me, "Now, now, Briar. You promised me you'd behave."

"Then stop torturing me," I whined. "I can't take it."

"You can," he insisted. "You've done it before, and I know you can do it again."

"I can't. You're making me insane."

He didn't seem to care because the pace of his fucking never changed. It was slow and steady as it had been when he started, his cock sliding deep inside of me and then out, pressing against my inner walls and sliding over a sweet spot that made me want to jump and turn, mounting Landon properly and take control.

"Then you understand how you make me feel," he growled. "I feel mad every time I look at you. With every move of your hips under your dress and every breath in your corset, all I can imagine is your breasts in my hands and your hips under mine. Day in and day out, I wish to tie you to the bed and keep you there. You'd service all of my needs, and I yours. I'd spend days between your legs, savoring your cunt and your juices, and then I'd spent another month with my cock buried deep inside of you, counting how many times I knot you and fill you. I'd fill you with so much seed it'd spill out of you, making a mess of our bed."

His words did nothing to help the squirming need inside of me. In fact, it made everything worse.

If not for Eris, I would demand we do that now. I'd ask him to forsake his duties and make good on his promises.

"You like that idea, don't you? I can feel how tightly you're gripping me. Your cunt is hungry for it. My omega is hungry for her alpha's cock."

"P-please," I tried to beg again. "Faster, alpha."

"Alright," he relented. "But only because you've been a good girl."

Immediately, his hips snapped into me, burying his cock deep, and then he pulled out to roughly slam into me again. The sound of wet flesh meeting flesh filled the seating room, Landon's heavy breathing in my ear and his fingertips digging into me, leaving their mark.

The hand he'd been using to hold up my nightgown slid further up and under it so he could roughly grab my breast, squeezing my chest, and kneading the small mound of flesh.

His cock twitched inside of me, the alpha clearly pleased with my small stature.

"So slight," he murmured, licking at the delicate space behind my ear. "Delicate and breakable. Mine to protect and keep safe."

I shivered, "Yes, alpha."

"I'll keep you safe," he promised, the words nearly desperate.

"I know you will," I assured him.

Groaning, Landon turned us, sliding my leg up and around so my back was pressed down into the couch, and he was bearing down into me from above. He took my mouth in a rough kiss, sliding his tongue against mine as he resumed fucking me in earnest.

The pace was rigorous and unrelenting, driving both of us to the edges of our tolerance.

"Landon, I'm close," I told him, nails scrabbling at his shoulders for a place to hold on.

His eyes flashed, glowing in the dim lighting, "I know, my rose. I know. I can feel it."

"Will you come with me?" I asked, no, begged.

It felt important that we did this together. Like a blessing for the battle I knew was to come. If we did this together, we could face whatever came at us tomorrow, I knew we could.

"I will," he promised me. "I'll come with you, my rose."

I smiled up at him, and his eyes met mine and never left, looking down at me, taking in every small shift in my expression. Relentless, his cock split me open and filled me over and over, until his knot began to swell, popping in and out of me until it reached its full girth and seated entirely inside of me.

It pressed perfectly against my sweet spot, the intense and steady pressure sending me over the edge just as Landon groaned, releasing inside of me.

Together we shivered, eyes locked onto the other, our orgasms binding us even closer together.

"God," he groaned, watching as I got lost in our passion. "You're perfect, Briar. The perfect mate."

"Landon," I sighed, sliding my hands up his chest, feeling the unsteady beat of his heart. "You're the perfect alpha."

"I try to be," he promised me. "Tomorrow, I'll make sure you're safe."

"You need to keep yourself safe too," I pointed out.

"Not as much as I need to keep you safe."

"No," I insisted, wrapping my legs around his waist, pulling him down so we were chest to chest. "We're *both* coming back here when it's all done. *Both of us.* Promise me, Landon."

He laughed, "I promise, my rose."

"You *will* keep yourself safe," I repeated, squeezing him.

"I will."

He didn't even argue, sensing how serious I was. I could only hope he could follow through on his word.

Chapter Thirty

When dawn broke, Landon woke me, and together we made the solemn march to the courtyard. There, in the protection of the castle walls, we prepared.

Landon donned his human form armor, the sheaths for two swords at his back, and then helped me into a spare set of leather armor that would at least protect me more than my gowns were capable of.

Elias arrived dressed as if he was attending a ball, in a fine black silk shirt, high-waisted leather breeches, and silver jewelry at his ears and fingers. The tips of his horns were capped with yet more silver, all of it gleaming in the morning light.

"Do you not wear armor?" I asked.

The fae shrugged, "I need to be able to move to cast well. It's better for all of us if I can do it without hindrance."

"Alright," I nodded. "Fair enough."

"Briar," Landon said. "If something happens, Elias is your go-to. Find him, and he'll make sure you get out of there."

"Nothing is going to happen," I insisted.

His blonde curls shook, "It doesn't matter what our intentions are. We are *going* to plan for every outcome. We *must.*"

"Alright," I capitulated, not wanting to argue. *"If something happens, I will find Elias."*

"We got this, love," Elias said. "Don't worry about it."

"I'll try."

Into the courtyard streamed Landon's elite squad, all of them dressed in human-sized armor, sheaths ready for their weapons. Behind them, a few soldiers I recognized from around the castle joined us, guards all of them, and all of them talented with a sword. Several page boys ran about the space, loading swords into the backs of the wagons, along with baskets filled with bread, cheese, water, and ale.

When they were done, Landon clapped his hands, gathering everyone's attention.

"Today, we ride for the mountain pass," Landon announced. "You all know what we fight for today. What we aim for. We will put a stop to the dragon attacks and free our land from the curse of the witch, Eris."

"Here here," the crowd rumbled, some lifting their fists, others knocking on their breastplates.

"This is the end of her reign of terror. We will take revenge for those we lost in the attacks, and we will take revenge for Briar, your princess. Today marks the end of Eris and the beginning of a new Fenestral!"

"Yah!" They cried, stamping their feet and howling their battle cry.

Together, they all piled into the backs of wagons, and Landon, Elias, and I went with them. In total, there were three wagons filled with warriors, all outfitted with armor and trained to know how to fight.

Landon hadn't filled me in on the nitty-gritty details of their plan, but I knew in my gut that he had prepared for as much as possible. He knew what he was doing, had waged battles before, and had a team of tacticians on his side.

I had to trust him.

We'd had our ups and down, but as I tightly gripped his hand and the wagon rumbled towards the mountains, I found that I *did* trust him.

He had come to believe me. He'd rescued me from Eris. And he'd not shown a shred of doubt in me since. We were finally on solid ground, and I prayed to anyone who would listen that we'd come out the other side of this on that same ground. We deserved our chance to blossom.

Once Eris was defeated, I'd make sure we did.

The trip was silent. All of us lost in our thoughts of what if. Of plans and backup plans.

At noon, we ate some of the bread and cheese packed away in baskets. That, too, was quiet, with only polite murmurings of thanks passed around.

When we pulled into the pass, I could feel the soldiers around me focusing. It was a tangible thing, their battle senses. Swirling in the air around us, observing and listening for any sign of trouble. The faintest beat of a dragon's wing or the crackling of malevolent magic.

There was none, and then someone rapped on the front of the wagon. Lan stood and went to the front, sliding open a small high-set window that allowed him to speak directly to the driver.

"We approach the springs," the driver said quietly. "The wagons can go no further."

Landon nodded, "Very well."

"It's not far from the path," I informed him. "Or, it wasn't."

"I'm sure it's still quick to get to." He turned to the wagon, announcing. "We depart."

Instantly, they flew into practiced, silent action. The wagon doors were thrown open and everyone filtered out. Shortly the other wagons followed, everyone stepping down onto the rocky path and then reaching for their weapons. Each soldier outfitted themselves with a silver sword, a steel sword, and a dragon lance, just in case they ran into serious trouble.

I personally grabbed a small knife, strapped it to my hip, and then slid another one into my boot. Just in case.

Then, Landon looked to me and nodded.

Nervously, I glanced at the sky, but when it was empty, I turned and began to lead them to the springs.

Landon was right. It was still quick to get to, though the path was now overgrown and hard to spot. Eris clearly wasn't taking any visitors at her springs. More evidence that whatever was going on here, she didn't want anyone disturbing her.

Landon took the lead ahead of me, his steel sword in hand, swiping away at the vegetation, clearing it away until we came to the face of the mountain.

There, where I *knew* a cave once yawned, was a sheer cliff face.

"What?" I asked, staring up the side of the cliff and then up the mountain, confused.

"Eris." Landon spat.

Elias came to my side, squinting at the rock, "This isn't a natural rockface."

"It's not?" I asked.

Stepping forward, I pressed my palm against the stone. It was cool and solid under my fingertips. It felt as real as any other mountain and just as immovable.

"Step back," Elias said. "Let's see how talented this Eris really is."

Doing as he asked, I stepped back, coming to Landon's side. Behind us, the soldiers watched Elias and the land around us keenly. In the bushes to our sides, I could hear Lan's scouts checking our flanks.

As we watched, Elias lifted one hand and frowned at the stone. In his palm, a blue mist gathered, and once he had a sphere the size of a globe floating above his hand, he launched it forward at the rock. The smoke hit the rocks and splashed against them like a wave hitting the shore, climbing up the sides and pushing against the craigs of the rocks, trying to find a way in.

As they spread, Elias grunted, concentrating hard on his work, and then, all at once, the smoke froze, and Elias smiled.

"Got you, bitch," he muttered.

The smoke moved quickly then, pushing into a small gap in the rocks, and then all at once, the rock face was gone, leaving the cave entrance I was familiar with.

"This is it," I told Landon.

He nodded, "Well done, Elias."

Elias dusted his hands as if he was clearing the magic from them, "Thank you kindly."

I walked towards the cave, trying to peer into its depths. Five thousand years ago, the cave had been well-lit, with a few vendors at the entrance selling various scrubs and cloths to bathe with and some clothing to change into should a traveler not have any.

Now, it was abandoned. The wind echoed through it, whistling past us and rustling our hair. It yawned darkly before us, foreboding and beckoning. A void ready to swallow us alive.

"Stay here," Landon said, turning to me suddenly.

"Here?" I asked, confused.

"Caves are dangerous," Landon explained. "I can't risk a cave-in from the battle crushing you or trapping you inside."

"The same could happen to you," I pointed out.

"Yes," he admitted readily. "It could. But I'm not pregnant. I don't carry the future of Fenestral. *You do.*"

Uneasy, I put a hand over my stomach, trying to think logically.

The mother inside of me, the woman who was just coming to be, agreed with Landon. But the rest of me, the part of me that believed in doing my duty and protecting my kingdom and the part of me that wanted revenge on Eris, protested.

I belonged there with the soldiers. I *needed* to witness her demise.

"I have to see it happen," I told him. "I *have* to."

Landon took me by the shoulders and looked deep into my eyes. "My rose, I will bring you her head. Stay. Here."

"Okay," I whispered.

His words were so firm I agreed immediately. If he was going to offer me her head, I would take it.

Landon stepped in close, kissed me gently, and then turned back to the soldiers. He lifted his hand with a closed fist, and then gestured towards the cave, beckoning them into the darkness. Without hesitation, they drew their swords with whisper-quiet precision and nodded at their prince.

Landon tipped his chin at them, nodded to me once more, and led them slowly into the cave.

Elias met my eyes, winked, and followed directly behind Landon, a small ball of blue fire in his hand to light the way.

One by one, they faded into the darkness of the cave, leaving me alone in the forest.

At first, I sat on a stone, trying to maintain my composure.

But as the minutes stretched out my only company was the chirping of birds, anxiety had me standing and beginning to pace. I strained to hear any noise from inside the cave, but still, there was only the rushing of the wind as it came through the chasm.

From experience, I knew the cave wasn't bottomless, the spring only a short walk into the depths. There, in the darkness, was a pool of water warm enough to steam in the cold cave air. The water itself was a pale blue and slightly cloudy, and I remember how torch light would spark off the surface when my mother and I had visited, creating flashes of blue and yellow in the dim.

At the center of the pool was a small island covered in moss, a single tree in the center of it. It bloomed beautifully, with pale pink flowers that reached for the cavern's roof, and dropped petals into the waters below. In its trunk, there was a gap, a hole from which water flowed out and into the pool below, keeping it fed.

I'd thought it magical when I'd first been there, but I'd considered what it was on its surface— a very unusual spring that produced warm, soothing waters. Never would I have imagined it something that could be used for ill.

Let alone control dragons.

As if summed by my thoughts, I heard the steady beat of wings sound down the side of a mountain, soft and distant.

"Oh *fuck,*" I cursed.

Whirling, I tried to look beyond the canopy to see where it was approaching from, but it was impossible to see past all the leaves. The beats grew louder and closer, and I whirled, looking for a place to hide.

I didn't know if this was a coincidence or if the dragon was arriving at Eris's bidding, but I knew the last thing I needed was dragon fire bearing down on me.

On instinct, I dove for a thicket close by, getting as far down and close down to the ground as I could. Then, I turned onto my back, eyes scanning the canopy. The beats of the dragon's wings grew louder, and the leaves began to shake in time with them. It was getting so close the branches bent under the wind, and then there was a crash as the dragon landed on the mountain face. I craned my neck and could barely make out a huge claw with sharp talons dug into the rocks above the cave entrance. The deep blue dragon roared with a huge deep cry that made my chest shake and my ears ache.

Oh gods help me, I begged silently.

The dragon had to know there was something wrong. It had come right to the cave, *right?*

Fear struck through me, and two things came immediately to mind. First, the dragons Landon knew, the dragons of this age, were aggressors. Second, the dragons I knew, the ones from my past, were protectors.

Which one was here before me?

I contemplated it from my spot in the dirt, craning my neck to see as much of the dragon as possible. It rumbled a low growl that had me shivering where I lay. Thankfully, there didn't seem to be any sign of Eris.

There was just a dragon to deal with.

Taking a deep breath, I weighed the options.

If the dragon remained here, then when Landon and the men emerged from the cave, they'd be ambushed and turned to cinders before they could mount a proper counter-attack. But I wasn't exactly outfitted to fight a dragon, either. I had two short knives and no combat experience. Rushing to attack the dragon was a suicide mission. I doubted I could sneak past it either and go warn Landon and the others.

That left only the *last* option.

The insane one.

The one I *really* didn't want to do. But I knew I had to.

I couldn't let them all die.

Gathering my wits and steeling my spine, I scrambled to my feet, burst out of the brush, and craned my neck to look up the side of the mountain and directly into the dragon's eyes.

"Hello!" I called. "Um, I'm not here to fight! I'd really like it if we could communicate somehow?"

The great beast blinked at me, blue eyes curious and slightly suspicious.

"I don't know if any of you remember Skyridge, but I am Briar, Princess of Skyridge. We used to have peace between us!"

The dragon chuffed, smoke billowing out of its snout.

"I know the witch, Eris, has corrupted you! I want to help! I want to go back to how things were. We can bring you offerings again. We can help each other!"

The dragon's head lifted, and he looked out to the sky. Then, he bellowed, loud and low. When he was done, he leveled me again with a look. This one was less suspicious and more openly curious. He leaned down, bringing his head closer to me, and inhaled deeply.

That confirmed something for him. I opened my mouth to ask what he saw in me, what he smelled, when two more sets of wingbeats echoed through the mountains. One huge deep red dragon and one who shone a more silver color came to join the blue dragon. They clung to the cliffs, glittering in the sun like jewels hidden in the stone.

It was *breathtaking*.

And I recognized the red dragon.

"You..." I whispered. "I know you."

He dipped his huge head, confirming it.

This was the same dragon who had been at the last ceremony my father had led. The last offering. He was even older now but moved just as well as the other two younger dragons at his side. They shifted on the rocks, glancing at one another, communicating silently.

"I... I want to make peace," I called after a moment.

Their heads swung to watch me.

"I know the witch is controlling you, somehow. Making you hurt people. I want to stop her. I brought people with me to help," I gestured to the cave. "They're in there now, looking for her."

The red one grumbled, head shaking.

"Is... is she not in there?" I asked.

He huffed.

Fuck.

"Where is she?"

Their heads turned all at once, pointing towards the sky.

"Is she coming?"

The red one huffed again.

"Oh, *gods.* Wait here," I begged them. "Or go, I don't want them to hurt you. We'll stop her, I promise. But if you can't help us, then please *go.*"

I didn't see what they decided because I was *running* full speed into the cave. I had to find Landon and Elias, and the others. I *had* to. They were in the wrong place.

I made it halfway to the spring before I encountered the first scout, a young man I recognized from guard duty around the castle.

"My lady," he said, confused. "Please, go back outside, Prince Landon—"

"You're in the wrong place," I panted. "The witch isn't here. She's coming now from the mountains. She's on her way."

"Fuck," he bit out. "Wait here, Lady Briar."

He went running deep into the caves, and I bounced back and forth on my feet, waiting for his return. I didn't wait long. A moment later, I took off running after the scout, too anxious to allow him to go on his own. I had to see Landon for myself. Tell him the news personally.

I barreled across the stone, feet pounding, and only stopped when I took the last bend and nearly ran straight into Landon.

"Briar," he said, steadying me. "You should not be here."

"Eris isn't here," I panted. "But she's on her way. She's coming from the mountains."

Elias came to stand beside us, "She knows something's wrong."

He'd rolled up his sleeves, and I gasped when I caught sight of the black marks and smudges covering his hands and trailing up his forearms.

"Elias, what happened?"

He shrugged, "I took care of some spells she had cast down here. You were right. She was using the springs to control the dragons. I dismantled what I could of her setup."

A shiver went up my spine, and on instinct, I turned to look at the once-beautiful spring.

The once pale blue waters were muddy and dark. Though I knew the pool was shallow, there was no making out the bottom of it. It was so tainted. Black swirls of something foul floated on the surface of the water, and the tree which fed the waters spewed forth more of the dark substance with every second.

"She destroyed it," I whispered.

Even the pink petals of the tree had turned brown and wilted sadly on the branch.

"She did," Elias agreed. "But hopefully, with time, the spring will heal itself. I removed most of her incantations and destroyed the *apparatus* she had set up around the tree."

"Apparatus?"

"We will explain all later," Landon assured me. "You said she is on her way?"

I nodded, "She is... also..."

He dipped his head to hear me better, "Also?"

"There are dragons outside."

"What?"

"They're friendly!" I promised, holding up my hands. "I already talked to them. I think they felt it when Elias did what he did. I think maybe they're free now."

Landon's head snapped up, and he narrowed his eyes on the dark recesses of the cave. "We need to move. Now."

A second later, I heard what he had: Another set of wings approaching.

Another dragon to join the others?

We all raced to the mouth of the cave, staying just under its cover as we observed the skies. Above us, the three dragons clung to the cliff face; their faces turned to watch the new arrival.

From the east came a great black dragon, nearly as big as the huge red elder, and on his back was a small, willowy figure shrouded in a red mist.

"Eris," I whispered.

Landon moved quickly, "We'll take her by surprise here at the mouth. Find a place to hide, weapons drawn. Wait for my signal." He gestured to the soldiers around him, *"Go."*

When they sprung into movement, Landon turned to me, "Hide deep in the spring."

"What about cave-ins?" I asked, pointing out his earlier concern.

"Better that risk than the dragon fire that's to come."

On that thought, I glanced above us. The red dragon's head dipped to look down at me, and something... instinctual passed between us.

"I'll remain here," I said firmly. "They'll help us."

Landon frowned, glancing between me and the red dragon, "I don't know, Briar, I think it's best—"

I shook my head and pressed my palm to his chest, "Please, Landon. I *know* they will."

My heart practically *burned* with the truth of it. It was in the elder dragon's eyes, and how he positioned his body. He hung off the cliff face, wings slightly out, shielding Landon and me from the sun, and the mouth of the cave from Eris's view. They were helping us.

Perhaps, with them, we could do it.

We could defeat Eris. Free the dragons.

Sighing, Landon relented, "Alright, my rose. Alright."

He eyed the approaching black dragon, its scales shimmering like spilled lamp oil, and then glanced around us, deciding on his plan of action. "Come, we'll hide here and listen to what the witch has to say. We need to know why she's here."

I nodded, and then looked back up at the older dragon, "Be safe."

He chuffed, and I swore it was a laugh as if he was amused by my well wishes.

I couldn't blame him. He was a huge, red dragon. One whose scales still shone brightly despite his age. He could take care of himself. The other two shuffled next to him, low, amused rumbles coming from them too.

Alright, then. The dragons would be fine.

As the black dragon and its rider approached, close enough now to see Eris's face twisted with anger, Landon and

I dove for the walls of the cave, finding an alcove to wedge ourselves in and hide from view.

Everything fell silent.

Save for the clattering of rocks dislodged by the dragon's talons and the beat of the black dragon's wings, not a soul could be heard. I swore Landon even stopped breathing.

We knew Eris had landed when there was a crash against the stone, echoing through the cave.

The witch called out loudly, "You, what goes here?"

I heard a lighter voice, the slighter dragon, respond with a chuff that was fairly non-committal.

They were covering for us.

Holy hells, it was *working!* The dragons hadn't immediately ratted us out to Eris, though they easily could have.

"There's something *wrong,*" Eris said, her voice growing louder, closer. "You beasts can feel it, can't you? I'm sure you can *at least* manage that much."

The dragons chuffed, and a new tone, deeper and rougher than the other dragon voices, cut them off with a sharp growl. They all fell silent.

"Fine!" Eris shouted. "Since you're of no help, I'll have to check on it myself."

She stomped towards the cave with loud angry steps and then stopped.

"Where is my glamor?" She asked, peering into the dark. I could just barely see a few wisps of her dark hair.

Landon's muscles tensed under my hands, and I could feel with how tightly we were pressed together in the alcove that he was ready to spring forth and begin the battle.

Wisely, he waited.

Eris snapped her fingers, "Dragoth, guard the mouth. You three, *don't move.*"

The dragons did not respond, except for Dragoth, who I assumed was the black dragon. He chuffed his assent and then growled as if he was warning the other dragons.

Eris's footsteps drew near, morphing from the heavy steps on dirt and rock to tread striking stone, echoing through the caves. I could see her entire form now, black cloak of night and dark hair and glinting red crown on her head.

Landon's hands flexed as we watched breathlessly as Eris wandered deeper and deeper into the cave. When she passed us, and her back was all we could see, Landon silently stepped out into the open.

Like a cat crawling after its prey, he made no sound as he moved, footsteps quick, and then he lunged, sword aimed for Eris's ribs.

The witch froze and then whirled, snarling, "Who—?"

She caught sight of Landon's blade and dodged it, turning to red smoke and then reappearing a few feet away.

Landon shouted, "Now!" and everyone sprang into action.

From the shadows, the soldiers emerged, their blades aimed directly at Eris. Elias moved with them, hands raised with blue smoke and bright sparks swirling around him. As one unit, they descended on the witch, whose eyes widened and then began to glow bright red.

"You *dare?*" She hollered, nearly shrieking.

"We dare," Elias said, throwing his first shot.

A ball of blue flame flew at Eris, and she lifted her hand, throwing up a protective circle that deflected the flame. It flew up into the ceiling, leaving a scorch mark behind in the stone.

"You brought another fae," she sneered. "How original."

"You have no idea," Elias said, hurling another attack at her.

Landon used the opening to launch himself at Eris, blade looking for a home. Several other men moved with him, striking out, circling her, and cutting off her exits.

Circles of red magic disappeared and reappeared around her body, deflecting blows nearly as quickly as they came. When the soldier's blades made contact with the magic, a field or red sparks erupted between them, casting the cave and the people inside in eerie and ever-changing lights.

Elias's own magic was might brighter than the witch's, and it streaked through the sword fighting, following Eris as she shifted and weaved around the blows she didn't outright deflect.

With each strike, Eris grew more and more furious, shouting and growling at those who faced her.

When Landon managed to sneak in a strike, opening a shallow cut on her cheek, she shrieked, *"Enough!"*

In an instant, she turned into red smoke and reappeared just outside of the cave, her head turned to the dragons.

I ran after her on instinct and adrenaline, trying to hear what she said to the dragons.

"Kill them!" She demanded.

Dragoth roared, bellowing rage into the sky and shaking the mountains. When the other three did not respond, she looked nearly inhuman with her fury. Her face twisted and became a shadow of its former self.

"Answer me!" She demanded.

The elder red dragon hummed, noncommittal even to my ears.

"You defy me?" She asked, shocked. "You defy your master."

The three dragons growled, and Dragoth growled right back at them.

I emerged from the mouth of the cave, Landon and Elias hot on my heels, and Eris's eyes went right to me.

"You!" She raged. "This is your doing. What did you do to *my spring?*"

"Me?" I asked. "What did *you* do to the spring? How could you defile it like that?"

She laughed, haughty and disbelieving, "Oh this is *rich.* The princess who knows *nothing* of the world where she lives is lecturing me on what. *Preserving nature?*"

"You used the spring for *evil,*" I spat. "Do you deny it?"

"No, I don't." She said, rolling her eyes. "But if you think that's the only power I possess, you're delusional."

Eris stepped back, Dragoth at her back, eyes narrowed on me, and all at once, everyone sprung into action again. The red, silver, and blue dragon lunged for Dragoth as Eris began to shift right before our eyes. Her elegant face lengthened, and her limbs began to shimmer and shift, her body growing and morphing. Within seconds, the Eris I knew had shifted, changing into a huge red and black dragon.

Soldiers rushed past me, and the other dragons launched into the air, battle erupting like a volcano all around me. I tried to take all of it in as quickly as I could, dodging as the Dragon Eris reached towards me with her huge jaws wide open. They snapped shut inches from my shoulder, and I rolled through the brush, scrabbling to get away from her.

"Briar!" Landon hollered. "You *fiend!* Leave her be!"

His lance in hand, he stabbed at Eris's chest, and she hopped to the side, tail swishing, trees cracking and crashing to the ground in her wake. Elias had to dodge her tail, and as he moved, he threw another bolt of blue magic at her, aiming for her head.

She dodged that too, knocking over more trees in the process.

"Woah!" I jumped to my feet and scrambled to the rock face, pressing my back against the stone to avoid the wreckage.

Above me, the four dragons were fighting, Dragoth moving quickly through the air as the red, silver, and blue dragon shot streams of fire at him. The heat made my cheeks warm, and as I looked between them and Eris, Landon lunged at her again, drawing her attention away from me.

With silent determination and anger that seemed to roll off of him in waves, he engaged Eris in combat. For now, the dragon-witch was content to leave me be as she focused on Landon. He was the more current threat, and so she focused entirely on fighting him.

Elias worked with Landon, sending bolts at Eris's side, opposite of where Landon was attacking, though the blue magic seemed to do little to her tough draconic scales.

Landon stabbed at her and Eris swayed to the side, more trees falling in her wake. The soldiers around Landon fell into step with him, their training setting. As a unit, they worked at Eris, and she returned in kind.

Her heavy and strong tail was as much a weapon as her claws were, and she used them both in conjunction. With precision, she struck out with her claws, swiping at anyone too close to get out of the way.

Two of Landon's men went flying, and Eris followed it up with a stream of fire, red and sickly, sweeping around her in an arch. Immediately, the underbrush caught aflame, roaring to life and devouring the fallen trees around us.

The arch of flames separated a few more of the soldiers from where Eris was. They were unable to get through the flames among the fallen logs, and Landon caught sight of it immediately.

Elias tried to shoot some of his magic to cool the flames, but the fire raged on, fueled by her hate and anger.

"Take the men and go!" Landon ordered Elias, throwing his arm out, and gesturing back down the trail.

"I will!" Elias shouted. "Get the bitch!"

Landon nodded, and Elias and the other men moved, immediately following his orders, leaving Landon and I behind with the dragons.

Above, Dragoth was letting his own streams of fire out, aiming at the other three dragons as they dove and swooped through the air. The sounds of their fight roared around us, echoing through the mountains.

It was *chaos*. And when Eris lunged for Landon, the sound of claws against steel joined the cacophony as the fire roared and soldiers shouted to one another, coordinating their retreat.

And then Eris whirled, tail swinging around her and coming close to where I was. I ducked, and it hit the stone wall with a *crack.* A rain of gravel fell from above, hitting my head and shoulders as I scrambled again, trying to get away.

I ended up inside of the cave, backing away from the fighting.

Landon glanced at me and then glared at Eris. He doubled his efforts, drawing his sword so he was double armed, and lunged at her.

Eris hissed, a snake-like voice coming from her huge head, "You're pathetic. You think anything you do can stop me? Whatever you did to my spring, I'll fix it. The dragons *will* be mine again."

With a growl, Landon came close to Eris's chest, trying to strike through to her heart.

"Fool," she growled.

Eris spread her wings and rose up above the trees, the beat of her wings joining those of the other dragons looping through the sky.

She opened her mouth, revealing huge white rows of sharp teeth, and rained down more fire on the ground below. Huge red flames carved through the wood and glowed against the stone, and reflected off the metal of Landon's armor.

Though he was dressed in full plate, he was still able to move with quick and sure steps, keeping himself out of the worst of the fire, though he did misstep once or twice, stumbling and catching some of the flames at his back before he recovered and rolled out of the way.

In the fray, he abandoned his lance, throwing it away from the fire towards the cave, and hefted his sword, shouting up at Eris, "Come down here, beast!"

"Beast?!" She raged. "How dare you!"

Swooping, she laid down another line of fire, going directly over where Landon was standing. Dragoth roared with her, and I gasped, hand over my mouth as I tried to find my mate in the vibrant red flames.

I couldn't see him, and Eris laughed, "Oh, how they fall so *easily.*"

She landed at the mouth of the cave as Dragoth and the others continued their battle behind her, the black dragon spinning in the air, claws aimed at his fellows. The silver and blue dragon deflected him, keeping their red leader safe.

"You have nowhere to run," she hissed at me, steam coming from her nostrils, surrounding us in fog and smoke. "Nowhere else to go, *princess.*"

I looked between her and the dragons in the sky, trying to determine what to do or where to go. Her dragon form was enormous, nearly as big as the mouth of the cave, and with the red flames behind her, she seemed to emerge from the underworld itself. Here to eat me and make me her pray.

"Dear gods," I said, stepping away from her.

Laughing, she chuffed, "Oh, now she crumbles. Without her prince here to protect her, she's *nothing.*"

"I am not," I shouted at her, glaring. "I'm *Briar.*"

"Oh, *pardon me,*" she said sarcastically, the words a hiss accompanied with more steam. "You are Briar. And look at all the good being here has done you."

"Better than being you!" I hurled back. "A woman so pathetic she has to desecrate a magic spring to meet her own ends!"

"Pathetic, or smarter than you lot? You had the spring for hundreds of years, and what did you do with it? Bathe your feet in it? *Pathetic.*"

I shook my head, disbelieving that she could be so callous about her actions. About who she was. Did she really have no shame?

Perhaps she was so old now she had no sense of who she was anymore.

I glanced again around me, realizing I was alone here.

With Eris the Dragon.

Shit.

She took another step towards me, savoring how I squirmed, and I glanced down, measuring just how far she was from me. Then, it caught my eyes. *Landon's lance.*

I looked back up at Eris's huge dragon head, met her eyes, and then *lunged.*

As quickly as I could, I threw myself forward and onto the lance, hefting it up into my arms and propping it up against the ground. It was so much heavier than I thought it would be, and I had to drag the end of it through the dirt as I hauled it forward, trying to aim the tip for Eris's chest.

She growled, readying herself to step to the side, when a blast of blue magic hit her in the face. Freezing with shock, her head whirled to see where it had come from, and I used the opening Elias gave me to *push,* running with the lance and lodging it as far into her chest as I could. It took all of my strength, my muscles straining as I tried to use the lance for leverage.

It was wickedly sharp and sunk into a space between her scales easily, the metal shining in the firelight as black blood oozed from Eris's wound.

Roaring, Eris reared back, and I had to drop the lance, scrambling backward on my behind.

"How *dare you?*" She screamed, letting a stream of fire into the sky, shouting her rage.

Another blast of blue fire hit her, close to where I'd stabbed her, and she cried again, clearly wounded. But it wasn't enough, not really. She reached one huge claw for the lance and yanked it out of her.

Behind her, Dragoth landed among the rubble and the fire, clearly there to back up his chosen master.

"Briar!" Elias shouted. "We need to go!"

He shot more blue magic at Eris, creating a shower of blue sparks where they burst against her scales. Dragoth growled at him, starting after him, only to be met by the other three dragons, red and silver, and blue, landing between him and Elias.

All four of them were worn but still full of fight. With Elias, the three good dragons lunged for Dragoth, dragging his attention away from me, leaving Eris on her own to face me.

As the dragons roared and Elias's magic flashed and boomed, Eris focused on me.

"Bitch," she hissed. "This is your end. No more Briar. I'll kill you today the way I should have a millennium ago."

I stood there, staring her down, and watched as she took a step for me, the wound in her chest still weeping dark blood.

And then Eris was shrieking, whirling to face something behind her.

Then I heard him, Landon snarling, "Die, witch."

The witch-dragon's head dipped and snapped out before suddenly she whined and reared back. High-pitched and keening, she weaved back and forth as if she was unsteady and then careened to the side, thudding to the ground.

Out of the top of her head, I caught the tip of Landon's sword sticking out, having been speared through her mouth, silencing her forever.

I looked at her with wide eyes and then looked up to see Landon rounding her side, coming towards me.

"Landon!" I gasped, running for him.

He folded me up in his arms, squeezing me tight to his chest, "My rose."

It was only a brief embrace, cut short by the continued sounds of Dragoth's own battle. The black dragon, who had followed Eris voluntarily, was flagging. The combined force of Elias with the other three dragons was wearing him down.

They bore down on him with bursts of flame and blue magic, and then with movements quicker than I thought possible, the huge red dragon bounded forward, jaws agape, and snapped at Dragoth's neck.

With a sickening crunch, Dragoth's neck was snapped, and he fell to the ground with another huge thud.

It was over.

Finally.

Chapter Thirty-One

With the body of Eris before us, Landon and I stood there, panting.

I was weary still and kicked one of her huge claws, looking for a reaction.

She had none. The great beast who was once a beautiful but deadly witch, was now dead.

The dragons were doing a similar investigation of Dragoth, sniffing at his body. Apparently satisfied, the red dragon threw his head back and roared his victory to the skies. The blue and silver dragon joined him, and from all around, we heard even more cries join them, a cacophony of sound that shook me to my bones.

The dragons were free now, and they were shouting their victory together. Announcing it to the world.

"Wow," Landon whispered next to me, eyes riveted to the beautiful creatures.

Elias came to stand aside us, agreeing, "They're a sight to see."

"I never knew," Landon whispered, guilt shining in his eyes.

"You had no way to know," I assured him, grabbing his hand. "Don't think of it."

He smiled at me briefly but then dropped my hand and approached the dragons.

They dropped their heads and eyed his approach warily.

"I want us to go back to how things were," he announced. "I am Prince Landon. Of Fenestral. I will return here on the solstice with an offering. If you'll accept it."

The red elder dragon eyed him carefully and then dipped his head, chuffing a kind of agreement.

I smiled and watched as the dragons considered their business done and launched themselves off the ground. As one, their wings beat, and they flew away, further up into the mountains to join their brethren.

"Well," Elias sighed. "Let me put out these fires. I'm ready to go the fuck home."

"Thank you, Elias," Landon said, clapping the fae man on the shoulder.

Elias shrugged, "Don't mention it."

Without Eris's magic present to feed the red flames, they died easily under Elias's blue ice magic, and Landon, Elias, and I were able to make our way carefully back down the path. It was a quiet walk, each of us processing the battle we'd just survived.

Landon's armor was nearly entirely black from dragon fire, and Elias had his own singes and cuts. I was in shock, stumbling down the hill with Landon helping me along. How had we all survived? Was this really the end of Eris?

Months of living in fear of her and worrying she'd appear to curse me yet again had made me jumpy. And now it was just... over.

"Is she really dead?" I asked Landon quietly.

He glanced at me and said, "She is, my rose. She is."

"Gods, thank goodness," I whispered, taking his hand and squeezing it.

His hand was warm in mine, and he squeezed my hand back.

"You did good, Briar," Elias said, smiling back at me from further down the path. "You really stuck her good. Gave the prince here just enough time to get his feet back."

"I thought he was..." I gulped. "Well, I'm glad he found his feet again."

Landon squeezed my hand again, and I smiled over at him.

Before I could thank Elias for distracting Eris enough for me to get at her, we emerged from the treeline and found Landon's soldiers there waiting for us.

"My prince!" One said, running for us. "You survived!"

"More than survived," Elias exclaimed. "Landon has felled the beast! We're free of the witch's tyranny!"

"Huzzah!" One person cried.

"Huzzah!" Shouted another.

"Huzzah! Huzzah!"

The cries of victory rang around us, and the soldiers swarmed us, clapping Landon's shoulders, bowing to me, or taking my hand and kissing the back of it. It was jubilant and relieved, and it wasn't a dream.

None of this was.

I was very much awake, and all of this was real.

My life, the one I felt like I'd had to restart over and over... was finally *really and truly* starting.

I was *free*. Free of Eris, free of fear...

Unbidden, tears filled my eyes and spilled over. I turned to Landon, tugging at his hand, and looked up at him.

"My rose," he whispered, taking my face in his hands. "All is well."

"I know," I whispered back. "I don't know why I'm crying."

He smiled and pulled me into his arms, squeezing me tight, "Let's get you home. Back to Fleur."

"Yes," I nodded. "Home. Please."

"Together," he affirmed.

"Together."

EPILOGUE

On the next solstice Landon and I made the track back to Skyridge, back to where it all began.

I was *very* pregnant, with a bump that was impossible to hide and an aching pelvis that made the ride out to Skyridge *very* uncomfortable.

Landon tried to ask me to stay behind, but I *had* to go. I needed to see it happen for myself.

Together we journeyed there, and seeing the ruins for the first time in nearly half a year made my heart ache. But it wasn't the ache I'd been expecting. Instead, it was a bittersweet reminder of all of my memories.

I still missed my family, my siblings, and my mother and father, but I was happy here with Landon. Our lives had settled into a routine, attending functions in the evening and preparing for our child to arrive. It was hectic, but in a way that was fulfilling. I got to do all these things along with Landon, and together we cemented ourselves into the court of Fleur.

The king had softened towards me, especially once Landon gave him my writings to read, and it was nice to have him look kindly upon me. No one could replace my father, but it was nice all the same to have a man look upon me in a fatherly way.

The carriage rumbled to a stop, and Landon helped me alight from it, holding my hand as I descended the stairs.

The dragons were already there. They were perched along the ruins of Skyridge and in the craigs of the mountain. The sunlight shined down on their scales, sparkling beautifully in the afternoon light.

"It's just like you said," Landon said quietly, looking up with awe.

"It is," I agreed, taking it all in.

It'd been so long since I'd seen this view that I savored it. This small piece of the past.

It was healing, in a way. Seeing them take over the ruins of where I once lived. I thought my father would be pleased to know that even if his kingdom fell, his castle was still of use to the dragons who protected us.

We made our way towards the castle, and then I pulled Landon to the side, taking him to the small clearing where we'd always made our offerings before. Behind us, people bustled, unloading wagons full of our offerings and rushing to where we went.

The small patch of grass between the castle and the mountain face opened up before us, and it was full of dragons. In every color of the rainbow, they gathered, waiting patiently for us to approach. And at the forefront of them all was the red elder, the blue, and the silver dragon from our fight with Eris.

They dipped their heads at us in greeting, and Landon and I returned the motion.

Then, the red dragon chuffed, seemingly in a laugh, and I smiled back at him.

"It's been a long time since we met like this," I called to him.

He chuffed again, as did the blue and silver dragon.

"Is this your first?" I asked, gesturing to the smaller two.

They both looked at me, nodding and grunting.

"Then welcome," I said. "It's my mate's first as well. And I hope it's the first of many."

The red dragon dipped his head regally, eyes closing, before he locked eyes with me again.

"Let's begin!" Landon called, gesturing the others forward.

One by one, Landon and I watched first the younger, smaller dragons take their offerings, and then the middle ones, large but still growing into themselves. And then the adult dragons came forth, huge wings and glittering scales that were captivating to watch. Then the older dragons, with wrinkles in their eyes and dents in their scales and scars along their tails.

One by one, they took their offering, and then spread their wings and flew away, disappearing over the nearest mountain.

Then, lastly, the blue dragon went. Then the silver. And, finally, the elder red dragon approached.

I stepped forward with Landon and watched with pride as the final dragon took his offering and flew away, following his brethren.

It was done.

And I could feel it. Feel how the balance was restored.

I smiled, looking up to the sky, and watched the huge red dragon disappear into the mountains, and then turned to Landon, "We did it."

"We did."

WANT MORE?

Join my mailing list for exclusive scenes, art, and more goodies! Plus, keep up to date with me and my upcoming books!

www.alodiathaliel.com/newsletter

Afterward

And that's White Roses!

Thank you so much for joining me on this journey! This book came so easily to me, and it was so much fun putting all of this to page and bringing Landon and Briar's story to life. I think I've always been fascinated with Sleeping Beauty because she represents hope. Hope that life can change, that no matter how low you may be brought, you will rise up again.

That in spite of whatever forces may work against you, love can always win.

Whenever you're feeling lost or down, remember that! Love is love is love. And it *always* wins.

Much love, and see you in the next one!

LET'S CONNECT!

TikTok - @alodiathaliel

Twitter - @alodiathaliel

Website - www.alodiathaliel.com

Mailing List - www.alodiathaliel.com/newsletter

Email - alodiathaliel@gmail.com

Made in the USA
Monee, IL
29 July 2023

40004566R00225